The

Raven King

E.J. McCracken

Black Rose Writing

www.blackrosewriting.com

ISBN: 978-1-61296-083-8

PUBLISHED BY BLACK ROSE WRITING

www.blackrosewriting.com

Printed in the United States of America

The Raven King is printed in Byington

To Lisa,
whose honesty keeps me sane.

To Madeleine—
My cross country & chem
buddy!
♡ Emily
E J McC

The

Raven King

1

When their world ended, there was only silence. The boy and the girl stared at each other in wonder. Behind them, smoke rose fleetingly into the pale blue sky.

They stood in a battlefield, or what was left of one, and the smoke still plumed from its wreckage. A city lay before them, torn to its foundations. The skeleton of a guard tower loomed just overhead. Its stone walls shot into the sky, rising forty feet before ending in a jagged platform. Just below its peak, metal hooks protruded from the stone. They curved upwards, as if praying to the Gods for their delivery. One of them was bent over, straining against the weight it supported. A body, newly dead, dangled in the breeze.

Rubble shifted beneath their feet. The girl picked her way between the remains of smoldering chariots, dodging the various swords that lay forgotten on the ground. Her black hair wavered in the smoke as she worked her way towards the center of the devastation. Death was everywhere.

She came to the last defense the city had offered, a river, still churning from the chaos. Its silted waters slapped against the banks, and her reflection was quickly torn apart. She watched as her pale face disintegrated into murky blackness.

Except that the water wasn't black. Not totally: something white flickered in the shadows of the bank. The waves rolled it against the mud, crashing it against the melting shore. She bent down, her fingers hesitating before entering the water. Her heart tremored, and she bit her lip. She had reason to fear.

She shook the thought aside, plunging her hand into the icy water. The object was small and metallic, and as she pulled it dripping from the water, she couldn't help but feel relieved. The locket glistened in her open palm.

Her fingers fumbled with the clasp, even though she knew its mechanisms by heart. She had once had one like it, small, intricately carved, and delicate. Arie had told her that it was made by the elves, but she hadn't believed him. Not then. Now, gazing at the pictures inside, she wasn't sure. The ink was blurred, but the woman was most definitely elven.

She gasped, prepared to hurl the locket back into the river. It was only her brother's memory that stopped her. She paused, fingering the delicate chain.

The locket was elven. That much was certain, and if the locket was elven, than the city had to be, too. No other species would harbor such a creature. She glanced over her shoulder, opening her mouth to call for the boy. They need to leave, and soon. The humans could be back at any moment.

Her words came out in a soft whisper. She didn't want to leave, not really, not after all she had been through. Where would she go? The Clan was lost to her now, only a distant memory, far off in the underground tunnels. They would never accept her back, not with Isen still as king.

She watched as the boy stumbled towards her, his face caked with dirt and exhaustion. If she looked closely enough, she could still detect hints of his golden hair beneath the grime. He looked like his father, and sight made her shudder against the breeze. She thought she had escaped Isen once and for all, but now it seemed that he was following her in the form of her best friend.

She shrugged, sucking in a deep breath before turning back to the locket. *He's not his father,* she reminded herself. *He's not Isen, no matter how much he looks like him.* She peeked over the edge of her cupped hands. The boy grinned back, and she felt a smile warming her lips. They were alone in Ivindor, but they were alone together.

Her fingers traced the edges of the locket a moment longer. Then she threw the chain over her neck, letting her cloak swallow the silver pendent. The locket wasn't hers, but it felt like it should have been. Her own locket was gone, left behind in the Clan, and with it had disappeared her last vestiges of Arie.

She crunched through a shattered shield, kicking aside the jagged pieces of metal. A plank bridged the chaotic river, and she stepped out onto the wood, her imagination filling the silent air with the screams of the raid. The humans must have been powerful, to overcome a city of elves. A torrent of ghost arrows whistled past.

The opposite bank had seen the worst of the plundering, and the girl strolled among the mess, peering into the huts that guarded the waterway. All were empty. Walls had crumbled to the earth, and animal pens hung open and vacant. Footprints trampled the blood soaked soil, dancing out the last flight of the villagers. A few feet further on, the first body appeared.

She gulped back the bile that rose to her throat. This

wasn't some ordinary raid. In the Clan, other tribes were attacked all the time, but no one was ever killed. Not even when Isen took the throne, and began his reign of terror. Killing angered the Gods.

She bit her lip, tasting the sweet slipperiness of blood. The stuff was everywhere: in the water, in the ground, rising in steam from the bodies. *Why the elves?* She didn't understand it. *What did the elves do wrong?*

"Alina!" The voice was harsh in the still air. She whirled to face the boy, his face flushed red with excitement. He motioned for her to join him. "There's something here."

Her pace quickened. She dashed down the narrow lane, past the boy, and into a small courtyard. The garden gate swung lazily on its hinges, creaking as she pushed through it. The boy followed her, his face now grim. He pointed at a small hut.

She paused just outside the door, listening. The humans seemed to be gone, but she wasn't about to take any chances. She couldn't afford a struggle.

A whimper. She froze, the color draining from her face. *Not now. Gods. Please.* She glanced questioningly at the boy, but he shook his head. No, he had not been in the hut. He had no idea what was in there, and the worry on his face warned Alina. She shook her head. *We can't just walk away.*

She pushed the door open. Inside, the dark air trembled with dust. The soft outlines of furniture, a rug lying motionless on the floor: all seemed ordinary, as if the house was totally removed from the bloodshed outside. She moved in, ducking her head to avoid the low archway. Her eyes adjusted to the dim light rapidly. In the corner, a figure was huddled.

Careful, now. Alina reached for her cooking knife. Holding it out in front of her, she crept forward. The figure shifted, and she raised the blade high above her head. "Who's there?"

The whimper came again, louder. She leaned over the figure, staring down at its still form. A face looked up at her, black hair mussed and crisp with blood. A child!

Hastily, she shoved the knife back into her belt. She knelt beside the boy. He was perhaps twelve years of age, skinny, with a waxy complexion that could only result from extreme pain. Several layers of rags were pressed to a wound on his stomach. Even in the gloom, she could see the blood seeping through. He groaned. "Please . . . "

"Hush," she murmured, leaning down. His face slid into a patch of light, leaving his delicate features to fall victim to the sun. Her heart went out to this boy, and as she looked into his eyes, she couldn't help but feel moved by the need to help. She peeled away the bandages, blanching at the sight of the hole gaping in his side. She pressed the rags back in place. Alina had never learned the healing arts—women of the Clan weren't allowed to, but she could see that this wound was far beyond even the most skilled help.

She heard Carn kneel beside her. The boy had clung to her side ever since they had been exiled from the Clan, and now his ragged breathing filled her ears.

"Alive?" He reached for the bandages, but she slapped his hand back. "Gods." He pulled Alina out of the hut.

They huddled in the garden outside. A few dead flowers poked up out of the weeds. The stalks waved in the breeze.

"Elven." He put his hand on Alina's shoulder. "We can't stay here, not if this was a city of elves. Some one's bound to come along. You can see the smoke for miles."

Their eyes met. Indeed, the smoke did spiral high into

the air. It was what had attracted them in the first place. At the time, they had thought it to be a cooking fire. Only later did they realize that it was much, much larger.

Alina nodded, not convinced. In the three days since they had left the Clan, she had learned to fear the world. She had reason to fear.

If the boy was an elf, then there was nothing Alina could do for him. In the past few days she had learned a lot about the ways of the world. The elves and the humans were to be left alone, to deal with each other as they wished. This was how it was done; yet Alina still felt a pang of remorse.

"We can't leave him here," she whispered. "He's just a boy. Our age."

Carn grimaced. "He's beyond help."

Alina glanced back at the hut. Even from here, she could hear the boy moaning. "He'll die without us." It was merely a statement to fill the air. Even with their help, Alina knew that the boy would soon be gone. He was an elf, and that was that. "There's got to be someone around here who's friendly, someone who can help. Like you said: someone will see the smoke." She glanced at Carn, who nodded. Simultaneously, they turned towards the gate.

Carn led the way out of the garden. A cobbled street opened at their feet, and they followed it cautiously, picking their way through the debris. They came into a square, its wide expanse gaping before them.

A row of stalls lined one side. Alina walked along them, staring at the broken shelves. Fruit lay spoiled where it had fallen, lying beneath the chunks of meat that hung tattered from hooks in the ceilings. Fragments of clay bowls crunched under foot. Against the backdrop of the city, her features were accentuated. Life underground had taken its toll on the race of the coremen, and her bony frame barely reached five feet in height. She kicked at a basket of fruit.

"It's almost as if they weren't expecting it." She turned to Carn. "Like they knew whoever did this."

"The humans?" Carn wavered. He staggered after his friend, shell-shocked. Too much had happened in the last few days.

"Who else?" Alina glanced at him. Carn had given up so much for her. He had been heir to the chief of the Clan, set to come to power at his father, Isen's, death. The jewels he could have inherited! The golden crown that would have adorned his brow, the worship the Clan would have paid him! But he had never been one for riches or glory. And for that, Alina envied him. Born poor, she was destined to long for the throne.

And the Clan! Not only had they left behind a chance at a good life, but they had also left behind their families. Alina's mother and twin brothers . . . She even missed Isen, for all that he hated her.

He had no reason to punish me like that! She bit her lip. The leader had always been disgusted at her presence, and Carn's friendship with her had not helped matters. The leader probably would have banished her anyway, even if her brother hadn't intervened. She shuddered. Arie's death had opened a range of possibilities.

They entered the outskirts of the city. Here, there was less evidence of the battle. Fewer bodies littered the ground, and half of the huts they came across were untouched. Carn lagged behind her, throwing open the doors.

"Just making sure."

Up ahead, a tree hugged the earth to its fallen side.

Alina settled on its slick surface. The bark tugged at her shapeless wrap, and she pulled her cloak more firmly around her shoulders. She waited as Carn sat down beside her.

"We need to go back." Her eyes flicked up to meet his. "To the Clan. We can't stay out here forever, not with this war."

"Are you crazy?" Carn looked ready to slap her. "We can't go back, Alina. Not after what your brother did."

"Arie . . . " She grimaced. "It wasn't my fault that he was caught!"

Carn licked his lips. "Caught during an assassination attempt? Do you really think Father was going to let you get away while Arie hanged?"

"I hardly ever saw Arie. And why are you complaining? If he succeeded, you would have been king."

They were silent for a time, staring out at the landscape. Carn had spotted the smoke the day before, and had suggested that they make their way towards it. There hadn't been anything else to do at the time.

Eventually, they rose to their feet. They had found no other survivors, no one to help them with the boy. *He's on his own.* She felt a pang of fear for the child they had left behind, writhing in pain and alone in the world. *But there's nothing we can do.*

She led the way out, picking her way back through the market square. She crossed the narrow footbridge over the river, and soon they were beyond the guard towers. She tried not to look back at the smoldering ruins behind her. Instead, she turned her attention to the wide road that snaked away from the city. Paved with flat stones, it was wide enough for two carts to walk abreast. It followed the river on its course downhill, weaving between farmhouses and water wheels.

On the edge of the horizon, she spotted another plume of smoke. This one was smaller than the one that rose from the city, but it was black with ash. At its base, she could just make out the vibrant red of leaping flames.

She quickened her pace. Beside her, Carn broke into a run. Alina hardly had time to think; she leapt to keep up with her friend. Together, they ran towards the smoke.

As they neared it, Alina slowed. A nagging worry tugged at the edge of her mind, and she reached out to catch Carn's arm. "That fire hasn't been burning for very long. How do we know that *they've* left?"

Carn understood immediately. He crouched on the ground, scanning the section of road intensely. Nothing moved; even the birds were still in the trees. The air was thick with silence, and with the smell of smoke. Long grass waved on the side of the road. The source of the smoke was hidden behind its weave.

They crept forward, hands scraping at the stone as they pressed themselves against the road. Alina inched slowly ahead of Carn. She slipped onto the shoulder of the road and slowly peeled the grass back. With Carn breathing over her shoulder, she peered into the scene beyond.

A house, or at least the frame of it, was just beginning to crackle under the flames. Alina could feel the heat radiating onto her angled face, even though they were a good distance away, and upwind. The door of the house hung crookedly on its hinges. Before it, a porch swayed under the weight of an old rocking chair. A blanket was crumpled at its feet, like the occupant had been dragged away from the comforts of a nap.

A sudden crunch of footsteps sent them sprawling on the ground. Someone, or something, was emerging from behind the house. Alina's breath caught in her throat.

There was flash of dark metal. Two men emerged, each dressed in full plate armor. The metal clanked as they walked, and must have been remarkably heavy, but this was not what held Alina's attention. The armor was the darkest of all blacks. It was the color of the night sky, once all of the stars had been extinguished. It was the color of a dungeon that has seen no light. She thought she could see death itself staring back at her from its depths.

One of the men led his companion into the space beyond the house. A deep purple cloak flapped at his ankles as he walked. With one swift motion, he tugged the helmet off of his head. Flaming red hair gave way to a full-throated beard. "No survivors?"

A flood of relief washed over Alina. These people were trying to help! She moved to get up, but Carn grabbed her arm. He yanked her back to the ground. "Wait," he hissed.

She turned her attention back to the two men. The second man had removed his helmet as well. He frowned. "Not that I saw."

"We should be certain." The red haired man tapped his sword hilt lightly. It hung at his waist, unsheathed. The blade gleamed red in the light of the fire.

The second man nodded. "The rest of the men have returned to camp. But I'll sweep the city."

"They're lazy; you are not. I value your service." He jammed his helmet over the mass of fiery hair. His sword clanged against his armor as he stepped away from the house.

Alina caught Carn's eye. There was something not quite right about these two men, something she hadn't noticed right away. She was glad that Carn had kept her from greeting them. She turned and began to follow the men back towards the city.

They passed through the gates without incident and continued on towards the heart of the city. The men marched through the market place. They showed no particular interest in the bodies that scattered the main street.

Coming to an intersection, they turned onto a side road. Alina and Carn crept around the corner. Alina's breath was coming fast and ragged now; she could feel her heart beginning to flutter with panic. She could only hope that the men weren't able to hear its pounding.

They continued up the side street for a ways. With a start, Alina realized that the street was familiar. She and Carn had walked up this same road only minutes before. Off to the right, she spotted the run-down hut where she had found the boy. Holding her breath, she hoped that he would keep quiet.

A single, screeching moan echoed from its depths. Alina's heart sank. She watched as the men stopped. The red haired man fingered his sword. "Better check that," he said.

The second man swung open the garden gate. He waited for the other to step through before latching it neatly behind them. Only then did he turn to enter the hut.

"Ah, yes. We've got a live one." His voice sounded strained, as if he were lifting something heavy. The moaning grew louder, and more intense.

The man emerged with the boy half slung over his shoulder. He threw him to the ground at the other man's feet.

"You know what to do." The red haired man had pulled off his helmet again. His nose wrinkled, as if he were regarding something faintly disgusting.

The other man nodded. "I just thought, since you were here, you might want to—"

"Very well." In a single motion, he whipped his sword from its place in his belt. He raised it high above the boy's head. The sword flashed, and blood spurted forth.

Alina gulped. She tasted bile in the back of her mouth, and worked desperately to keep it down. Her entire body was trembling. Tears threatened to overflow her eyes.

"Come on." Carn grabbed her hand. He began to crawl back up the street. Alina followed, not daring to look back at the scene in front of the shed. When they reached the corner, they broke into a run.

They wandered downstream of the city, following the water as it meandered towards a larger river. Birds flitted along the banks. An occasional deer spooked as they crossed a meadow, but for the most part, Alina and Carn were alone. They walked quickly, glad to be away from the horrors of the city.

Towards noon, the high grasslands morphed into the thin forest of the riverbank. Huckleberry bushes and salal scratched at their legs. Oregon grape, just baring the first of its yellow flowers, pushed through the undergrowth, coming to a head at the base of vine maples and aspen. The sound of the river rushing between rocks could be heard over the tweets of golden finches. The stream hastened onwards.

Alina stepped into the icy water, biting her teeth

against the cold. Wading through the brush was too much work to sustain for long, though traveling by stream was not without its ill effects. Between her scratches and thorny scars, Alina's legs quickly turned red. Her feet went numb. Behind her, Carn gasped as he slipped into an eddy, splashing cold water onto his tunic.

The stream deepened. Alina kept to the shallows near the bank, but when the water curved, even this area was fraught with unseen pits. By the time the stream crashed into the waters of the river, both Alina and Carn were soaking.

Carn stepped up onto the bank. He held out his hand to Alina, pulling her up as well. In front of them, the river water boiled against the incoming stream. Huge boulders clashed with the forces of the water, and the spray misted their faces. Alina frowned. She glanced downstream, where the brush of the forest lightened. Eventually, taking that path would lead them back into the meadows. It was also easier for traveling. *But we're more likely to meet someone if we go that way.*

She turned upstream. Fallen trees sprawled in the beds of emerald plants, their branches sticking up at odd angles. Blackberry vines crept up the remaining trees. Alina glanced at Carn. He shrugged. Either way, they were on their own.

It wasn't until the sun began to sink in the sky that Alina felt the first pangs of hunger. Her two-day fast came to a head in an instant. Water had been plentiful, but she hadn't thought about food until now. Her stomach grumbled.

She scanned the multitude of plants at her feet. She recognized none of them. In the Clan, they had eaten only the meat that the men caught near the earth's surface, small voles and the occasional badger. Vegetation had been a rarity. Sometimes the women would find plant tubers, and when the Clan emerged from their tunnels in the fall, they would gather fallen apples and other fruits. Alina hadn't tasted anything green in years.

This posed a major problem for Alina as she prowled the forest. There was plenty to eat, like the little red berries that hung from the plants with square stems, but she had no way of knowing if they were edible. She reached out and plucked one. Its tart taste sent her reeling back. She spat the berry into the water near her feet.

Carn could hunt, if only he had a weapon to hunt with. A multitude of small birds and rabbits clung to life in the forest, and as they walked, the animals darted into hiding. She watched Carn tense as each animal appeared. "You could trap them," she suggested.

Carn shook his head. "Only if we stayed put."

Alina bit her lip. Stopping for a few days was a possibility, and it would allow them to catch their breath and regain their strength. It seemed like a good idea, if they weren't so close to the destroyed city.

"No one's going to come looking for us," Carn said, watching her consider the options. "Those men didn't see us, I'm sure of it."

"And if they did?"

Carn grinned. "Can you imagine that man walking this far? He must have weighed as much as a horse!"

Alina's eyes brightened. She laughed. "More like a rhino, with all that armor." She inspected the landscape. "I guess we could stay."

Carn beamed. He bounded ahead, snatching up a long stick as he went. A suitable bush came into view, and he approached it cautiously, the branch held before him like a sword. He delivered a hacking blow to the side of the bush.

Alina snorted with laughter. She grabbed her own makeshift sword and swung it at Carn. He blocked her blow, letting the sticks clatter together. "Not so fast, Guard!"

"What am I guarding?" Alina spun. Suddenly, she lunged forward. Carn's sword dropped, and for a moment, he was unprotected. She lightly tapped his chest. "Gotcha."

Carn was not to be deterred. He sprung forward. "Just a scratch!" His stick caught on Alina's tip, and with a quick flick of the wrist, he sent both sticks flying. "Who's the master now?"

Alina's smile faltered. The boy's moan of pain seemed to echo in the branches of the trees. "It's so easy to kill."

Carn sensed the mood change instantly. He let his play sword lie where it had fallen, instead putting a comforting hand on Alina's shoulder. "There was nothing we could do, you know."

Alina's voice was halting. "If we had shown ourselves . . . Maybe we could have stopped them."

"Are you kidding? We would have been killed, too. You saw that man—he didn't care about life. Killing was easy."

"Still." She stepped over a rotting log. "I don't think I could do it."

"Well," Carn smiled, "Let's hope you never need to. Come on, though. We're free; we're safe. Let's find a place to set up camp."

Alina nodded. She pushed the thought away, turning to follow Carn as he tromped through the undergrowth. They found a clearing to rest in for the night, and in the morning, Carn promised to cook rabbit stew.

2

When they went to check the traps the next morning, they found nothing. Alina stared at the place in the undergrowth. There was no trace of the thong snare. It was like it had disappeared off the planet.

"I swear . . . This is the place," Carn said. He circled away from Alina, kicking at the plants. "Maybe I made a mistake," he admitted when he returned from his search empty handed. "But I really thought—"

"Could a rabbit have run off with it?" Alina asked. She bit back the hunger that was rising in her throat. "You know, broken the anchor?"

Carn shook his head. Silently, he led the way back to the clearing where they had spent the night. Alina followed him. She knew better than to ask about the other snares.

Their clearing still smelled strongly of wood smoke. Alina hadn't wanted to light the fire, but Carn had insisted, saying that it would keep the wild animals at bay. Alina had finally given in. The prospect of sleeping without a fire was too much to face.

Now, as she scattered the ashes in the forest, she regretted her weakness. *It would be so easy to track us,* she thought. *Those snares didn't just vanish.* A branch cracked to her right. She spun, just in time to see a raven flap away. *I'm being silly. No one else is here.*

She broke a branch from a nearby tree. The sap was sticky on her hands, but she stripped the wood of its remaining twigs anyway. She bent and used the stick to stir the bed of leaves where they had slept. The imprints of their sleeping forms evaporated into a sea of debris.

Carn watched all this without a word. He hunched his back and reached for his toes. Then he yawned, rolling back to standing. His sleepy eyes smiled blearily from beneath his tangled hair.

Alina smiled. A leaf sprouted out of his mass of blond hair. She reached for it, pulling it free from the tangles. It fluttered to the ground. "Ready?"

Carn nodded, and they were off. Free from packs and equipment, they moved lightly through the forest. Before long they were back beside the rolling river, and they strolled on the rocky bank. The water churned beside them. Alina thought she could hear the rocks rolling beneath its waves. The crunch of the collisions beat rhythmically in her head. Bird songs wove an intricate, continually changing melody. The sounds were comforting; they reminded her of the music of the Clan.

Arie always loved the music, she remembered. Her brother, five years old at the time, had spent hours in front of the Clan musicians. When Alina was born, he would drag her along too. Neither were allowed in the audience— Alina was girl, and both were born poor, but Arie had managed to weasel them in anyway. Isen had banned music a few years later.

Alina snorted. That had been the first of many bans, and like the others, there was no real logic behind it. Isen took over the Clan with a supreme ideal in mind, and he moved quickly to cultivate its base. Women were reduced to mere slaves, and the men vied for their leader's attention. Arie never became a favorite. By that time, he had turned to other activities.

Her mouth twitched slightly. She picked her way around a pile of fallen logs, waiting as Carn climbed over the top of them. The river curved away from their bank. Soon, their path of stones was reduced to a mere dribble along the edge of the water. Alina splashed in the puddles as she walked.

She turned her mind to other subjects, leaving behind the painful topic of her brother's death. It seemed like everything brought up his memory. She was beginning to get sick of the constant grief.

Behind her, Carn marched slowly. His blue eyes twinkled, reflecting the color of the water beneath him. He had torn the sleeves off of his tunic for the snares, and his pale arms stuck awkwardly from his shoulders. The skin was beginning to turn a faint pink.

Alina frowned. She pulled her cloak tightly around her, despite the heat she felt. Carn had thrown his own cloak loosely over his shoulder. She wished that he would put it on. *Sunburn is the last thing we need to be worrying about.* She didn't mention her worries to her friend– Carn hated worry warts.

They walked steadily onwards, watching as the river shrunk at their feet. The change wasn't noticeable at first, but after crossing several tributaries, the river was hardly more than a wide stream. Alina glanced across to the other bank. The trees were thinner there.

"Think we should cross?" Carn had followed her gaze.

Alina shrugged. "I don't know. We're not actually going anywhere, so it won't make much difference." She threw a stick into the water. It bobbed for a moment before being washed away. "It might get deep in the center," she cautioned.

Carn smirked. "Afraid of getting wet? Come on, we could use a swim anyway." He waded into the river. When the water was up to his waist, he turned and waited for Alina to follow.

Alina rolled her eyes. She slipped into the river, feeling her wet clothes sag in the current. When she was near Carn, she dove into the water.

She came up sputtering. Carn grinned and followed suit. Together, they began to swim to the opposite shore. Alina's long, smooth strokes pushed her ahead, but the current was strong. She watched her chosen landing place sweep by, and behind her, Carn was beginning to slow. She no longer heard his hands slapping the water. His panting was hardly audible.

"Almost there." She felt her toes scrap the rocky bed. The current was still too strong to stand, but the sign encouraged her. She pushed forward, though her limbs were beginning to go numb. She hauled herself onto the warm stones of the bank.

Carn dragged himself in beside her. They lay for time, letting the sun dry their clothing. Alina peeled a twig to comb through her hair. The swim had exhausted her, but because of her numb stomach, she could longer feel the pangs of hunger. She felt her eyes droop. The warmth of the sun cradled her into sleep.

She wasn't sure what woke her. The gentle hum of voices was startling, but so was the scent of smoke. She drew in a deep breath, and though the smoke wasn't chokingly thick, it was disturbing. She crawled out of its path. In her half asleep mind, it didn't occur to her that both the voices and the smoke were out of place.

Luckily, Carn was ahead of her. He dropped to all fours beside her, hushing her with a warning glance. "Someone's here," he whispered.

"Well that's obvious," Alina shot back. The details of their situation came flooding back to her. Cautiously, she stood.

Carn followed her lead. They crept towards the edge of the forest, where the smoke was thickest. The gentle flicker of a campfire came slowly into focus. Alina pushed a branch out of the way, and the leaves rustled. The voices stopped.

"Probably a squirrel," came a man's voice. He spoke slowly, choosing every word.

"What else could it be?" His companion asked. "We're in the middle of nowhere, on the very outskirts of our territory."

Alina peered through the bush. Several men sat with their backs to her, turned in towards the flames. A young man, his pale blond hair streaming with water, poked at the fire with a stick. His green eyes stared sulkily at the rising ashes. Another man watched him intently. "So you saw nothing."

The young man waved his hand. "What was I supposed to see? Like I said, we're in the middle of nowhere. Nobody's going to be out here—"

"If Alvardine caught wind of a disturbance, then it's our duty to investigate it." The man snatched the stick. He snapped it cleanly in half, tossing the pieces into the forest. "If you'd paid closer attention, maybe you would have noticed." He waved another man forward.

The man shifted hesitantly. "Of course, it wasn't very noticeable, so I wouldn't expect you to see it," he began, "but there was evidence of a campfire. The ashes were scattered on the edges of a clearing. Across the river, of course."

"And?"

"Well, there was this." The man pulled a strip of leather from inside his cloak. With a start, Alina recognized the snare Carn had set the day before. "It was set not far from the clearing."

"Ah." The man turned to the boy, smirking. "And what do you make of that, Leif?"

The boy frowned sullenly. "Alright. How many people?"

"Two. Small, almost like children."

Alina drew back. She met Carn's eyes. These people were searching for *them*! She turned and began to crawl back to the beach.

A twig snapped underfoot. Almost immediately, the men were on them.

Alina screamed. "Carn! Run!"

She had been in this situation before. She felt the blood coursing through her veins, heard the shouts of the men behind her, and remembered. Then, it was Isen who had chased after her. His hands clutched at a dagger. Arie swung from a noose, his body still twitching—she wasn't even sure he was dead, just that he was gone. There was no one to save her now.

She heard Carn's panting breath behind her. Even he had been the enemy, then. She slipped up a rocky embankment, heading toward the river. If she could just reach the water, maybe she would be safe.

This was not to be. She stumbled on a log and fell. Her hands scraped the earth, and she threw herself back onto her feet. When she looked up, a man was blocking her path. His eyes narrowed.

She spun, vaguely aware of the man drawing his sword behind her. The river was blocked, and she turned towards the forest. Men were streaming towards her. She saw the blond boy veer to meet her. She swerved. Something hit her back, hard.

Without thinking, she reached for the wound. Blood stained her hands. Still, she pressed forward. She ducked another blow, her head spinning with the effort. She couldn't out run them forever.

But stopping was not an option. Ivindor was full of raiders, and these men were out for her blood. It was either run or be killed. She spotted a narrow trail off to her left and spun into it, her feet slipping on mud. A branch tore at her hair. She felt it scrap against her cheek.

The path widened suddenly, and she darted across the glen. A doe looked up from the grass, chewing slowly as it watched her. She scurried past it.

"This way!" A shout from behind her spurred her on. The men were gaining. She heard their feet slap against the dust. Another trail forked off to the right, and she crashed through a pile of brambles as she raced towards it. Her feet hit solid ground. She took off.

Her breath was coming in ragged gasps now. She turned her gaze forward. At the end of the trail, she saw the glisten of river water. She pounded onto the beach. The stones grabbed at her toes. Even here, nature was against her.

The water was cool against her skin. She plowed into the river, her hands splashing in the current. The men shouted a warning. She heard something dive into the water behind her.

She whirled. The man was crashing towards her, sending up a spray of white foam. She saw Carn on the beach. He dodged the blond boy and twisted towards the water. Another man was there to catch him. He struggled, but the arms were strong. Carn was caught fast by the enemy.

Alina did not think. Within seconds, she was back on the beach, leaving her swimming pursuer far behind. She whipped the water from her eyes. A man dove for her. She step sided him. Her hands found a heavy stone as she scrambled up the bank. She hefted it. It thudded against the blond boy's head.

She watched him fall. Carn took the opportunity to break away, and he raced towards her. Taking her hand, he dragged her back to the water. "Swim!"

She did as she was told. Her arms spun wildly against the waves. Her feet kicked flurries of spray into the air. It didn't take as long as she expected for them to reach the opposite shore.

Alina waded onto the bank. Beside her, Carn gulped down air. His wet hair streamed water into his face. She shook the dampness from her own hair. Safe.

"Alina!" She heard the warning a moment too late. Hands grabbed at her arms, spinning her back towards the rivers. The man was huge, and his arms bulged as he fought for control. She felt a knife press against her throat.

She froze. Beside her, Carn did the same. He whimpered.

The man laughed. "Give it up, kid." He yanked the two coremen together. His companions grinned.

"Tie them up." The blond boy staggered from the water. He clutched at his head. It was with some satisfaction that Alina saw a welt rising there.

She felt a rope being pulled tight around her wrists. She kicked out, hard. The man grunted, but the bonds were tied.

Another man threw a loop around her feet. The rope burned against her ankles. Escape was now impossible. Alina wobbled and fell to the ground. Her body ached from where she hit the stones.

Carn was thrown loosely beside her. She tried to catch his eye. "If we can get to the tunnels," she hissed.

He shook his head. "We'll never make it!" He gulped down the rest of fear. She saw the knife wound on his throat gape like a fish. "Stay quiet. Once they see we don't have anything—"

"Silence!" The man, panting hard, leaned against a tree. He glared at them and wiped the sweat from his brow. His sword dripped water onto the sun-baked beach.

He dried the sword on a bit of dry clothing. "Gods. This is just what we needed." He strode over to where Alina and Carn lay. His foot connected with Carn's ribs. Alina heard her friend gasp. "We don't have time for this."

The blond boy smiled. Alina shivered. "I say we kill them. Now."

Another man shook his head. "You heard what Alvardine said. All intruders are to be brought back. Let the elf deal with them."

"He'll let them off." He clutched at his golden hair, rubbing the spot where Alina's stone had hit. "Kill them. No one will ever know."

The man frowned. "We can't do that, Leif. What if they're—"

"What if they're what? They're spies. We all know the punishment for that," the boy called Leif growled. He slid his sword from his sheath. "We're on a time budget here." He took a step forward.

Alina couldn't tear her eyes from the blade. The metal glinted with water and sunlight. He shifted the hilt in his grasp, and the tip slid closer to Alina's throat.

"Leif!"

"If you're such a wimp, you can go wait with the horses." Leif took another step forward. He raised his eyebrows. "All of you. This won't take long."

The man seemed about to protest, but his companions nodded. They glanced at the captives. One sheathed his sword. He headed towards the river, wading until the water was up to his waist. He began to swim with long, clean strokes. The others followed him.

Leif watched them go. When the last man had reached the opposite shore, he turned back to Alina. His sword quivered. The tip traced the underside of her cheek.

She shuddered. The metal was cold against her skin, and she felt the blade rip several strands of hair. She closed her eyes. Better to face death without the distractions of the outside world.

"No!" Carn squirmed beside her. He whispered something in Alina's ear, but she couldn't tell what. She wished he would be quiet. There was nothing he could do.

The blade shifted, and Alina felt it leave her neck. Carn hissed.

"I'll just take care of you first, then," Leif growled.

"No." The voice was firm. Carn stiffened against her shoulder. She snapped her eyes open, staring around wildly for the stranger.

"Put the sword down, Leif." The man slipped silently onto the beach. He scanned the scene with silver eyes. His black hair swung loosely against his high cheekbones.

Alina sucked in a deep breath. She watched as Leif sheathed his sword before turning her attention back to the newcomer. His lithe body shifted as he gazed down at the captives. He pushed his green cloak away from his face. One thing was for certain. The elf was not feeling merciful.

3

The campfire swirled in the wind. He watched the sparks rise into the night sky, stars ascending to the heavens. Smoke drifted across his face.

He turned away. The night was cool against his skin, but he didn't notice. Even the dew, just forming like crystals on the grass blades, was inconsequential. The Raven King was slipping out of his grasp.

No. He wouldn't let that happen. They needed the Raven King, needed him more than anyone could know. Without the Raven King, all would fail. Without the Raven King, they were stuck. He watched the cool air float from the girl's mouth.

Killing them wasn't an option. He wouldn't have their blood on his hands, even though it would save time. Alvardine wasn't a murderer. Not if he could help it.

He stood, stretching beneath the wool of his cloak. That still left the Raven King. The man would need to be found, and soon, before things got out of hand. King Rolan was on the move.

He sighed. Twenty-seven years ago, he never would have dreamed this would happen. His best friend had turned enemy, and the only thing to stop him was a legend. A mere legend, taken from a book in the school library. The prophecy of the Raven King was slowly coming true.

But Rolan wasn't supposed to be on the receiving end. Alvardine still couldn't get over that fact, though he had had twenty-seven years to get used to it. King Rolan would be destroyed.

He strode around the campfire, crossing to where the captives slept. The girl was silent, her face obscured by her cloak. The boy, however, rumbled with snores. Alvardine smiled softly. They looked like children.

No. He knew better than that. They were coremen, not children. Shorter than most men, with agile bodies to squeeze into cracks, they looked like children. Except that they weren't.

He bent to tuck a stray hand beneath a blanket. The girl shifted, her black hair slipping over her closed eyes. He smiled.

"She's not a spy, you know."

Alvardine nodded. He turned to face the speaker, a young woman huddled inside a grey cloak. Her golden hair spilled out from a tight braid at the nape of her neck. "Neither is the boy."

The woman folded her arms across her chest. Her blue eyes glinted in the starlight. "So what are you going to do? We can't leave them here." She crouched beside the sleeping forms. Slowly, she drew the blanket up around Alina's chin. "And no matter what Leif says, you can't just kill them."

Alvardine nodded. "I know. Leif spoke in anger—even he doesn't think we should kill them."

Elewyn frowned. "Sometimes I don't understand him," she muttered. "What is he doing here in the first place? He joined so abruptly—"

"Oryth's doing. He likes the boy."

"Oryth? What does my father have to do with anything? He's just here because you're here. You know he doesn't believe in the Raven King."

"Shhh." Alvardine held up a hand, silencing her instantly. They both glanced at Alina and Carn, but neither stirred. They slept on, oblivious to the hushed voices above them."

"He doesn't believe in the Raven King," Elewyn continued in softer tones, "and you know it. He's here to support you." She stepped closer to Alvardine. "And we both know why you're here."

Alvardine grimaced. His face twitched, and for a moment his set face was broken. He reached for his pocket.

He pulled out a crumpled piece of parchment and unraveled it. A portrait stared back him, its paint cracked and worn. The woman's face was serene. Black hair was swept across her delicate brow. Clear grey eyes sparkled with a hint of blue. The woman's hands fluttered near the edge of the frame. Alvardine stroked their fluid lines.

Elewyn smiled. She watched as Alvardine's face calmed and his hands stilled. On one of his fingers, a single golden band spoke of his ties to the woman.

"Cere would have understood," she whispered to the elf.

"Would she? It's been seventeen years. She never even knew about the Raven King." He paused, sucking in a choking breath. "And now, well—"

A time will come in Ivindor
When rivers flow with blood.
And at this time, the Sacred Lore,
Will, torn, lie in the mud.

But from this dark shall come a light,
The Raven King, alone,
To lead the men, their king to smite,
And sit upon the throne.
Two times these words shall come to pass,
Two kings shall be removed.
The noble and his brother's mass,
Before the strife is soothed.

Elewyn waited for the last whispers of the prophecy to still. "It was enough, to know that you loved her."

"Was it? Sometimes, I wonder. Who would she have chosen, if she was given chance? Me, or Rolan?"

Alina's eyes snapped open. She shut them just as quickly, her heart pounding. Elewyn's touch had awoken her at first, but as she lay there, she couldn't help but overhear her captor's conversation. Carn had told her about King Rolan, and the devastation he had caused. The King hated the elves.

"Father says she didn't love Rolan. That it was obvious, back at the Academy. She chose you."

Alvadine bowed his head. His voice grated with emotion. "Even so. With Liam, I couldn't help it, and— Maybe neither were good enough for her."

Elewyn ignored this last comment. "Do you think there's hope?" She wasn't talking about Alvadine's wife.

"If we find the Raven King, maybe. It all depends." He watched as Oryth's form shifted in the shadows.

The old man stepped lightly to crouch beside his friend. His white beard caught in the campfire smoke, and for a second, Alina thought he had crept too close to the flames. She froze. If they discovered her eavesdropping— No. She wouldn't think about it.

"The Raven King is too old to lead a war," Oryth whispered. "He wasn't young the first time."

"What, when he overthrew the elves? Age doesn't matter. He's the Raven King. The Gods are with him." Elewyn stared at her father. "The question is: will he be willing to go against everything he's worked to do? He spent years trying to pull the elves from their thrones and put the humans in their place. Will he really want to undo that?"

"It doesn't matter what he wants. He was given a duty by the Gods, and King Rolan must be overthrown."

Alina bit her lip. The last time the Raven King had acted, things had been bad in Ivindor. The elves had forgotten their duty to the Gods. Now, with Rolan making the same mistake, she was sure the same group would act. "The Wanderers," she mouthed to herself. She clenched her jaw. These were rebels; they would not be forgiving to her or Carn.

"So what will you do with them?" Elewyn's eye had been drawn by Alina's sudden movement. She watched the girl, but Alina let out a slight snore, she turned back to Alvardine. You can't kill them.

"And you can't just leave them here, if they really are spies." Oryth glared at his daughter. She lowered her gaze.

"I don't know. We can't go back to the Wanderings and leave them with Rohananon. Maybe Leif could take them back?"

"And 'accidentally' kill them on the way? I don't think so."

"Well, what do you propose, Elewyn? That we accept them into our midst?"

"Yes." Alina's voice rang out from the shadows. She stepped into the firelight. "King Rolan—he has red hair."

36

Her voice quavered, but she held firm.

Alvardine nodded cautiously. "Red hair is uncommon in Ivindor. I've only known one family to posses it."

His words only confirmed what Alina had been thinking. She thought back to her discovery of the ruined city, and the red haired man that had walked its streets. Then the image of the dying boy came to her unbidden. She hardened her resolve. "I want to find the Raven King."

4

Leif jerked awake. His blond hair was mussed from sleep, but his eyes were wide and angry. He stood, throwing his hand onto the hilt of his sword. The naked blade flashed in the moonlight. "Alvardine!"

The elf smiled. He paced in front of the fire, his cloak swaying dangerously close to the embers. "It's your choice."

Alina breathed a sigh of relief. She stood up to face her tormentors. At her side, Carn pulled himself upright. His face was pale.

"You must understand, Leif. This is the only option."

"Apart from the logical. I say we kill them now!" Leif reached for his sword.

"No!" Alvardine stayed his hand. "We can use them. You have to know what you're getting into, though," he said to Alina. "Both of you. Sir Alleyn won't come willingly."

Alina nodded. She was startled to hear Alvadine use the Raven King's real name, but she hid her surprise. "Why does it have to be the same Raven King? You say that he's old—"

"The Gods chose him." Leif brushed Alvardine aside, coming to stand in front of Alina. "I wouldn't expect you to understand.

Alina bristled. "The Gods can choose again—"

"And they will." Alvardine sighed heavily. "Don't you think I've thought of this? Even the prophecy suggests it. 'Two times these words will come to pass.' The first time was when Sir Alleyn overthrew King Loren, the last of the elven kings. Now it has to happen again, but this time with King Rolan. Sir Alleyn can't be expected to serve twice in the same lifetime."

"So why doesn't one of us become the Raven King and be done with it?" Alina asked.

"Because it's not our choice. The only people with the power to decide on the next Raven King are the Gods, and they speak to the Raven King alone. We're going to need to find him if we want to know his successor."

Alina nodded. She watched as Alvardine stirred up the fire, sending sparks shooting into the air. They danced away on the fingers of the wind.

"They still can't come," Leif announced, striding forward. He shook himself awake, and his hair fell neatly into place. His footsteps were loud against Alina's ears. "They're spies."

"Leif," Elewyn reproached. She gaze the boy a chastising glare. He sneered back at her. She tossed her head. "Alvardine doesn't think so."

"Alvardine is a fool." Leif took a step forward, positioning himself so that he stood directly over Alina. Even though his back was turned, Alina felt a glimmer of terror rise to her throat.

"We can't trust them. Not now, not ever. We were better off killing them in the first place. Now," he growled, stepping backwards, "we'll have to kill them without any light. After *he's* fed them!" His foot slipped over Alina's hand. She gasped as he pressed down.

"I don't know about that, Leif." A hunched shadow

appeared from the other side of the fire. The man's cloak billowed around him.

Alvardine reached for his sword.

The man stepped into the firelight. "Alvardine trusts them. That should be good enough for you."

Alvardine laughed. He relaxed his grip. "Oryth, my friend! Gods, you gave me a scare!"

Oryth smiled. He pulled his hood down, revealing his grizzled white hair. A snowy beard wagged down the front of his chest, nearly obscuring his twinkling blue eyes. His fingers twitched on his staff. "So the newcomers are welcome. Good. I was beginning to worry that our manners were going downhill."

Leif glared at him. "That doesn't fix anything, old man. We cannot bring them with us."

"And why not?" Elewyn asked. "They don't seem like spies to me. And besides. We don't even know if the boy wants to come."

All eyes turned to Carn. Alina shifted uncomfortably. Arie had died in just such a rebellion. When she left the Clan, Alina had sworn never to get involved. Now she wasn't so sure. The image of the dying boy flashed in her mind. She remembered the ruins of the city, and the red haired man. "We have nowhere else to go," she pushed out. "And the Raven King must be found." She glanced at Carn, who shrugged.

"Where Alina goes, I follow."

"Then that's settled!" Oryth clapped his hands together. "Alina and Carn come with us!"

Elewyn laughed. "Gods! We were needing a couple more hands." She reached for a sack at her feet. The buckles clanked together as she rummaged in its depths. When she emerged, she clutched several biscuits in her breast. She handed them out to Alina and Carn.

Alina bit into the flaky bread. Her stomach rumbled hungrily, and her first food in days lay rich upon her tongue. She closed her eyes, trying to savor the flavor.

"It is not settled, Oryth." Leif's voice was an unpleasant interruption. She swallowed the biscuit with a lump of air, grimacing.

"I still don't trust them. And to make matters worse, just look at them. No weapons! Alvardine, you know we don't have enough swords to just hand them out."

The elf nodded indulgently. "Doubtless we can pick some up in Falator."

"In Falator?" Leif stamped his foot. "We don't have any money! Or have you forgotten spending it?"

Elewyn glared at him. She took back the biscuit she was offering him. "We'll scrounge something up."

"We always scrounge something up. Even in the Wanderings, we always scrounged something up. But what if this time we can't? There aren't any back ups here, Elewyn."

"Enough, Leif." Alvardine set his biscuit aside. He motioned to the young man. "Just tell us. What do you have in mind?"

"We need horses."

"We have enough extra pack animals."

"Then the swords." He seized on the idea. "I propose an arms raid. Daedalyus isn't far from here, and its full of smithies. There's got to be thousands of extra swords there!"

"Daedalyus is also swarming with Black Knights." Alvardine stretched, reaching for his biscuit once again. "King Rolan's patrol men," he explained to Alina and Carn. "Reckon you've heard of them."

Alina nodded. She had grown up listening to stories about the fearsome warriors. Mothers in the Clan used them as a sort of boogie man, scaring their children to sleep at night. Once Arie had even dressed up like one. Alina had been scared out of her wits.

"Very well. We'll raid Daedalyus." Alvardine shook his head. "It shouldn't be too much of a problem, not with all of us working together."

"Wrong," Leif interjected. "We're not all going. Just Alina and Carn. They need to prove themselves."

"You go too far!" Alvardine jerked upright. His eyes flashed. "Remember, Leif, who is head of this company!"

Leif blushed scarlet. He lowered his gaze, but he held firm. Slowly, he raised his eyes to meet Alvardine's. "We need to know who they are."

"I trust them!"

"And I don't!" He straightened himself, staring down Alvardine. "We need to know."

For a moment, it looked like the two were going to draw their swords. They glared at each other, Alvardine a good six inches taller than Leif. The boy narrowed his eyes.

Alina gagged on a bit of biscuit. This wasn't working out at all how she had planned. Volunteering had seemed like a good idea at the time. It was either accompany the group on the search for the Raven King, or likely face death. There was no two ways about it. Now, she wasn't so sure. An arms raid didn't sound like the safest option.

"Fine." Alvardine broke the long silence. "Alina and Carn will go to Daedalyus. But I'm going with them. Leif, I'm sure you'll agree. They need looking after."

Alina frowned. She didn't like the sound of this one bit. If she didn't know any better, she would have thought that Daedalyus was just an excuse for getting rid of them. But of course, that wasn't true at all.

5

Alina brushed aside the tattered hem of her cloak. The horse Alvardine had found her to ride was not an intelligent beast. Alvardine called him Mandan, after a hero in the Cavern Wars, but the horse hardly lived up to his namesake. He was a dull animal, with a dusty coat of spattered tan. His mane looked like it had been hacked with a dull knife. The edges wobbled as he walked, and the black strands floated in uneven heaps. He dragged his feet against the trail.

Alina flicked the reins. The leather straps still felt uncomfortable in her hands; there had been no horses in the Clan. She bit her lip. When she had volunteered, she hadn't realized that they would be traveling by horse. She braced herself against another jolting step. The pain was enough to make her regret her decision.

No. She shook her head. *I volunteered for this journey. There's no turning back.* She glanced behind her at the darkness, as if she was expecting to see the comforting lights of the Wanderings there. Instead, the gloom of early morning filtered through the pressing trees.

She didn't like to admit it, but the darkness scared her. It was a different sort of darkness than in the Underworld; this air had tasted light, and craved the glow of the sun.

Alina pressed her feet to Mandan's flanks. The horse snorted under the new pressure, stepping lightly over a rotting log. Alina bit her lip. The air sucked at her skin, and she shivered.

Two horses trotted along the path in front of her. Carn's stocky figure bounced high on the back of a pony, Alvardine a slender shadow beside him. The elf shifted atop his painted mount. In the dim lighting, he looked like some strange creature, half man, half horse. Alina shuddered, and this time it was not from the cold. Half demons were cursed were by Nora, the greatest Goddess of all.

She lifted her hand to her forehead and traced the bridge of her nose with her middle finger. The God were not to be crossed, even in the imagination. Her mother had told her so, when she was just a little girl.

Five Gods of Ivindor. She ticked them off slowly in her head, letting each name wash the fear from her body. *Nora, Great Goddess, and her king, Zyl. Soul, daughter of the underworld God, Ragor. Cyn, the last of the Gods. The God of fire, the God of death.* She shuddered again, retracing the bridge of her nose with her finger. Normally, the Gods weren't named separately. They were a team, the body of a parent spirit. Only Nora, Cyn, and Ragor, siblings at birth, were ever worshiped separately.

She paused at this. Her fingers tapped against the reins as she counted off the days. Midwinter was the celebration of Cyn; the men of the Clan had feasted that day. The celebration of Nora was approaching rapidly. At mid-summer, all of Ivindor would lay out a meal fit for the Gods themselves.

Alina licked her lips at the thought. There would be roast haunches of deer, acorn pies, and her favorite, pastries of honey. The women would spend days hunting for the hives, straining away the comb, and baking. Alina had helped with the preparations the year before, though the heat of the ovens had nearly made her faint.

Of course, the women would cook *lorkats* as well. The morning of the celebration, boys would hurry to the ponds. Every fish in the area would be caught, scaled, and sprinkled with salt. The raw fish would be stuffed into bread and served whole. Alina's stomach turned over at this. She had always hated the dish, even though it was Carn's favorite.

And I'll be gone this year. She didn't pause to remember that she would be gone every year, that she would never taste lorkats again. Not that she would mind, but . . .

She strained to see up the trail. Mandan had fallen far behind the others, and she could no longer see the lantern. Carn was slipping through her grasp. Not even the pungent order of lorkats could lure him back now.

Don't be silly, she told herself. She dug her heels into Mandan's ribs, and the horse jumped ahead. He broke into a limping trot, each step throwing Alina into the saddlebags behind her. She gritted her teeth and pressed on.

Carn's voice drifted towards her. She leaned forward. Mandan responded to her movement, lengthening his stride into a canter. She threw herself upright. The horse slowed as he reached the other horses, grunting a greeting to his companions. Alina awkwardly patted his neck.

"And so I said: 'what do you mean my goat? I ate 'im for supper two nights ago!'" Carn's voice echoed against the silence of the trees. He bent over in fits of laughter. Alvardine chuckled appreciatively.

"Very funny. You've got a future as a story teller, young

man." Alvardine patted the flanks of his mount reassuringly. He had dressed himself that morning in soft silks and a thick elven traveling cloak, all of dark coloring, so that he was almost invisible atop the soot rubbed coat of his stead. He hadn't bothered to saddle or rein Haranee, in the traditional habits of the elves, preferring to feel her muscles rippling along her back. The mare moved gracefully and without hesitation—she trusted Alvardine. The two had ridden together since Haranee was just a filly, and both were aware of the other's thoughts. It was as if they were interconnected, the way Haranee turned without being told to, speeding up and slowing down without a single signal. She was perhaps the most beautiful creature Alina had ever seen.

Mandan moved stubbornly between Haranee and Siv, Carn's chestnut mare. Alina nodded approvingly. This way, she was shielded from the all-encompassing darkness. Carn had told her stories of the creatures of the forest, and none were beasts that Alina had any desire to meet.

"Hey. You decided to catch up to us." Carn cast a grin in her direction. He slipped out from under his hood. "Took you long enough. What happened?"

"Mandan isn't one for speed."

Alvardine glanced at the gelding with a knowing smile. "Oh, he's fast enough when he feels up to it. I expect he wasn't too excited about being woken up at two this morning to go on our little excursion. Mandan used to be a race horse in his prime."

"Really?" Both Carn and Alina looked up in surprise. How had the Wanderers managed to get their hands on a retired racehorse?

"Yes. Mandan was King Rolan's favorite horse. He won more than enough races for the King, some against

Wanderer horses, for money, so we 'confiscated' him. He's made us a wonderful packhorse."

"It's a shame," Carn said. He reached over to scratch the horse's ears affectionately. "To see such a talented horse put to waste like this. But it's good to know that Alina can get away if she needs to. Especially with Daedalyus ahead."

Alina nodded gratefully. She had been trying not to think about the raid. Her stomach clenched. When she spoke, her voice quivered, but she held firm. "Daedalyus. Why would Rolan name it Daedalyus? It's a strange name."

"A strange name for a strange place. It's been called Daedalyus for centuries, since before Rolan came to power. I can remember when I was a little boy; my father used to take me there . . . " He trailed off. "Rolan uses it as a massive smithy. There are furnaces all over the city, and the Knights keep them fired day and night. Daedalyus is the weapon factory of Ivindor."

"Which is why we're raiding it," Carn noted. "At least its not called Fromth. That's the goblin name for sewage pit!" He let out a nervous laugh.

"There would be no reason for Rolan to name a camp 'Sewage Pit' . . . " Alina reproved.

"You'd be surprised, Alina. Daedalyus stinks from here to the heavens. Those Black Knights aren't too fond of bathing!" Alvardine nudged away Siv's inquisitive nose with a gentle a hand. Haranee was known for her dislike of close contact with any creature, both man and horse. Being this close to Siv and Mandan was making her nervous; Alvardine was quite aware of her rolling eyes and impatient snorts. He had to be. He was the only person Haranee would let close enough to ride, and he had to be constantly aware of their surroundings. One wrong move by either of his companions could send Haranee into a fit of flailing rage.

The trio rode on in silence, confronted by the fluttering of the leaves. Overhead, the wind howled like a pack of wolves, but it was louder and more chilling than any Alina had ever heard. Mandan stumbled along as if he was blind. Alina had to correct his course every few moments to avoid bumping into Haranee or tripping over a cliff. Her eyes drooped despite her pattering heart. She felt herself sliding off of Mandan, and shifted to correct it. Her early start that morning was beginning to take its toll.

Alvardine rode ahead of the two coremen, his hands caressing the silken fur of Haranee with exaggerated movements. He hadn't been especially eager to accompany Carn and Alina on their raid of Daedalyus, and he always was reluctant about starting a journey, but now that there was no turning back, he was quite pleased to be on horseback once more. Horses were a comfort from earlier days.

He sighed, bracing himself as Haranee dipped under an overhanging branch. The horse fidgeted under his touch, feeling the anxiety in the flex of his hips. He laid a hand on her neck to comfort her, forcing himself to think of anything but the raid ahead. Seventeen years among the Wanderers had done nothing to calm his nerves.

A pace behind him, Alina twisted to look at Carn. He had pushed his hood back, letting the light rain condense on his cheeks. His cropped hair hung in limp clumps. Alina resisted the urge to smooth out the tangles. Carn's knuckles were white as they gripped the reins, and his blue eyes scanned the trail ahead. *Even Carn is nervous.*

She felt the hairs on the back of her neck stand on end. Carn was her rock, her steady island when the surrounding waters got choppy. She had never known him to grow anxious, though there had been plenty of opportunities in their sixteen years of friendship. She bit her lip, hard enough so that a drop of blood colored the saliva in her mouth. *Carn's never scared. Even when Isen was about to kill me, he knew what to do. And now. . .* She stole another glance. Carn rode stiffly beside her, his face frozen and expressionless. She knew him well enough to know recognize his emotions. *If Carn's nervous, then I should be collapsing of fear.*

Yet, her body felt strangely absent of emotion. Warmth tingled in every corner of her body, releasing her clenched stomach. Her face felt flushed with blood, and below her, Mandan crept slowly forward. She could no longer feel his halting steps forcing the saddlebags into her ribs.

She settled back for the long haul. Daedalyus was a good day's ride away, and if Alvardine's plan went accordingly, they would spend the night in the forest. She tucked a strand of dark hair behind her ear.

Alina was small, even for a coreman, but her slender frame was almost completely obscured by her shapeless cloak. Piercing black eyes stared determinedly from beneath her hood. In the light, they would glow an uneven gray. Alina had always liked her eyes. Carn said that they were her best feature. For the moment, though, she had to fight to keep them open.

She turned her attention to the passing trees. The sun had begun to rise in the east, and its cold morning rays echoed against the branches. Shadows danced in the undergrowth. She watched as the darkness swirled around her. Her head felt surprising heavy. A branch cracked. She spun, and there he was.

He leaned against a young sapling, studying her as she rode. His black armor flashed the sunlight into her eyes, and she had to squint to see him. A shadow fell across his face, and her sight narrowed in on his hair. Bright red, the color of fresh blood. A sword flicked into view. She started in horror, remembering how the same blade had pierced the boy's flesh, back in the ruins of Ferrington. It swung towards her. Behind it, the red hair sprung into flame.

The image changed. The man disappeared, replaced by a gangly boy of twenty. Dark hair swung to shoulder length as he bounded forward. His black eyes twinkled mischievously. His hand went to his belt, and she saw a curved dagger tucked within its folds. She watched as he pulled out it. The blade glowed a faint pink.

"Arie," she whispered. Her hand extended towards him, but the boy laughed. He held the dagger out of reach, and she saw the fierceness of his gaze. He stared into the distance. She watched as his expression went slack.

She spun, following his line of sight. A hobbled man stood beneath a rowan tree, his hair bleached white with age. His cloak swirled around him. The dark fabric flickered with silver embroidery. The man reached into its depths and suddenly all she saw was his hands, pulling forth a moonlit sword. The blade glistened with morning dew, and she noticed the engraving in the steel. She leaned closer, catching a glimpse of a raven on the hilt. Then the cloak shifted, and the fabric washed over the blade. The last vestiges of the dream dissipated into darkness.

"You think she'll wake up in time?" The voice drifted into the black mist. Hazily, Alina thought she recognized the speaker, but she couldn't be sure. She tried to remember, but the air around her was thick. She gave up, laying back into the comforting arms of sleep.

"We can't wait much longer." The voice interrupted her once more. She rolled over, hoping that the person would leave. It was so peaceful here, in the land of dreams. But the voice refused her silent plea. "We could just leave her here."

That was it. She blinked, and slowly the world swam into view. She was lying on her back, staring up at the crisp blueness of the sky. A few tree branches swayed overhead. Somewhere in the distance, a horse snorted. She heard it rip its teeth into the grass. Her arm ached, and she became aware that she was lying on top of it. She shifted her weight.

"That's the ticket." She twisted her head. Carn was staring down at her, his face flushed with concern. He grinned, and his hand snaked towards her. She took the water bag gratefully. The liquid was cool against her throat.

"We weren't really going to leave you." She rolled her head back towards Carn. He winked at her, and then frowned. "I'm sorry that's not warm milk," he said, nodding towards the water. "There's none in the packs."

Alina nodded. Carn was being silly, but her mouth still watered for the taste of hot cream. Her mother had always prepared the drink for her when she was little. It helped her wake up in the mornings. She closed her eyes and tried to pretend that the water was thick and steamy sliding down her throat. It didn't work.

She opened her eyes. Alvardine came into view, settled off to the side. He sat cross-legged, fussing with something in his lap. His fingers flicked in and out of the yarn as he spun the sock into his lap. She watched as the garment emerged, stitch-by-stitch. "I didn't know you could knit."

Alvardine glanced at her. "Sit up. It will help."

Alina pressed her palms into the ground. Her head whirled, but in the end, she had to agree with Alvardine: sitting up did help. She plucked a piece of grass from her dress. "I fell off, didn't I?" She didn't need Carn to figure out the answer. "The horse. I fell asleep."

She twirled the stalk of grass in her fingers. Her face flushed red in embarrassment. "Sorry."

Carn shook his head. "You mean, why did you fall asleep when the rest of us didn't." He pulled the piece of grass from her hand and tossed it aside. "We're not in the Clan anymore. A lot has happened in the past week, what with your banishment, watching that boy get killed, and being caught by the Wanderers. And you did just volunteer your life to a cause you know nothing about." He watched Alina carefully, but her face didn't change expression. "You're still grieving. Arie—"

Alina blanched. She tore a tuft of grass out of the ground and scattered it to the breeze. "I don't want to talk about it."

"Sorry," Carn amended. "So you fainted. Or fell asleep. We did get up early this morning, way before the crack of dawn."

She managed a small smile.

"It'll work out anyway. Alvardine and I were talking. He doesn't think we would have made Daedalyus before sunrise even if you hadn't fainted. We would have been caught on the outskirts of the city with nowhere to hide. So really, you just saved us a lot of trouble."

Alina grimaced. "We're still raiding the city?"

Alvardine tossed set his knitting down in his lap. He

looked up, catching Alina and Carn's eyes. "We'll take the city by nightfall. Until then . . . " He shrugged, holding up his knitting. "As Leif likes to say, we'll just 'hang out.'"

Alina grinned at the thought. She couldn't imagine Leif using the modern term. He was only a year younger than her, but still. He seemed to have so much power. She shook her head. There was obviously quite a bit about Leif that she didn't know.

She shrugged this off. Wobbling to her feet, she found herself in a small clearing, more of a gap between the overhanging branches than a meadow. The road traced a faint outline behind the overgrown brush. A cluster of young saplings bent under the weight of a fallen branch, and she drowsily moved to relieve them. Birds twittered their warning calls as they darted away from the new threat. A young stag blinked at her from the gloom of the forest. She held her breath as he stalked away, his noble head held high. The forest was at peace with the newcomers, and it was hard to imagine that troops of Black Knights marched only miles away.

She shook her head, trying to clear her thoughts of the dark mists that swirled at the edges of her mind. The forest wasn't untouched. She could see that now, in the sharp angles of the fallen trees. Strange abrasions marred the bark of the trunks, as if something very large and metal coated had rubbed against them. The animals that she saw were the last in the forest, the survivors of years of hunting. She heard the stag crash in the bushes as he leapt away. The last of her dream dissipated, and she looked out over the landscape with fresh eyes.

Ivindor had changed greatly since she had last come to the surface, when a young girl could wander the hills without fear of kidnap. The earth had been roughly shaken from its peaceful slumber by a series of violent earthquakes. What had once been a quiet river valley was now a gaping canyon, jagged teeth lining its edge so that it resembled a dragon's mouth. Streams crashed over boulders in roaring waterfalls. The forests were looming caves full of monstrous beasts. The People of the Faeries no longer darted between the trees or hid beneath the petals of flowers. They had once been a numerous race, but Alina failed to see a single one on the edge of the clearing. There were no pixies in the wild roses, nor were there garden elves peering out from behind the fallen logs. Everything was silent and still, lost in the haunting depths of King Rolan's reign.

The king had yet to organize an attack against any other than the elves, but the Wanderers were sure that it wouldn't be long. Everyone in the Wanderers, except for Alvardine, that is. Even as the Black Knights swept through the countryside, destroying all in their path, both humans and elves alike, Alvardine maintained that Rolan's grudge was against the elves, and no one else. Perhaps the elf knew something that the others didn't. After all, he had been trained in the finest school in Ivindor. But as Alina stared at the mangled land, she couldn't help but think that he was mistaken. The people of Ivindor had disappeared. The Black Knights, under Rolan's command, were ruthless in their quest for widespread genocide. A depressing darkness had settled over the kingdom.

Alina fell to her knees. She couldn't remember a time when Ivindor had been at peace, but that fact drifted away. She had survived sixteen years with Isen breathing down her back. She would survive the raid into Daedalyus. Her fingers twitched against her thigh as she settled into the ground. The Gods would continue to wreck havoc on Ivindor, but for the moment, she was content to wait.

Carn crept slowly in the shadows of the evening. One hand dragged against the stone wall, feeling its comforting coolness at the tips of its fingers. His other hand picked nervously at his travel stained clothes. Where was Alvardine? The elf had said he would meet him here, on the right hand side of the gate out of Daedalyus. Was there another gate? In his mind's eye, he searched the map that Alvardine had shown him earlier. *No. Just one gate. So where is he?* His eyes flicked towards the stream of people entering and leaving the city. It was market day, so crowd was large and noisy. He blinked at the unfamiliar faces.

Behind him staggered a drunken beggar woman, her cloths all in a tatter, her head covered by a ratty shawl. She had been following him all morning long, but he didn't mind. The woman didn't talk much, and her presence was a comfort to him in this strange place.

She scowled when he paused to step over the flea bitten legs of a beggar man, lost in the depths of a drunken sleep. "Disgusting. Utterly disgusting." Alina's voice sounded hollow beneath the beggar woman's clothes. "You'd think these people would show some concern for their health!"

"Shhhh! You'll give it away! You're one of them, remember?" Carn stooped over the man, the better to see his true condition. "Besides, I don't think many people here have much of chance to purge themselves . . . Here, this one's out cold. He won't be much help."

Alina tugged her skirts out of the way as she stepped

over the sprawled legs. "What do you think happened to him?"

"Happened to him? Alina, this isn't a murder mystery! He's drunk. Stoned. Nothing happened to him!" Carn motioned vigorously for her to continue on. "We don't have much time. Alvardine said he'd meet us here before the night market started, and the baker's wife is already setting up her booth. Keep your eyes open."

"Keep *my* eyes open! That's your job! I don't have to do anything until Alvardine gets here—he said so." She paused long enough for a sigh to escape from Carn's tight lips. "Where is he?"

"No idea," Carn said roughly. "Come on, let's get going."

They moved silently on to the next line of sleeping men and women, their breath congesting the putrid air. *How can people live like this?* Alina kicked away a clump of feces, nauseated. Her eyes caught the sight of a young family huddled together at her feet. Three helpless children, starving to death, and their parents even more emaciated because they had given up all of their food to the son and daughters. The father had draped his cloak over the shrunken body of his son, but the boy still shivered uncontrollably. Tears rolled down his sisters' cheeks as they slept on, completely unaware of the young man and woman that passed by their poverty stricken figures.

A little ways beyond the family lay a still form swathed in rags. The sheet covering his face had been blown away, and Alina recognized the young boy's twin, eyes clouded and vacant like the eyes of Alina's siblings after the plague had passed over them—lifeless. And beside him was another body, and another, all covered with rags. A grandmother prayed over the skeleton of her granddaughter. She glanced up as Alina passed, but it was with sudden horror that Alina drew back, for the old woman's eyes were almost as vacant as her grandchild's.

A warm hand clasped Alina's shoulder briefly. "And now you see what we are up against. These people are just the tip of the iceberg of King Rolan's reign." Alvardine led them both away from the makeshift cemetery. "Don't cry, Alina. I have seen terrible things in my lifetime, but I'm afraid that you will be exposed to much worse. These things will only get harder to look upon as we journey closer to Twedrig and Rolan's palace, but we have to continue. That little boy back there, his family, the grandmother—they all depend upon us succeeding." He looked at her strangely for a moment. "I must admit, I wasn't quite sure why you agreed so suddenly to join us. I wondered at your intentions, but I think I understand now." Alvardine nodded to himself before turning to Carn. "Have you found out anything yet?"

"Not much, just that Alina really likes to imagine all the worst case scenarios for every drunk we come across. You'd think she's a really pessimistic detective, the way she thinks!" He sobered at Alvardine's sharp look. "Other than that, no. We haven't come across anyone who's awake."

Alvardine smiled, his eyebrows rising in mock shock. "Good thing I had enough sense to round up our man. This, my friends, is Galore."

A man stepped out of the shadows. He was a tall, stocky man, perfectly capable of swinging a sword in the defense of his employer or hauling heavy trunks from the docks on the River into Daedalyus, which he did on a regular basis. His hands were callused from constant use, but his brain was weak and flabby. Alina doubted that he had ever been to school a day in his life, and his clothes showed it. He wore the greasy uniform of the dock staff, a black tunic tucked hastily into his trousers. He raised his hand solemnly in greeting.

"Galore will be watching our backs during the raid. His job often brings him to the storerooms, so he won't be questioned. Are we ready?"

"I suppose," Carn said at the same time Alina pulled up her hood. "Yes."

Galore and Alina set off at a rapid pace towards the storerooms stationed along the wall. They nodded curtly to each other as they approached and then wandered away. Alvardine and Carn followed, slowly making their way in the shadows to the back of the stone building.

"Sword out, Carn," Alvardine breathed. He had lent his dagger to the boy, but for a coreman the small blade was a thick sword. Carn drew the knife from its rawhide sheath at his waist. Alvardine loosened his own blade, Areslaine, in her scabbard, and then held a finger to his lips. "Watch."

Alina had taken her place. She was slumped over beside the door to the storeroom, seemingly drunk. Her stomach fluttered with butterflies. Galore sauntered by. *What did two fingers mean again? A guard or a captain?* She would have to act differently for each person, so it was important to know who was coming towards the storeroom.

"Drunks. They're everywhere! By the name of our lord, there seems to be more and more of them every day!" The officer paced beside Galore. "You be careful with that trunk, you hear? One slip and it'll be the worse for both of us."

"Yes sir."

"Say, I haven't seen this beggar woman before. Have you?"

"Yes sir."

The captain paid no attention to the large man's mumble. He nudged Alina with foot none too gently. "You. Who are you?"

"A drunk," Alina whispered. Now that the time for action was upon her, she was faint with dread. How in the world could she pull this off?

"'Yes, I can see that, but what's your name?"

"I am a drunk." Alina got wobbly to her feet, staggering against the wall as if to keep her balance.

"Name, girl!"

"Drunk . . ."

"A drunk without a name. Brilliant. Just like every other beggar in this hellhole. Well, I don't believe a word of it. In fact, I wouldn't be surprised if the next thing this girl tells me is that she's about to punch me over this wall," the captain said to Galore. "Can't trust drunks—"

"You're right, you can't!" Alina cried. Her fist flew through the air, landing with a heavy thunk on the captain's brow.

"See, I was right . . ." the captain mumbled. "Guards!"

Alvardine leapt into the scene. Areslaine gleamed in the air like she had been blessed by the gods themselves, swinging in and out of the sparse sunlight as her wielder rushed to block the gates. Behind him, Alina could make out the vibrating mass of over twenty guards rushing from their posts. Their feet kicked up dirt as they ran, so that by the time they reached the storeroom, no one could see a thing.

"Go on! Areslaine and I can hold them back. Get the trunk—inside, bright red! Galore, I've got a game for you."

"I've already killed two. That's more than you've gotten done."

"Right then. Rules, Galore, rules! First one to knock fifteen wins. Understood? Go!"

"Three . . . four!

"Ha, five!"

Alina grabbed Carn's hand and dragged him towards the storeroom. She shoved the door open, threw her friend in, and bolted the door behind them.

"Gods, Alina, if the rest of the journey towards the Raven King is like this, I don't know if I'm going to make it."

"Well, I don't think it's going to get any easier."

Inside the small storeroom, the air was choked with the overwhelming scents of pine trunks and oil paints. There was no light, as the guards normally left the door open while inside, which didn't help matters. It was warm and damp and sweaty and cramped and a whole lot of other things that could go on and on, but Alina thought the storerooms could be best described as the small chamber she had shared with her siblings before they had died. Both were claustrophobic spaces, but the storerooms were perhaps worse, sense it was obvious that they hadn't been opened in ages.

"Do you see it?" Carn's voice sounded eerily far away in the cramped quarters. He leaned forward. "I think I've got some sort of trunk here . . . "

"Ow! Carn, that was my foot!"

Carn put what he had though was the leg of a trunk stand down hastily. "Sorry. I thought—"

"Oh, never mind what you thought. Let's just find that trunk and get out of here!"

"And how are we supposed to do that, Alina? There's no light! I can't see a thing!"

"Wait a second—I've got some sort of chest here.

Alvardine described a crest to you. He said it would be inscribed on the lid. Would you be able to recognize it?"

"I think so." Carn groped about for the chest Alina had mentioned. His hands found the smooth wood of its lid and he stroked it softly. "No, this isn't it," he said as he felt the small indentations in the pine. "It's too small anyway."

"Alright, but at least we know how we're supposed to find this thing. Try another one."

They worked methodically through the stacks of crates and boxes, Carn feeling the wood until his fingers were riddled with splinters, and Alina straining her eyes so hard that her head ached. The figure of a roaring lion was burned into Carn's mind. He had been surprised when Alvardine showed him the symbol. After all, Rolan wasn't very lion-like. A vulture might have suited him better. Carn straightened up. His fingers throbbed.

"Carn!" Alina tugged on his arm. "Carn! Come on, we have to hurry!" From outside the oaken door came heavy thudding sounds. The wood crackled in the effort to keep the intruders out, and then buckled under the pressure. Glimmers of light shot into the dark room. Through the cracks, the friends caught the hurried movements of the guards outside. "This one! Is this one it?"

Carn brushed his fingers over it impatiently. "No. Another one! Quick!"

Alina tossed him yet another box. Its reddish wood shone in the streams of light like a beacon atop a lost hill, signaling for the entire world that it was here, that it had been found. Carn didn't even bother to feel for its identification engraving. He threw himself over the trunk and into the dark corners beyond. Alina followed, and they fumbled with the straps of the chest in the attempt to drag it away from the light that would surely enter at any second. Carn ripped his tattered cloak from his shoulders and threw the cloth over the chest moments before the door crumpled.

The huge silhouettes of the remaining guards filled the empty doorframe. Swords held high, they stepped over the threshold.

"We sure did a number on that giant outside!" The captain chuckled harshly. "Won't be getting up for a couple of hours at least, and by that time we'll have him and the other rascals safely locked up in prison."

"Got the other two cornered right pretty, haven't we boss? No way out of the storerooms. We did a good job, huh sir?" The guard standing closest to the captain shuffled his feet eagerly. His dark voice echoed in the small chamber.

"Well enough. I want the last of these vermin bagged before midday. Understand? Well, go on then. After them, man!" The captain strode away.

Alina and Carn drew back against the wall as the huge man strutted in. Both could hear the other's panting breath. Alina bit her lip. The guard was right—the storerooms were a dead end. And even if there had been back door, they wouldn't have been able to pry it open and sneak outside whilst dragging the huge crate of weapons behind them.

The guard was drawing closer to their meager hiding place. Trunks were lifted and shaken roughly for the loose rattling of someone hiding inside and then were tossed single handedly against the walls. Wood shattered, sending shrapnel flying in all directions. The guard threw aside Carn's cloak and hefted the crate of weapons in his huge palms, considering. He wound up for the throw like a stellar ball player. His eyes flicked along the wall, and then he found the corner.

"Hello," Alvardine cried. "You're in luck today, man. We have a special offer for you, and all you must do to win this special prize is answer one question. Now then, would you like one hit or two?" He raised a club menacingly. "Very well. Two clubbings on the house!"

The guard was felled after only one blow.

"Alina? Carn?" Alvardine crept into the storeroom cautiously, feeling his way along the structure's frame. Areslaine still glinted dangerously in his hand, and he didn't bother to sheath her blade. The need for speed was upon him now, brushing at his mind like a demon on the wing. It wouldn't be long before the remainders of the guards in Daedalyus became aware of their presence. Once the escaped captain bragged of his adventure to his fellow Black Knights, all hope would be lost: every Knight in the city would be on the alert. There would be no chance at all of escaping then.

Once Alina and Carn had ventured out from their tucked away hiding place, Alvardine quickly verified that the red trunk did in fact contain the weapons they were after. They dragged it through the dust to the edge of the wall and strapped a cloak over it. Even in the rapidly dimming light, a bright red trunk would be suspicious.

Alvardine splashed a bucket of water over Galore's still form. The giant moaned a little as the icy liquid dribbled down his chin, and Alvardine propped him up in the shadows of the wall. He brushed an oily lock of hair from Galore's brow with great tenderness, his fingers a gossamer touch on the waxy skin, like a breeze fluttering through the trees on its way to rest. A cool rush passed through his fingertips and into the temples of his friend. He smiled faintly when his patient struggled to sit. "Hush friend.

Sleep. May the world of dreams encase your mind and carry you far from this place, far into the realms of healing. May the elder gods watch over you."

Alina started. Alvardine didn't call people 'friend' very often. In fact, she had only heard him use the term once before, when he was talking about finding the Raven Song at the Academy. Even Oryth wasn't given the distinction. She stared at Galore. She couldn't imagine him in an elven school.

But 'friend.' Who had been with Alvardine when he discovered the Raven Song? Surely that person remembered the prophecy. They were probably engaged in the war. Somehow, Alina didn't think Alvardine's friend was a member of the Wanderers. She shrugged. She would have to keep a close eye on the elf as they traveled closer to Rolan's palace.

6

Oryth glanced up sharply from the twisted wood of his staff, blinking in the early morning light. His cloak was thrown loosely around his shoulders, still clinging to the fabric of his tunic as it had since Elewyn had placed it there. His teeth ached from clenching them against the chill of the night. Someone had drawn his silver hair away from his face and plaited it neatly across the smooth roundness of his head.

He rubbed the staff, deep in thought. It was a comforting object, passed down from his great great grandfather to his son, and so on and so on until his own father had laid the staff firmly in Oryth's then young hand. The wood, worn smooth by the generations of sweaty fingers that had handled it, was of the deepest, purest white imaginable, glowing as if lit with some mysterious light from within. At its tip was set a heavy black stone, a perfect sphere of empty space in the cluttered cupboard of Mother Iris's kitchen. His fingers brushed across its surface lightly, unconsciously, and then more purposefully. His thumb ground against the obsidian. The strange sensation of the energy gathering into his soul passed through him, his fingers aching with a sudden longing to clench themselves, as they always did when he brought the powers of the Realm of the Faeries onto mortal earth, but he ignored them both. He had spent too many years huddled in the corner of his master's storeroom to stop his work now, when it had only just begun.

His mind went blank. With a conscious effort, he drew himself into the Realm of the Faeries. The birthplace of all magic, it was a separate dimension, full of swirling mists and cloudy skies. Once this land had been open to any who wished to enter. Now only wizards could pass its heavily guarded borders, and even they couldn't bring their bodies. Oryth's shade floated freely in the Realm. The faerie creatures—the giants, ents, trolls, every creature that was only slightly human, breathed in the magic softly, staring as the wizard pushed his way into their world.

His feet touched down on a murky path. He strode ahead, eyes focused on the air in front of him. If he fell off this bridge between worlds now, he would be lost for eternity.

Finally, solid land was under his feet once more. He glared at the landscape, hard. Had it changed? He couldn't tell. It had been so long since he walked its soil. One thing was certain, however. The Realm of the Faeries was empty.

It had been this way since the elves left, banished by the Gods. The Realm had been torn apart by the action; creatures weren't meant to leave this place of magic. And when they left, the rest of the magical creatures went with them.

Now the elves wandered the lands of Ivindor. When they had first arrived, they had been welcomed with open arms, but as the centuries grew longer, the people turned away. Strange things happened around the elves. Men disappeared, and pure water was turned foul. Before they knew it, the people of Ivindor were under elven rule.

And so the people had revolted. One man in particular, Sir Alleyn, the Raven King, had led the charge. He seized power, and set about punishing the evil race of elves.

Oryth shook his head. Things had changed. Now the elves were peaceful folk, living in palaces high up in the forest canopy. More than once they had come to the aid of man. The elves had fought and died alongside the humans. Surely they had earned their forgiveness?

No. King Rolan continued to punish them. His men swept Ivindor, killing every magical creature in their path. No one was spared, not the nursing mothers, not the infants on their backs. The bodies were piled high. And up above, the Gods wrinkled their noses in distaste.

Oryth shoved his staff into the mists. The wood clanked heavily. He reached forward, fingers searching in the cloud in front of him. Suddenly, he caught hold, and a door swung open.

The Realm of the Faeries, gateway to all mortal lands. He looked down at the landscape, at its rolling hills and wide valleys. From here he could see all of Ivindor. The wind whipped his face.

He crouched down, straining to see through the haze. "Not here," he muttered. He reached out, and the landscape swiveled. A city came into focus. Its white towers stretched up towards him. Small figures could be seen walking its borders, clothed in shiny black metal.

"Black Knights."

He turned away from the city. *They should be here. . . ah, yes!* A small group of people was walking in the shadows of the forest. He zoomed in, and a dark elf came into view, along with a boy and a girl. *They've done it.*

He pulled back, throwing his vision out farther. The

three cities came into view. One, charred with rain and smoke, caught his gaze. "Finestal, the last city of the elves." He did not bother to zoom in; he had seen devastation enough. Finestal had been his home, and he had been there the night King Rolan attacked.

"Twedrig." He leaned out over the clouds, maneuvering the lands until the coast of Ivindor came into focus. Seawater splashed against rocky cliffs. Seagulls screeched as they dived towards the water. An island floated just off shore, its lands full to the brim with buildings. A palace stood on its hilltop, more Black Knights pacing its foundation.

With a nod, Oryth slammed the door shut. He had seen enough. King Rolan was on the move. His troops, a swarm of darkness, were gathering. His spirit flitted back to mortal earth.

He hit the stone pavement with exceptional force. Getting up, his hands rubbed at the soreness in his backside. Pedestrians blinked curiously from the edges of the street. Oryth grunted. He still hadn't gotten used to the non-magic folk. He grabbed his staff and slipped into the doorway behind him.

Mother Iris's kitchen was not a roomy space. Cluttered with pots and bits of moldy cheese, it appeared in every way to be the common home. Cupboards lined the back wall like a line of ragged soldiers—crooked and soiled. A cooking hearth littered the center floor with its wispy ashes. Holey curtains fluttered at the open windows.

The wizard nodded. "Very nice. Clean. Well executed.' He was not talking about the contents of the room. "Alright, out you come."

The cupboard farthest to the right creaked open. The hearth rose up for a moment as a trap door was briefly revealed. A rather large soup pot clattered when its occupants exited. All this happened at once, and in a few moments the entire company was assembled about the now blazing hearth. Potatoes, kept warm by their cloth wrappings, were passed out by a very smelly Leif (the butter churn, where he had hid, hadn't been cleaned since its last use). Elewyn started a kettle of water boiling at her feet as chatter filled the previously deserted room.

"It was good, wouldn't you say?" Leif grinned despite himself. "No warning."

Oyrth nodded. All morning, they had practiced hiding in case Black Knights invaded. The kitchen would not be able to withstand an attack. A few sword flings and the cupboards would fall off the walls.

Elewyn frowned at Leif. "I'm going to take a look around." She got briskly to her feet, tossing her grey traveling cloak well behind her in a sheet of fluttering cloth. Her hair fell in a thick wave just behind. Looking straight at Oryth, she left the room.

Outside, the girl stood on the rocky steps, breathing in the fresh air with obvious relish. Her clear, cerulean eyes took in the surroundings with detached interest. Carts drawn by scrawny horses clattered over the cobblestones a mere few feet away, but she didn't flinch, not even when a pair of heavily flogged mules rattled past, their eyes rolling. It was all coming back to her now; why she hated the city. Why she had been secretly glad when she and her father had moved away into the mountains, though it had taken the death of her mother and the loss of her younger brother to convince her father that the city was worth leaving.

She supposed he was dead now, her brother. He had been a thin, rail like boy when she lost sight of him in the crowd. She had seen his leaf shaped face, his namesake, squeezing between the stomping hooves of the Black Knights' horses. Mother had told her to keep an eye on him, but suddenly he had disappeared, and Mother was dead. Afterwards, Elewyn and her father had combed the streets for hours, but it was impossible to distinguish what body might have been his. So many young children had been trampled during the raid that every street was strewn with bodies. A few soldiers had walked about, turning them face down.

Elewyn cleared her thoughts with a suppressed sigh. There was no point in thinking about what she could have done to keep him close—he was gone now. He was but a memory amongst her thousands of others, a piece in the puzzle of her life. Her brother had only been four at the time, and she six. How on earth was a six year old supposed to keep her brother safe from armed soldiers? She knew it wasn't her fault, but she blamed herself for slipping his hand. If she had held tighter . . .

No, she remembered that he had squirmed, told her that was she was surely crushing his fingers. He wouldn't have let her hold on much longer.

But if she had! So what if he had bit and scratched like a wild animal. He would be safe now, at her side on this journey. And he wouldn't hold the grudge. Even now she was sure that he would have forgotten his anger in moments. Toddlers were like that. They were stubborn, but they recovered quickly.

"Out of my way!" She was startled from her remembrances by a sharp tang of cuss words. A carriage was flying towards her, drawn by four glossy horses. It was with a paling of the face as she realized that there she was, standing in the middle of the road, with what was surely a royal personage hurtling towards her. Yet she did not have the any way to remove herself from its path. The sides of this bit of street were lined with crowds of people, most of them hostile enough to shove her back into the street if she were to dive towards them. She was frozen in time, except that everything else was moving quite rapidly, especially the carriage. If she stood here long enough, she would have the chance to rejoin her brother.

But that wasn't an option. Determined eyes faced the charging horses. It took more than courage to stand in the way of a certain mauling. It took foolhardiness, but Elewyn had been born with more than her share. She reached for the trailing reins of the nearest horse. The horse lunged, but by that time Elewyn was gone.

She perched on top of the sweaty animal. Her fingers entwined themselves in the dark mane. The very bones of her knees throbbed from the constant motion, and her golden hair, torn loose from the braid at the nape of her neck, whipped across her face. She brushed it aside.

"Fool! You'll be killed!" The driver stood up in his box, waving his arms furiously. He had dropped the reins, and they fluttered near the wheels. Elewyn watched them for a moment, though she paid no heed to the driver.

She focused on the world swirling by. It was a mass of color, and she had to strain to make out her surroundings. The palace flew by in a flash of white and gold. Next the market place, roaring with voices. The horse jolted beneath her. His eyes rolled nervously, and he leapt forward. No one seemed to notice Elewyn's feet prodding him on.

There. She caught sight of a rolling hill, rising above the city, and leaned towards it. The horse veered onto a side street, his movements so abrupt that Elewyn nearly lost her balance. She tipped precariously for a moment, but her hands grabbed at the mane. By the time she had pulled herself upright, the horse had slowed considerably.

She wrapped her fingers more tightly in his mane. The horse snorted and threw himself into the harness, his muscles bulging as he galloped up the hill.

Elewyn looked up. A sharp turn in the road was flying towards her, and even then the cart had begun to skid. There was no way she would be able to ride through it. The horse would have to slow down, or risk wrecking the cart. She glanced back at the driver. It didn't look like he would mind.

She braced her legs underneath her, tearing her hands away from the mane in the same instant. The full force of the wind hit her as she rose from her shelter behind the horse's head, and for a moment, she teetered on her perch. Then her feet thrust out beneath her, and she was flying.

The leap was almost perfectly timed, and as she fell away from the horse, her legs jolted on the landing. It was all she could do to stay upright. Her bones ached, but she straightened up. The ground was a dizzy solid mess after the thrill of the ride.

She found herself on the steps of a white building. Dozens of people loitered in its doorway, and their curious faces peered out at her. She drew a deep breath. *They'll go away soon enough.* A small boy tugged at his mother's hand, pointing with his other grubby fist.

Above him, the temple soared into a peaked roof. She took a moment to look upwards, breathing in the blueness of the sky before weaving her way through the slender columns. She paused before the massive doors– it didn't feel right to enter in her condition.

She quickly released her hair, letting it fall into a wave down her back. Her nimble fingers worked through the tangles. Then, in a rush of movement, she neatly plaited all of her hair back in place.

This done, she slid into the doorway. The people had disappeared, just as she had predicted.

A flood of cool air hit her. She felt the scent of incense sting her nose, and she flared her nostrils briefly, wondering if this had been a good idea. Temples in the city were nothing like those in the mountains. She closed her eyes, remembering the small hut perched on a cliff side, its walls wind swept. Half of the floor hung out over empty space, and beetles had long ago eaten the roof. The temple's very existence had been a miracle.

This building was different. The temple was cold and dark, a long hallway more than anything else. Near its end, a giant statue loomed over the sparse worshipers. The marble walls echoed her footsteps as she approached.

She took a moment to steel herself before looking up at the statue. A marble woman glared down at her, her hair long and sterile. She was dressed in a simple toga, and a massive crown shaded her eyes. Even these were cold. Elewyn shuddered. This wasn't what the Goddess was supposed to look like.

Nora was Queen of the Gods, and since all gods were powerful, Nora was even more so. Elewyn squeezed her eyes shut against the statue, letting a new image filter in. This Nora was beautiful, with a delicate silver crown and snow white dress. A black raven fluttered on her shoulder. The symbol of wisdom, she was hardly ever without it. This was the Nora that Elewyn had been raised to believe in, not this brute, who stared with glare powerful enough to make her on lookers burst into flames.

Elewyn's eyes snapped open. She did not look at the statue again, instead bending over the alter in front of her.

Her knees screamed in protest as she lowered herself to the ground. The marble floor was cold and hard.

She reached into her pocket, pulling out a crumpled scrap of parchment. Words etched across its surface, but she had written it so long ago that she wasn't sure if she remembered their meaning. It didn't matter. She smoothed out a few of the wrinkles. The parchment fluttered onto the stone altar. Thousands of other prayer scraps swallowed it up, and her own wish was lost in the sea of pleas. She stared at the scraps.

It had been here, just a year before, when *he* had come. Tall, muscular, a graceful stag in the crowds of people. Many had gathered around her after she fell, but he had parted the crowd with just one sweep. He had strode towards, picked her up, carried her into the grove of trees. She sighed. How she missed him!

"Move, girl!"

Her eyes snapped open. A tall man was standing beside her, his foot tapping impatiently beneath his sweeping robes. She scurried to her feet, glancing at his face as she did so.

"You idiot!" She flew at him, throwing her arms around his narrow shoulders. "What are you doing here? When did you get back?"

The elf chuckled. He swept his hood away from his eyes, letting fall around his shoulders. "I thought I might find you here."

Elewyn frowned. "And you presumed that I would want company. Well, I am glad to see you, Alvardine."

Alvardine flashed her a brilliant smile. He nodded towards the door. "Oryth was getting worried—he sent me to find you."

Her frown deepened. "My father worries far too much.

He's . . . overprotective. He has been since—"

"He wasn't happy about the child, then?"

"What could I do, Alvardine? I wasn't going to let the girl starve!" Elewyn stood abruptly, yanking her cloak up around her ears. "Of course he wasn't happy. He thought that Liam and I had—"

"Yeah. I figured that out myself, thanks. The girl's gone now, though. Surely he's realized—"

"Realized what? He's Oryth, and he's stubborn. He'll never get over that shock. He hates Liam, and he's worried about me." She strode back towards the doors, letting Alvardine hurry to keep up. "We should get back."

Alvardine nodded, holding the door for her as she swept past. He shrugged and pulled his hood back up over his face. It didn't look like they would be talking much on the way back.

On the steps outside, however, Elewyn spun to face him. Her face was drawn with concern. "Did you get the weapons?"

"Yes. Alina and Carn—"

"Do you trust them?"

He frowned. "I already said I did."

"Yes, but . . . We didn't know anything about them, then. Now . . . Well, you've seen them work. Can we trust them?"

Alvardine paused. His eyes glinted in the shadows of the temple. Slowly, he nodded. "They're unexpected, and ignorant, but they won't betray us. The girl has suffered too much. She understands the cause. As for the boy . . . He'll do."

"You're not sure about him."

"How could I be? His father was a chief! He's royalty. Considering the nature of our task . . . We'll have to watch him."

Elewyn nodded. "We should head back to the others. Leif will want to open the trunk."

Alvardine shrugged. "Led the way, child." He hoisted himself off the damp ground. The cloak swished as he waited for Elewyn to catch up to him.

He led Elewyn away from the temple. The street was swarming with civilians out for their daily shopping, and Elewyn had to work hard to keep up. Rich ladies hung about the gates in gossiping clusters. Towards the center of the street were masses of beggars, their rags swarming with fleas. They darted to and fro beneath the stamping feet of mules. The last of the horses were gone; the rich men had already made their commutes. Instead, the people dragged their carts themselves, using mules whenever possible. A few slaves were visible in the crowd.

Slaves. She shuddered at the thought. King Rolan owned millions of them, captured from his raids on elven villages, and he gave them as gifts whenever he pleased. Each slave was marked with the brand of his master. Cotton groin cloths and tunics died bright red served to further alienate them, but it wasn't necessary. The slaves were identifiable by their starved looks and sunken eyes. No one dared to speak to such a creature, much less look at him or her. And who would want to? They were proof of the government's corruption, something the people had tried to forget in the decades of King Rolan's reign.

Elewyn glanced at them as she strode past. Most of them weren't ugly, even with the horrid black scars on their brows. Some of the slaves still retained handsome features of the elves. But the spirit was gone, that glittering of the eyes and leaping of the heart. They no longer smiled, nor sung the legends of old in their clear voices.

But now is not a time for singing, she thought. The world was too full of evil for poems of banquet feasts and heroes. It was just as well that the elves that still remained did not have the hearts they used to have; a revolt would surely spur Rolan into killing them all. *At least they're still alive. With luck, they might even survive. And then we'll hear the songs once again, sung high in the trees for the creatures of the forest.* She smiled wistfully. Maybe the trees would grow again, and the forests, now dry and sullen, would spring back to life. She longed to hear the sound of the birds rejoicing at first dawn.

They had reached Mother Iris's kitchen. Elewyn shook her thoughts aside. Her mind had run this path a million times. There was no need to brood over it. Instead, she glanced around the room. The butter churn was over turned. Some one had lit a fire in the hearth, and its flames cackled merrily.

Her eye caught the sight of a bright red trunk resting in the corner of the room. She hurried to it, brushing the dust of the road off with a sweep of her hand. "Thank the Gods."

Alvardine smiled. "Carn got it."

Elewyn turned to face the flushed boy. She looked him up and down. "I misjudged you."

If anything, Carn's face blushed a deeper red. "I had help . . . Alina was there."

Alvardine shook his head. "Whether Carn got it or not, here we are, with the trunk in front of us, with no idea what is actually inside it."

Elewyn stared at it. "You think it's the one?"

Leif and Oryth crowded around her. Alina and Carn hung back, but soon they too were hanging over the chest.

Alvardine knelt before it. He picked at the lock. It

cracked open.

He motioned for Oryth to open the lid. "The honor is rightfully yours, my friend. You are the elder of this group, and your wisdom does not go unnoticed."

"I know that, Alvardine. But you captured the trunk— the right is yours."

"I didn't capture the trunk. That honor belongs to Carn. He will open it."

Carn stepped forward, a frown creasing his young face. "I did find the trunk . . . " He jammed his fingers beneath the lid. Rotten wood splintered away as he strained. It came up so suddenly that he stumbled backwards.

Alina watched as he reached into the gaping mouth. To her, the trunk looked like a hungry beast, spewing flames of dust and ready to clamp down upon her friend's arm at any second. Her traveling cloak, ripped from the encounter with the Black Knights, hung in shreds around her boney frame. She pulled the edges closer—it was definitely colder above the surface then below it, in the Underworld. Had they grabbed the right trunk? She shuddered at the thought. What if they hadn't? They would have to travel all the way back to Daedalyus, and a raid would be impossible, now that the Black Knights had most assuredly tightened the security of the city. She leaned forward, peering past Carn's shoulder and into the settling dust.

Carn's fingers darted along the interior of the trunk like spiders. He closed his eyes in concentration. He could feel forms shifting in the sawdust. The cold scales of metal rubbed against his skin. He turned around, drawing a sword out with him.

The blade that had occupied the trunk was not an extraordinary thing. It had no jewels embedded in its metal. The blade was of sliver steel, the hilt of the same material. It was carved with vines of leaves snaking up the handle, flicking tongues of life onto the blade itself. Elven letters danced across the blade base.

"The sword Hildeharande. 'Hear my voice ring.'" Alvardine said softly, reading the words out loud. "A noble blade. She was forged, I believe, in the fires of the Govannon. And here is the inscription, 'Aneirin.' There was a king called by that name—he fell in the Cavern Wars." He smiled. "A noble blade for a deserving friend." He bowed, and taking the sword from Carn, offered it to Leif. "The blade Hileharande, borne by Sir Leif of Finestal."

Leif took the sword. He fastened her sheath onto his belt, a slight smile emerging from his sullen face. He nodded a grudging thanks to Alvardine.

Carn was back at the trunk. Now that the dust had settled, the contents were visible. He brushed the wood shavings away, revealing four daggers of varying sizes. Another long sword rested at the bottom of the jumble. He untangled it, letting the other weapons fall to cushioned landings.

"This one will do nicely, I think, in the hands of Oryth," Alvardine said. He examined the blade, gently testing its strength. The metal was so thin, Alina was surprised that it stood up to any pressure at all. The hilt was made of solid steel, with heavy white crystals embroidered in the metal. There was no writing upon it, but the sword was recognizable all the same. Alina had never seen such fine craftsmanship, had never seen such a sharp, unnerving blade.

Oryth nodded. He took the sword up, and without further ado, snapped it onto his belt. "Yes, this one has magic in it. I can feel it quiver, now, against my leg."

Indeed, he could feel the sword trembling. It was as if the very essence of the metal was trying to escape. This sword had a life of its own. He peered down into the darkness of its sheath. A faint glow shimmered from its metal.

"What will you call her?" Carn asked.

"Moonlight. That is, until I can recover her real name. But I think Moonlight will fit her nicely. Yes."

Three of the four daggers were passed out to Alina, Carn, and Elewyn. To the coremen, such daggers were long enough to be short swords. Elewyn pocketed hers without comment.

"Two fine knives," Alvardine said to Alina and Carn. "Hornet and Oakenwhite. Matching blades."

Alina buckled Oakenwhite on, and turned to help Carn with Hornet. The weapon felt strange against her skin. It was cold and clammy. *Like the death it pursues,* she thought. *But I'll get used to it. A blade with a name like Oakenwhite can't be dreaded. This blade is the bringer of light and good.* She stroked its hilt.

"Good. We're all armed." Oryth glanced at Alvardine, who smiled and patted his sheathed sword.

"Areslaine is all the sword I will ever need."

Oryth put his hand up. "Good. Then we'll sell the last dagger for supplies. Alvardine, you'll take care of that? I think a bit of clothing might come in handy." Oryth's eyes twinkled. "Especially for Alina, who seems to have worn through her dress. I've never seen someone so hard on clothes."

Alina blushed.

7

The horses trudged wearily up the steep path. Towards the east, the sun's first rays loosened the night's grip on the plains, and the pink was chilly compared to the noonday sun. The grass departed their dew on the fringed hooves. Leather straps snapped in the breeze. Not even the birds had bothered to leave their warm nests, and Alina didn't blame them. She would rather be asleep as well, but that wasn't an option. She drew her cloak more tightly around her shoulders, shivering.

Rolling hills spread out before them, giving way to mountains in the far west. The northern lands were bordered by forest; the trees were visible even from here. Eagles circled overhead, searching for their first meal of the day.

Alina's stomach growled. Had they eaten before they left? She couldn't remember. The last walls of the city had fallen away well before dawn, leaving the group alone in the wilderness. There was a slight amount of food packed in their saddlebags, but Alvardine had warned them not to eat it yet. If they were lucky, they would be in Abrelyon before nightfall.

Abrelyon. Alina had learned about the city years before, in the legends and tales Carn had told her. The only elven city on this side of the Tortallion Mountains, Abrelyon was nestled beside the Lake of Mists. Huge trees guarded its northern borders. It had once been the capital of the elves, a great trading city. Now, it was little more than a village, pillaged by countless parties of Black Knights.

The thought of King Rolan's servants sent a shiver down her spine. She leaned forward slightly, urging Mandan to catch up with the rest of the group. She had heard stories about the Knights, tales mothers used to put their children to bed in the Clan. As a child, she had admired them as heroes. Now she frowned. The Knights had destroyed Ivindor. It had been a Black Knight who had accompanied Rolan when he killed the boy in the ruined city. She bit her lip in disgust. She had not been on the surface for long, but she had learned the truth about them. The Knights were warriors without souls.

She trotted up beside Carn, and he pulled Siv back to wait for her. Several saddlebags had been added to his load, and they rose high behind him. His cloak was spread over them, regal.

Carn. She smiled, thinking of her friend. He had always been there for her, even in the Clan, when his own father was against her. He had risked his life for her more than once. Now he was risking it again, except this time he had had a choice. And he had chosen to come.

He shouldn't have, she thought, knowing all too well that if Carn were still traveling with the Clan, she would be dead. *He had a future back there, a life. A throne with a golden crown, and a group of people who would fight for him. Carn would have been the best leader the Clan has seen in a long time. He could have turned things around, stopped the killing.*

She sighed, clucking to Mandan yet again. *People have given up so much for me, and what did I do to repay them? Volunteered to risk my life again.* The idea of a journey had been a novel one while still in the comforts of the Wanderers territory, but now that there was nothing between her and the Black Knights, Alina wasn't so sure.

The riders had reached the peak of the hill. Alvardine slid from Haranee's back. He slipped a small package from one of his saddlebags and then slapped the horse's rump. She moved away to graze on the sodden grass.

Once the rest of the horses had been turned loose to graze (Mandan had to be tied to Oryth's pony so that he wouldn't run off), the group settled on a rocky outcrop. An old cloak was quickly spread out to cushion the damp. From the leather bundle emerged a dozen travel biscuits, presoaked in lard to keep them from becoming moldy. A packet of sugar was tossed to each person. Alvardine uncorked a flask, sipping it slowly to savor its taste. He passed the rations around the circle.

Greedily, Alina bit into the flaky bread. The taste of the lard was surprisingly welcome—she had expected the biscuits to be slimy, but the fat had been absorbed long ago. Instead, the biscuits were of a delicious moistness, a real treat compared to the hard tack the Clan had eaten while traveling. She shouldered deeper into the fabric of her cloak.

"Dreogan will give us the supplies we need. And if worse comes to worse, he'll provide an army." Alvardine spoke urgently to Oryth. Alina knew she shouldn't listen, but she perked her ears anyway.

"You think it will come to that?" Oryth huddled closely beside his friend.

"How could it not? No one has seen Sir Alleyn since he

stepped down from the throne. That was nearly five years ago. He's disappeared. Vanished."

"We don't stand a chance without the Raven King. Rolan is too powerful. I've seen his troops. They're getting larger every day, and what's more, they're moving east. Towards us."

"Then we'll skirt around them. Send word to the Wanderings. Tell them to start patrolling the countryside to recruit volunteers. If it's a war Rolan wants, it's a war he will get."

Alina pulled away. She didn't want to hear anymore. When she left the Clan, she had thought she was fleeing from civil war. Now she was caught in the middle of one, and this time, there was no escape. Her heart pounded in her chest. *Even Alvardine doesn't think we stand a chance.* She slipped a crumble of bread between her lips, tasting the stale salt on the tip of her tongue. Beside her, Leif huddled next to Carn. He laughed as he ate, all the while watching Oryth pace in front of him. Alina caught fragments of the conversation between her mouthfuls.

"At least Elewyn will be welcome. Doubtless someone will be eager to see her." Leif grinned at Carn. His feelings towards the newcomers had changed drastically since their raid on Daedalyus.

Behind him, Elewyn blushed a deep scarlet. She hurriedly bit into her bread, burying her feelings in the act.

"Speaking of which," Oryth broken in sharply, "I've decided that you will stay in Abrelyon, Elewyn. This journey is going to be much too dangerous."

"Father!" Elewyn stood. "We've discussed this. I'm coming. This is my decision to make. And Liam will be going too, once we leave Abrelyon. What else is there for me?"

"Quite a lot, if you would have accepted Dreogan's offer. He'd make a good husband."

"A husband twice my age! Liam's father? Are you kidding me? I wouldn't touch him with a ten-foot pole! And what's more, it's said that he travels around a lot, if you know what I mean . . ."

Oryth stood abruptly. His staff banged on the ground, and sparks shot from the tip. One of them, bright purple, landed on Elewyn's hand. She jumped back, brushing it away.

"I will not have such profanity coming from my daughter's mouth!" Oryth towered above Elewyn, his height growing with every word. His eyes sparkled dangerously. "You are free to do as you like with Dreogan, but with Liam? I've made my views clear on this, girl. He is not for you!"

His daughter returned his icy stare. Then she stood, whipping her cloak behind her as she made for the horses. She swung onto a white stallion's back, knowing that the others would follow her. Oryth slammed his staff into the ground, but by that time, Elewyn was out of earshot.

She bowed her head over the glistening neck of her mount. She knew that her argument was immature. She regretted it, now that the moment was past and her anger had cooled. What a fool she had been! Oryth was her father; it wouldn't do her any good to argue. In the end, he always had the last word. If he wanted her to stay and marry Dreogan, then there was nothing she could do about it. Accepting his judgment was the right thing to do, but she had chosen to fight the losing battle. How sorely he had lost!

She twitched the reins, causing her horse to break into

a gallop. His smooth gait massaged her tense muscles. No matter how many times she mounted up, the thrill never lost its flavor. Youth in the mountains had given her a lonely childhood, and the horse had been her only friend. She had spent her days bent low over her colt's back. She had grown up with the wind teasing her hair, the earth constantly moving as she was swept away by the pounding hooves. She had captured this horse during a raid; he had been just a colt at the time, and Elewyn had learned to train him with her own hands. They moved as one, the pure white stallion kicking up dust.

He carried her past Alvardine, out into the wide grasslands where she felt entirely alone. This was the sort of riding she loved, without caravans or hindrance. Here the horse was free to do as he liked, to stretch out and run like there was no tomorrow. She closed her eyes. If she concentrated enough, Elewyn could almost imagine a pack of wolves running at her flank like they had when she was young. Oryth had been good friends with the leader, a majestic beast called Braveheart. The wolf had been like an uncle to her, and he had kept her safe during those long days in the open air. She could almost hear the proud creature running before the flying hooves. He would raise his head in an arching howl, and his comrades would answer back. The gray bodies swept around the fleeing Snowberry.

Except that they weren't there. She was alone on the prairie, a few horse lengths ahead of her father's stern glare. Her face rose to meet the wind. Its soft scent played across her face, teasing tendrils of hair away from her tight braid. She yanked the horse to a slow trot, and the wind faded. Her hands guided Snowberry in a sweeping circle, until she was back where she had started, trailing behind her father.

Elewyn sensed Alina's approach long before the girl reached Snowberry's sweeping flank. She gripped the reins tightly. She could flee. She didn't have to talk to the girl. Her face contorted in her embarrassment. Alina's presence was yet another reminder of the argument she was trying so hard to forget.

"Elewyn." Alina slowed Mandan's gait so the two horses drew alongside each other. They were close enough to make the saddlebags chaff together. "You okay? Oryth was pretty harsh on you back there." Anxiety played out over her face. She respected Elewyn, and had been trying to approach her for days. Her heart pounded in her throat. She licked her lips nervously. She wasn't sure why it was so important for Elewyn to like her.

"I should have expected that. Father doesn't change his mind very easily; he's always been stubborn. If I had any sense at all I would have let the matter drop." Elewyn's brow furrowed. "Or he would. There's no way I'm staying in Abrelyon."

Alina shrugged. She wanted this girl as a friend, but with almost no practice in talking to people her own age, she hesitated. In the Clan, Carn had been the only other teen. "You want to help the Wanderers?" Alina could have smacked herself. *Of course she does, you idiot! She's here, isn't she?*

Elewyn waved irritably. "It's more than that. Father's had his sights set on Dreogan for years now." She leaned forward to stroke Snowberry's neck. The horse snorted in delight, and a faint smile spread across Elewyn's lips. "Dreogan is Alvardine's son. Father would give anything to have me marry him."

Alina clucked encouragingly to Mandan, who had

paused in hopes of a sugar tablet. The two horses grunted to each other as they walked. "Why?"

"He's heir to the throne of Abrelyon. He'll be a disgusting king, but that can't be helped. You've heard of the trolls? Well, imagine one of them, but taller with a lot more warts. That's Dreogan for you. He's got the temperament of a wounded dragon." She whipped her hair away from her face in frustration. "And he's got quite the appetite. For both food and women. " Her face softened against the wind. "But I don't blame Father. He hasn't any idea what Dreogan's really like. No one does."

Alina nodded with empathy. In the Clan, girls were expected to marry by age seventeen, tying the knot with whomever Isen chose. She shivered. Isen's triumphant words echoed in her mind. Marriage was inescapable. Another month, and she would have been joined with the lowest beggar of the Clan. *At least that's behind me now.* She waited while Elewyn's silence stretched on for an eternity. Mandan fidgeted beneath her weight.

Finally, Elewyn opened her mouth. She pursed her lips, releasing a stream of hot air. "But enough about me. I'm complaining too much, and you can't be that interested. You really should tell me when I get like this; I'm trying to cut back." She laughed nervously. "What about you? Any lovers waiting for you to get home?"

Alina blushed. She thought of Gulzar, and the excitement she had felt when her mother told her of Isen's decision. The excitement had quickly drained away to be replaced by dread. Gulzar's warty face loomed before her. Even in her memories, she could smell his filth. "No," she told Elewyn. "No one's waiting for me." She wasn't lying, not exactly. Gulzar wouldn't be without a wife for long.

Elewyn smiled. Her face went slack, and her eyes

misted as she stared off in the distance. "Love. Don't you hate it?"

Alina nodded. She had kept the news of her upcoming marriage secret, not even confiding in Carn. She couldn't begin to imagine how violent his reaction would have been. Yes, she had to agree. Love was a terrible thing.

Elewyn jolted her from her thoughts. "Can you ride? I've never heard of the coremen taking any horses with them to the Underworld."

She started at the abrupt change of topic. "I'm riding right now, aren't I? Sometimes the boys in the Clan captured a wild horse. They had contests to see who could stay mounted the longest."

"No. I mean really ride. Not just sit and let the horse follow the leader."

"This is my first time anywhere near a horse. You're right; coremen don't take horses with them when they leave the surface. They'd be useful though."

Elewyn snorted. "As pack mules you mean. I'm glad the coremen don't drive horses into the depths of the world. You can't cage a free spirit like that . . . It would die." She shook herself, turning to grin at Alina. "Let's see how naturally this comes to you then. Come on!" She threw herself across Snowberry's back, draping her arms around his neck. The horse sprang forward with a delighted whinny.

Alina shook herself from her surprise. She leaned tentatively forward, nudging Mandan's ribs with her heel. She felt the great muscles quiver. They bunched, and she flew after Elewyn. Her knuckles gleamed white to match her face.

The two girls darted ahead of the party once more. After a few moments, Alina dared to glance up from her trembling hands. A great gust of air tossed around her. The ground sped by in a blur of green and gray. She gasped, her heart nearly exploding from the exhilaration of the ride. She had never dreamed of flying so effortlessly above the sea of tumbled grass. Only dragons could move with greater agility, but their jerky movements hardly matched the sleek stretching of the horse beneath her.

Mandan began to show his true colors from the times when he raced for money. His legs were longer then Snowberry's and he flung them forward until he was stretched out to full length. His limps and whines disappeared with each bound, leaving Alina to glide over the prairie like water in a riverbed. The black mane streamed in the rush of air. He carried his burden without any effort on his part; Alina was so small that she resembled a thin child in weight. Even his jockeys could not have been so light. He ignored the uncomfortable stiffness of his rider. If her weight had to begun to slip, he might have slowed, but Alina was stuck on like a burr. He arced his tail, letting it catch the breeze in a waterfall of gleaming black.

Elewyn cried out, causing Snowberry to strain at his halter. The stallion dashed for Mandan, drawing level with him just as his own breath began to come in short gasps. Elewyn leapt lightly from his back. She settled herself behind Alina.

"That's probably enough for right now. The others will be worried." She entwined her fingers in the reins. Mandan cantered to a halt.

She slid from Mandan's back, lightly tapping the ground before catching up Snowberry's halter to swing herself back onto her own mount. She turned to grin at Alina. "You're not the worst rider I've ever seen, that's for sure. Fun, isn't it?" She yanked Snowberry into a slower pace as they walked back to the company. "Loosen up a little. Bunching into that little ball makes it harder for the horse to carry you. That's it. You see how the steps roll up your spine? You should be loose, but a little firmer. You're not a lump up there. The horse is relying on you to keep an eye out for sharp stones and the like. You can't afford to get lost in your imagination. Good." Elewyn tapped her fingers against her riding blanket. "This is how riding should be. Free."

Alina nodded. She wasn't in the mood to disagree with anything right now. The gallop across the prairie had the effect of a drug on her. Her head felt like it was floating in the clouds; her heart had already burst and was now a cauldron of liquid gold. She couldn't imagine how she could have spent her entire life not knowing how wonderful freedom could be.

Isen would be furious, she half thought. Women of the Clan weren't allowed to engage in wild dashes in front of the men. They were expected to stay quiet, meek, and eager to obey. If a horse was captured by the Clan, the women wouldn't be allowed anywhere near it.

Alina caught up Mandan's reins in her clammy fists. Now that she thought on it, she didn't really care much for horses. She could see why the Clan had avoided them: though useful, even a pony towered above her tiny frame. No, it was the freedom that she reveled in. She drank it like honeyed mead, fresh and strong. Her heart swelled under its effects. She was drunk with the feeling of power, the feeling that she could command her own body without fear. Her eyes sparkled with a new light, a light that seemed to glow from her very soul. There was no hesitation in her movements, just the swift, impulsive darts of her fingers through Mandan's mane.

Even the horse seemed to enjoy the new sensations. Alina cocked her head at that, but she accepted it without a fuss. *He's not unlike me,* she thought, *penned up all day, expected to do whatever his master asks. He hasn't had any more choice in his life then I have, and I've had quite a bit more than Mother would like.* She chuckled, and the horse perked his ears. He trotted into the folds of the company.

Carn greeted her as she rode up. His eyes were twinkling; she decided that he had also learned the joys of riding. *I never could keep anything from him.* With a start, Alina realized how little she had seen of her friend in the past few days. She bit her lip. She missed him.

He seemed to be thinking the same thing. He clopped her on the back, and Alina winced. She pulled Mandan a few steps to the right. "There's no need to hit me!"

It didn't seem possible, but Carn's grin widened. "You rode like a demon! Are you sure Cyn hasn't sent one of his death angels to possess you?"

Alina chuckled in spite of herself. "Of course not. You'd know by now. You would know the moment I came to rip your throat out!"

"How do I know that you haven't come to do just that?" Carn asked. "It's entirely possible. Didn't Cyn once possess the mind of elven king, Lucifer?"

"I guess. I've never heard the full story, but—"

"Never heard the full story of King Lucifer? The elf that drove the Gods mad? Then I'll tell it to you."

"I don't think that's really necessary—" She looked to Alvardine for help, but to no avail.

"I think we have all grown weary of travel. The story of Lucifer is a classic. It won't hurt to hear it again. Actually, I'd appreciate it. I hear Carn has a knack for stories."

Carn bowed his head modestly. "I used to love listening to the storytellers. But the tale of Lucifer. I haven't heard that one in a long time. Where do I start?"

"The beginning is always a good place."

"Alright." He cleared his throat.

Two worlds there were when time began,
One old, the other new.
The largest made of gritty sand,
Smallest had skies of blue.
The Gods arrived soon after that,
Though when I can't recall,
Upon the smallest world, they sat
And circles built of wall.
This world they called the Faerie Land,
And here they made their home.
Full of people and castles grand,
Across the world, they roamed.
Those creatures of the evil sort,
To Ivindor they sent,
Hoping perhaps, to evil thwart,
And lessen Cyn's descent.
Alas, 'twas not to be the case,
For now a proud race grew.
Tall and skilled, a most noble race,
Thousands of peers they slew.
These were the elves, the blessed ones,
And yet corruption came.
A greedy king ruled with his sons,
And to the God brought shame.
Thrown out, they were, to Ivindor,
The land of mortal lives.
To wait until the oath they swore

Was met through work and strife.
But this was not in stars foretold,
Instead, they spoke of war.
The elves built up an army bold,
Conquered from shore to shore.
Swirling and grey, the elven king,
Atop the mountain high,
Looked down upon the deathly ring
Of his peers, bold and wry.
His sword he raised, blade gleaming bright,
And so the war began,
The first race of the human knight
Against the elven band.
The men did roar to see the elves,
Bows taught with strong sinew.
They shook their spears and held themselves
Up, though the arrows flew.
When it stopped, the world was quiet,
The ground was soaked in blood.
Men lay dying from the riot,
Their corpses mixed with mud.
And so, Round One had finally finished,
The men, they had prevailed.
Race of elves, it was diminished,
Last ship of elves had sailed.
First battle won, many to come,
The earth was ruled by man,
Until such time that beats of drum
Once more filled up the land.

"And so the elves came to Ivindor," Carn said softly. "It is only a part of a longer tale, the history of our world."

"Well, you do have a knack for stories," Leif said. "I've

never heard the tale of Lucifer told that way before. Jadar always said that Lucifer was corrupted by love."

"Jadar?" Oryth sat up a little straighter. His wizened face peered curiously from beneath his hood. "Jadar? Of Ferrington?"

"Yeah. Who else? He raised me since I was a little boy, since my father abandoned me. But now Ferrington's gone, and Jadar . . . " Leif drew a deep breath. "I suppose he's dead. And what of it? He wasn't my *real* father. Like I said: My *real* father abandoned me."

"I'm sure your father didn't abandon you, Leif. Those were hard times; it was impossible for many parents to care for their children."

"He kept my sister," Leif grumbled, jerking his horse's reins up sharply. "But I don't care. I don't need anyone."

"You were four years old then." Oryth said. His voice had grown soft, and Alina had to strain to hear. He rubbed at his eyes, blinking. "You're lucky someone took you in. Most orphans were left on the streets."

"How do you know how old I was? Jadar never told a soul that I was a foundling. I was his son, understand?"

"I think I know your father closer than you will ever know. But that's no matter now. There's months of traveling ahead, time enough for me to explain. I don't think I'll start just yet." He hitched the hem of his robes up higher as mud spattered from beneath his pony's hood. His fingers absentmindedly stroked the wood of his staff as he rode.

Alina tore her eyes away from Leif's glaring face to smile at Carn. "How come you've never told me that story before? You've told me every other god-forsaken tale.

"I guess there never was an opportunity. You know how Isen was about stories." He twisted, waving his arms around him. "Isn't this wonderful? All this open space? You'd never know how big Ivindor really was in the Underworld. Not with all those tunnels. And the sun! It's brighter than I remember."

The sun was, indeed, a brilliant yellow that morning. It shone like liquid gold in the quilt of blue and white that made up the sky. The coremen occasionally caught glimpses of its rays streaming through cracks in the earth, but to see it in its full glory was a wonder they saw only once a year. It filled the sky with the Gods' light, that soft glow that can only be seen in the first hours of the morning. It was tinged red with the blood of Ragor's wounds, torn open afresh by Cyn's singing blade. If Alina stared at it closely, she could make out the dark scars amongst Ragor's golden hues, but they disappeared almost as quickly as they had come, leaving her with spots swimming before her eyes.

"It is bright," she answered cautiously. They had come to the edge of a forest, and its dark shadows preoccupied her mind. She couldn't help but think of the beasts that lurked within its depths. Big cats weren't common in eastern Ivindor, but they were present, and would attack if provoked. Lumbering grizzly bears were known to wander the outskirts of wooded areas. Alina glanced at the early summer sky, and hoped that the Gods were watching. She pressed Mandan forward.

On her left, Leif nodded briefly to Alvardine. He dismounted, swinging onto the marshy ground. His fingers curled around the hilt of his sword. Then, taking a few quick steps, he melted into the forest around them. Alina listened for his footsteps as he crept away, but all was silent.

She stared at the trail that curved away from them in the gloom. Trees swayed on its flanks, quavering from the movement of a passing squirrel. She traced its path as she waited. The animal leapt lightly from branch to branch, its bushy tail held high for balance. It chattered a warning call. Alina gasped and turned her attention back to the trail.

"Leif's back."

She squinted into the haze, trying to make out what Alvardine's sharp eyes had seen. Leif jogged towards them. He exchanged a few muttered tones with Alvardine, his eyes shifting continually back to the forest. He had lost his cloak in the few minutes he had been gone, and muddied his boots on the trail.

Why am I noticing this? Alina shook her head, as if trying to rid her mind of the illogical thought. Her hands trembled on Mandan's reins. She tugged the horse a few steps forward. Her feet itched. She wanted to run, gallop away from this place. The darkness scared her. She sucked in a deep breath and tightened Mandan's reins. The horse stomped in them mud. She tapped her fingers impatiently.

Leif nodded to Alvardine, mounting up on his stallion with the grace of one well used to riding. He clipped his sword back into its sheath and smiled. "The city's fine." He waited for the sighs of relief to fade. "The Knights haven't managed to break through its defenses. They have a camp on the other side of the lake; Dreogan says that there are six, maybe seven Knights there at most. The elves took care of the rest." He spoke quickly, relaying the information he had memorized just minutes before. His eyes twinkled at Elewyn, who scowled. "Come softly. If we stick to the trail, we may pass into the city unseen." His heels dug into his horse's ribs, spurring the horse into a silent stalk.

Alina fell into line behind Carn. The trail led them

deep into the forest, and before long, the sun disappeared from view. She was reminded of the forests Carn spoke of in legends, where the trees were larger than houses and the ground was blanketed with moss. There were only three such forests left in Ivindor, the Northern, the Hawthorne, and the island of Shaw. The rest had been logged and carted away. This forest, the Arrowhead, was not nearly as old, but it was not for lack of trying.

Carn had told her stories about the Arrowheads, repeating facts from the books in his small, pilfered library. The trees were mostly beech and ash, she remembered, but as she passed, she also saw the springy wood of rowan and yew. It was no wonder that the elves called the Arrowheads home. The forest was full of wood for bows and arrows. Stags and their harems of does roamed freely, and the river was full of playful otters. Near the center of the forest, The Lake of the Mists provided the elven city on its shores with fresh fish. Abrelyon itself, the only establishment in the forest, was almost perfectly isolated from the outside world.

Alina turned her attention to the stream that played beside her. Its waters traced the trail as it wound towards the Lake. She didn't need Carn to remember history of the waters. After all, it had only been ten years since the entire Lake was red with blood. She closed her eyes. She hoped that it wouldn't turn color again.

A stone wall appeared out of the trees. It rose into the canopy layer, where birds twittered on its stone ledge. Closer to the ground, a gate of twining vines guarded a gap in the defenses. They swung open at their approach.

Inside, trunks the size of small houses spread across the forest floor. The gnarled roots etched across the path. There were no people to be seen, but their presence was evident. Crude baskets hung from hooking branches, filled to the brim with berries and the like. A small doll lay abandoned at the foot of a sapling.

Leif led them to the largest of the trunks. Its mahogany wood was a sight to behold, and it glowed like freshly cut wood, though it must have been in that condition for centuries. A doorway had been cut into its center, a large piece of bark fitted into the space as a door. A small hole had been bored into the bark at eye level, or at least, what must have been the eye level of the elves. Quick slash marks marred its smooth shape.

Alvardine held up hand for halt. He tucked his cloak back behind him. He was a tall man, but he had to stand on tiptoe to reach the eye hoe, which he stared into with some reservations. His hand wavered before he knocked. The sharp sound echoed in the chamber beyond the door, bouncing against the walls and shooting back through the eye-hole. He glanced at Oryth. "Empty."

"That's not too big of a surprise. This is just the watch house, nothing more. Dreogan has fallen into the habit of neglecting his guard duties." Oryth clucked his tongue in disapproval. He strode around the edge of the trunk.

Alina followed, anxious to keep everyone together and out of harm's way. What she saw was beyond her wildest imagination.

More than a hundred tree trunks stood before her. The tops of the trees had been cut off, leaving blocks of wood each a good ten feet high. Thatched roofs were lashed to the tops and coated with red clay. A doorway had been chiseled into the wood of each trunk, and, occasionally, a window stared blankly from the recesses. Smoke stacks rose above them in the form of hollow logs, guiding the swirling matter into the canopy above. They were little cottages, built directly into existing trees. Towards the center rose a curling tower of an oak, its wood dotted with dozens of windows. The branches had been woven together to create narrow runways with hemp railings. Where they led she could not see, but the highway above the ground promised many days of exploration.

A cooking hearth smoldered near the foot of the tower. Pots of fragrant stew brewed among the embers. There were several small bowls lying about, half empty, with spoons carved into the most marvelous creatures. A few had scenes of legends painted on them, scenes of the Ancient Ones, and of the Gods themselves.

Alina stepped towards the nearest, curious. They couldn't have been left for long; the stew was still quite warm to the touch. Even the spoons still bore the faint heat from their owner's chubby little fists. She stooped, plucking one from the ground. It was marvelously smooth. *A lot of love went into the making of this,* she thought. If that was true, then why had it been so carelessly flung on the ground? She froze, feeling the dread wash over her. Something wasn't right here. It hadn't been in a long time.

A child's thin wail pierced the air. She spun, heart pounding. She felt Carn place a warm hand on her shoulder, and drew back from the trees, confused. There weren't any children traveling with them!

"We're not Black Knights," Leif called. He ignored Alvardine's warning look, staring into the trees eagerly. "We are but a small clan of travelers seeking refuge, nothing more."

Oryth hissed at him. "Get back. You have no idea what might be causing that sound. More fearsome creatures than a lowly child make a wailing noise. Pulmorta, the Knights' horses, for one, and where they are, the Black

Knights are never far behind."

Alina gulped. She turned back to face the trees. What if it was Knights? There was no way their stolen swords could protect them.

"Oryth?" A voice sounded from the trees. A haggard man stepped out, his clothes ragged and unkempt. Twigs clung to his dull hair. "Oryth? Is that you? By the Gods man, I never expected to hear your voice again!"

"You look like Dreogan." It was an accusation. "How am I to know that you are not a Black Knight in disguise, or a shape shifter?"

The man flinched. "And how am I to know that you are not the same? Come now, my friend, I *am* Dreogan. And it's dangerous to speak of those creatures in these woods. There are many among us who would have you hanged for speaking of them so freely." He waved his arm impatiently. "You've always been cautious, but this?"

"The name of your mother, Man Who Resembles Dreogan?" Oryth asked.

"Cere, wife of the elf Alvardine, who I see travels amongst you. My father."

"Hardly." Alvardine clapped the man on the back.

The two men embraced, and Alina saw that there was a slight resemblance. Dreogan's black hair shone brightly around his pale face. Back to back, the two men were the same height and both stood with an easy elegance. Only the eyes were different. Alvardine's black eyes searched his son's grey ones.

"When did I saw you last? You were still in diapers, or close to it. I wouldn't call that being a father. You've grown!"

"I would hope so." Dreogan swept his arm again. "I welcome you, Father and friends, to our humble abode." He twisted to half glance at the trees. "Lisa! Fetch mead for our thirsty guests! And will someone call Liam down from the loft? Some one is here to see him!"

Several women stepped from the trees, closely followed by a great clustering of children. They stepped gracefully into the clearing. Wide dark eyes evaluated the visitors. One, her face soft over her high cheekbones, motioned for the others to follow her. A few boys clutched uneasily at nimble bows. They aimed them upwards, as if fearing an attack from the squirrels that chattered above. The woman gestured again, and they disappeared into the nearest hut. Smoke began to curl from the chimney. Moments later a girl scurried back out, calling for the boy, Liam.

Dreogan shrugged apologetically at Alvardine. "The women have never been ones for chatter. Not since the Knights came, anyway. A bit of mead might loosen up the boys' tongues, though."

Alina considered this for a moment. No men had appeared from the shadows; she wondered if any inhabited the village at all. But no, that was a stupid thought. Of course there were men in Abrelyon. There had to be. How could there be children without men? They had to be off hunting, she decided, but her stomach twisted. There had been battle here against the Knights, and the casualties must have been numerous.

"It's no matter." Alvardine was saying. "I'm sure that we'll make enough talk for a thousand women. Leif here especially."

Leif blushed a deep scarlet.

"But come, you mustn't have them go to a great trouble on our behalf. We've been traveling for only a day's time. I dare say we can stand another rationed meal."

Alina caught Carn's moan, sharing his mood. Why

spend the night with growling stomachs when the feasting was abundant? She personally was looking forward to a good meal of roasted meat, preferably young pig. And honeyed bread, completely lathered in butter, swigged down with rich soups . . . she had her mind set on the feast of legends, the feasts that only happened in Carn's stories.

"Of course, Father," Dreogan said with a slight smirk. "But you wouldn't deny yourself the luxury of a warm meal. Not when you have a long journey yet to begin." He smiled lightly. The expression suited him, Alina noticed. "No, you will be comfortable tonight. And tomorrow . . . We'll decide then." Motioning for them to follow, he turned and led the way to the largest hut. He pushed open the bark door.

Inside, the warm air crept into their lungs, easing their breathing. Plush hides were arranged in a circle at the center of the room. The depressed seats were worn from years of wear, faded to a sickly yellow where generations of buttocks had rested. Dreogan seated the travelers, instructing Alvardine and Oryth to sit on either side of his own cushion. A glowing ember was coaxed to life in the hearth at the back of the building. It crackled merrily as the group settled into a comfortable silence.

Dreogan withdrew a slender pipe from a shelf beside the door. He tapped it with expert fingers, ridding its cone of ash. He leaned back and took a long draw. Smoke rings slid from his mouth, curling around his head until his features were obscured. He handed the pipe to Alvardine.

"What brings you to Abrelyon, Father? The last time you were here you vowed never to return."

"I assure you, I have not forgotten that vow. I wouldn't be here if it wasn't so important. Time's are changing, son.

Not all of us are able to live in such a care free manner."

Dreogan coughed. "Care free? Father, let me remind you that I run an entire city! There is no 'care free' involved. It's hard enough finding food for three hundred people, but now we have to contend with the Black Knights. Our women fear rape when they go to fetch water. We can't afford to send our children out to learn the ways of the hunt. Care free? Father, our culture is slowly being wiped out!" he snatched a flask from is hip and drained the last dregs. "Don't tell me that times are changing, Father. I know better than anyone."

"And no one said you did not," Oryth muttered. The pipe had come to him, and he worried the end like a nervous dog. Smoke shapes flashed in the air in front of him, changing color with each new breath. Dragons and wolves charged from the cone. They were so realistic that every hair was visible. The dragons blew miniature smoke rings, tiny versions of themselves, behind their faint roars. The wolves' howls bit at Alina's ears. Both types of smoke rings charged around his head and disappeared in great puffs of smoke. He watched them with a smile of satisfaction. Occasionally he reached up and stroked a grey back with an arthritic finger.

"Will you stop making such a racket? It's driving me nuts!" Leif sprawled on the mat beside Oryth. He had removed his sword from his belt, and it balanced precariously on his knees. He ran his fingers up her blade, pushing her to the hilt. She slid backward into his outstretched hand. "I think your smoke creatures are amazing, I really do, but isn't there some way for you to make them without the sound effects?"

Oryth glared at him. No one had ever dared to tell him to be quiet. Most people were scared of angering the old wizard, and with good reason. He shot a string of snarling wolves at Leif. They broke upon impact, leaving the young man to choke on the remains.

"That's enough." Alvardine slapped his leg to get their attention. "We don't have time for such silly arguments. Or have you forgotten what we set out to do?" He turned to Dreogan. "What's this about Black Knights? There was a time when the elves would have fought them off. When I left, we were a strong race."

"When you left, the other elves were still providing us with protection. They're not doing that anymore—they have to protect their own people, and rightly so. The Black Knights slipped past our guards—"

"There were no guards this morning."

"No, but we had guards posted the night the Knights slipped through. They killed over a hundred of our men. What were we to do? We were strong enough to drive them outside the walls and bar the gate, but we don't have enough warriors to drive them from the forest. They've been in the Arrowheads for nearly a year, chopping down our trees to light their fires and stealing our crops."

"It was a good battle, though," a voice said from the doorway. A young man stepped boldly into the room. Unlike the majority of the elves, his hair burned a brilliant red and his blue eyes glowed beneath a high brow. He walked towards his father with a muscular grace that belied his skill with a bow. "We fought well, but the Black Knights are fierce warriors. They're hard to fight off." He smiled at Alvardine. "Hello, Grandfather."

"Liam!" Alvardine leapt to his feet, clutching the boy to him.

Liam grinned at the embrace. His strong arms enveloped Alvardine's body. "You're my grandfather- You're supposed to old!"

"Ah, but elves age slowly, boy," Alvardine said, releasing him from his grasp. "Let me look at you. Weak, too pale for a seasoned warrior, but that should improve over time. That is, if you are anything like the elven boys your age. Your reputation proceeds you; I have already heard all about your heroic exploits. You've done well. I don't think you'll be worthless, at least. Not destined to be a scribe. No man of my name is! Maybe a hunter, maybe a warrior, if you can keep up your strength." He glanced Liam up and down one last time. "I've seen worse."

Dreogan grimaced. "You've seen worse! The boy eats enough to fed ten men. All that food has to be going somewhere. And he's fast, too. No one climbs as swiftly or as silently as Liam. He runs farther than anyone else. He's the best man in the city."

"He can run, huh?" Alvardine asked. "Running is a great talent, but only if you are running towards the scene of trouble. Too many men run away from it. Tell me Liam, are you courageous?"

Liam blushed. "I would like to think so. I was the first boy of my age to make a kill on the hunt. A boar. You know how dangerous they are. We all do. I was the only boy to take a boar for his first kill."

"Good. I can see that you are being raised in experienced hands. Did you know that I also killed a boar for my first time? A small one, but a boar all the same."

"Liam killed a sow and one of her piglets, the most dangerous of all boars. She was a big one, too. Fed us for three days solid."

"Did you save the pelt?" Alvardine's question was directed towards Liam, who had regained a bit of his dignity in hearing the praise.

"I did. It's hanging above my bed until I can fashion some sort of cloak from it."

"I'd like to see it very much, I think." Alvardine nodded to Dreogan. "You've done well, son. I must admit that when you first found him, I was a little worried. You'd never shown much aptitude for rearing young ones before, and with his human blood... No matter. He's turning out well."

"Thank you." Dreogan glanced at Alvardine, and for a moment, father and son were silent, holding each other's gaze. Alvardine flicked his eyes towards Liam. Dreogan nodded. "Now, for the feast!"

The door swung open to reveal a line of women, each bearing a well-laden dish in her hands. Fragrant loaves of bread were set before each diner. Soup was ladled into stone bowls and left to steam heavenly scents into Alina's nose. Spoons appeared out of nowhere, and she eagerly dipped into the meal. Creamy broth soon filled her mouth. Chunks of roasted beef, cooked until the meat almost dissolved at a touch, dribbled down her throat. The honeyed mead was delicious. She could hardly stand to put the goblet down after each sip. She tore the bread apart and was rewarded with a pat of butter, already inserted into the loaf. The wheat soaked up her soup rapidly, and she quickly learned that it was much faster to use the bread instead of a spoon. Her bowl emptied almost instantly, only to be refilled with a rib of pork.

Carn waved his spoon enthusiastically, helping himself to another loaf of bread. His face was a gloating grin smothered in stains—Carn had never been a neat eater. His plate was stacked high with crust remains and bones in minutes. "I never thought food could be so good!"

Alina nodded, not bothering to empty her mouth enough to give an intelligible answer. The food of the elves was a rich mixture, and it took some getting used to, especially since Alina was used to coremen fare. The underground race ate mainly dried fruits and honeyed ham, sweet foods that often left your teeth rotting. In the fall they would gather maple sap, boiling it down into syrup. They used it to preserve almost all of their foods. The food that filled Alina's mouth now was a combination of tastes entirely new to her, and she reveled in this world of sensory.

As they ate, the talk fell to the achievements of the local young men. Liam, of course, was widely praised to the most accomplished in the village. He was a born shadow. No one could see him when he chose to lurk, the faintest crackling was foreign to him when he stalked. He was the artist of many pranks and various mischief and was rarely caught. The elves valued him as a scout, sending the nineteen year old out alone to locate prey. And now that the Black Knights were a constant threat, Liam often went out to track their movements.

"He hasn't been discovered yet; sometimes I think he actually has some elvish in him!" Dreogan laughed, but Alvardine's eyes flashed warningly. " I see no reason to keep him home. And he is a big help. We would have been raided weeks ago if it weren't for Liam."

"Yes, but he could be discovered any day! Have you forgotten what the Knights do to spies? He'll be flayed alive! One of these days you'll wake up to find his head being nailed to your door." Alvardine gave any involuntary shudder. "The work he's doing is important. I don't doubt it, but this is my—" He snapped his mouth shut. "—Grandson we're talking about! I just don't want to see him die so young."

Liam, whose presence had been momentarily forgotten,

cleared his throat. "I *am* very careful, Grandfather. The Knights don't even know that I'm there. And if they did, well, I know these forests better than anyone. I would be away like the wind before they had a chance to strap on their swords."

"My boy, they would not need to 'strap on their swords.' They would unsheathe them and butcher you alive. That is how the Knights are. They are a threat like we've never seen before. You can't be too careful." Oryth nodded. "It is a noble task to be sure, but I agree with Alvardine. Spying on the Black Knights is too dangerous for any man, but especially a boy—"

"I'm nineteen!"

"*Young* Man, then. But not even the best warrior in the world would be able to stay hidden for long. The Knights might not be able to see well, but their horses have a wonderful sense of smell. They're worthy opponents, and they've earned many honorable titles."

"Including Bone Breakers, Night Death, and The Blood Letters," Alvardine said grimly. "Their reputation is very well known. People all over Ivindor fear them."

"The Black Knights are formidable opponents, to be sure," Leif agreed. "However, they are mortal men, and can be killed. Tell me, Liam, when do they sleep? We can creep up and attack them. They'll be caught off guard, and with the elves we'll have more than enough warriors."

"And die right then and there! The Knights don't sleep, idiot. They won't be caught unawares, no matter if we do have the cover of darkness to hide us. No," Oryth concluded, "even if we were able to kill one or two, the others would surely escape, and soon we would have the whole of Rolan's army breathing down our necks. This is not the time to be foolish!"

"It never is, Father." Elewyn forked a leg of mutton onto her plate, resting it on a mountain of mashed potatoes like a Greek temple. She paused for an instant, admiring the scene she had created, and then tore into the flesh. "Delicious."

"I'm glad you think so, lady. Liam speared that sheep yesterday." Dreogan smiled. "It was tough kill, that mountain sheep. They're agile beasts. But you've never seen one before—they're hard to come by."

"They were plenty abundant in Grisholm, where I was raised. A local man took me out to hunt them once. You're right. They're extremely fast. They scented us long before we got anywhere near them."

"Yeah, we had that problem too at first," Liam nodded. "We learned to come up from behind them, uphill. If the wind is blowing just right, you can get within throwing range."

"You spear hunt, then?" Elewyn asked. "Or sling? But no, I suppose a sling couldn't bring down a sheep." She avoided looking him in the eye. She was sure that if she did so, the game would be up.

"Bow and arrow. A few men use a bola, but I haven't learned that yet." He leaned back against the wall of the building. In the dim lighting, Alina could see that his eyes were hollow from lack of sleep.

Alina turned to Carn, who was shoveling down his third plate of food at a furious rate. She rolled her eyes. "Don't you ever stop eating? What's a bola?"

"Type of hunting weapon."

"Yeah, I got that far."

"It's a collection of stones wrapped in hide with rope to swing them around. Why do you want to know? You don't hunt."

"No, but she could." Elewyn frowned. "Just because she's a girl!"

"I never said that! Girls can hunt as well as any boy. I thought modern society had agreed on that."

"Carn," Alina admonished. "There's no need to be sarcastic." She paused. "Not in these times, anyway. What if that was the last sentence you ever said? Would you want to be remembered as a sarcastic know-it-all?"

"Geez, Alina. Only you would think of something like that."

Alina scowled at her empty plate. What did Carn know about such things? Was it possible that he didn't realize how fragile life was? There were Knights right outside the wall, a flimsy wall, and Carn was joking? *I could kill him right now and he would laugh about it. Joy is great, but there are times for seriousness.* She tapped her fingers, feeling the anxiety flooding through her core. *The Knights are just out that door... Listen! You hear the footsteps? They're coming!* She ducked, only to realize that the 'footsteps' were just the heavy knockings of Oakenwhite against a bowl.

Her eyes leapt to the other faces in the room. *Thank the Gods no one noticed! They would think I'm an idiot. Probably leave me behind because they think I'm such a coward. Well, I'm not an idiot, and I'm certainly not a coward. Didn't I stand up against Isen in the Clan? I braved those stupid tunnels and kept my wits in Daedalyus. I can't be a coward. I wasn't raised that way.*

She tugged at her dress, noticing that it was fraying around the cuffs. She would have to make a new one soon, or at least figure out a way to drape her cloak like Elewyn did. Somewhere in the saddlebags was a bit of gold, enough to buy a new wardrobe. That was emergency money, though. She couldn't use that on a silly dress! Maybe Carn would lend her a tunic and trousers. They'd be more practical for travel anyway.

Carn's right. Only I would think of something like this. Why am I so paranoid? She stretched upward, straining her back against the very notion of the thought. The mats had been comfortable at first, but they had long since worn down to an uneasy flatness. She could feel the floor rising up through the layers of leather. A stone dug into her hip. For the first time, she noticed that the floor was at an angle, sloping backwards from the door. The hill hadn't been noticeable from the outside, or maybe that was just her imagination. She couldn't recall. Her eyelids drooped downwards. Through half closed eyes she watched as the women appeared again, clearing away the dishes.

"Bed!" Dreogan cried. "Liam will show you to your rooms. I hope you don't mind; we're going to have to put you two to a chamber."

8

The girl slid out of the shadowed doorway. Her bare feet carried her lightly across the worn path, her lean body shimmering in the moonlight. A light traveling cloak fluttered about her feet as she walked. Up above, the stars twinkled against a backdrop of the deepest blue.

She slipped around the edge of the last hut and into the darkness beyond. She did not carry a lantern, but the moon was shining brightly enough for her to see her way. Her blue eyes stared searchingly into the dark forest the surrounded her. She had moved into the outer rim of the forest now, and the trees stood like centuries all around her. Heavy brush snagged loose tendrils of her blond hair as she swept by, but she did not seem to notice, so intent was her focus. She padded along the soft path, one hand trailing on the smooth stone of the outer wall.

She came to a clearing and paused. At her feet, a narrow creek bubbled eagerly through the tall grasses. She settled down beside it to wait. Her fingers played in the water, dipping in and out of the liquid like otters on the sea.

A crackling in the bushes to her right caught her attention. Her fingers stilled as she froze. Her keen eyes darted through the brush. Was it him, finally come? She tugged her cloak nervously. He had said that he would come. He always did. This was their meeting place, the secret grotto that enveloped them whenever she could sneak away. It had been so long . . .

But that did not matter. She was here in Abrelyon, finally. It had been over a year since she had last sat beside this stream. He had been only eighteen, with the first hints of a beard growing as soft, downy fuzz. He was older now, stronger, a seasoned warrior. She had seen the grace with which he strode through the village, had seen the powerful flexing of his muscles when he leapt into the treetop homes. He wore a sword now, a huge, heavy weapon that only the most skilled man could wield, made of thick steel sharpened to its fullest. She shuddered to think of him using such an implement, but its masculinity suited him. He had grown a lot over the past year, and she had fallen for him all the harder.

The stream sang to her desperation, She let her fingers trail in the water, interrupting the steady flow into miniscule rivulets. The cool liquid caressed her skin. She stared into the river rock, fully aware of the presence behind her. He filled her thoughts as he stood, silent and observing. His scent flooded her nostrils, and still she did not turn. This was a dream; it could not be real . . .

And yet it was. She could hear his soft breath sifting through the air. The gentle smell of pinesap, collected from days in the trees, hung in her conscience. She waited for him to move, to come to her, to wrap his strong arms around her and hold her close. She prepared herself to go limp in his arms. But he did not move, and his warmth, just a few seconds ago so real, dissipated into the twilight.

She turned back to the clearing. Her eyes closed on the emptiness, swelling her mind with tears. Had he forgotten?

No. She could hear distinct footsteps now, the soft, barely audible sound of his bare feet padding on the needle carpeted earth. His strong frame pushed branches aside silently, and yet the rustle of his passing was quite distinct to her. *He is coming.* She whirled back to the stream, so that only her long, shapely neck was visible from the edges of the clearing.

A voice rang out in the cool air, its notes cascading to meet the stream.

Meet me by the tree
So tall and oaken white
Growing in the land of cold.
A stone ring circles it,
A girth for its mantle,
A bowl for its blood,
When it spills.

Meet me by the tree
Where we will be given
The chance to repay our sins!
Strange things happened there,
Once upon a night.
My love, meet me there again.

He stepped out of the brambles just as she had imagined, his bow slung loosely over his shoulder as if he was hunting. But she knew better. His prey, the brilliant white stag that he was stalking, was *her.* He had already aimed his great arrow, sending it arcing through the air to pierce her heart. Now he followed his wounded prey, ready with his soulful eyes to tether her to him. But she did not struggle, indeed, she did not flee. She was a willing prisoner of his soul. He approached her pale frame, a ghost to the sleeping forest.

His tunic flapped in the night air. He saw her still frame and paused. His eyes drank in the graceful curve of her neck. It had been so long . . .

When he had last seen her, she had been hardly more than girl, exuberant and full of life. She had been beautiful then, yes, but her beauty had not ceased to grow over the intervening year. She had matured as well; he had seen the quirk of a woman's wisdom in her eyes. He could see that she had blossomed into a young woman, though she tried to hide her new curves beneath the bulk of her cloak. She had never been one to enjoy a woman's life, but he didn't expect her to. She was like her mother, strong in mind and body, skilled with the sword and comfortable with horseflesh between her thighs. Her father was wise to keep her close; she would be a catch if the proper bait were obtained.

He lingered for a moment, taking in the soft trickle of her golden hair as it cascaded down her back. She had released it from her customary braid, and the curls were loose as a result. The cloak had slipped down from its high perch about her neck, revealing one delicate shoulder. Her fingers, hardened from years of riding and softened by her loving character, dappled in the cool creek water. He smiled a slow smile. This was the position she took up when they came to the clearing.

And as the position was expected of her, the actions were expected of him. He crept forward on stealthy feet. He brushed a lock of hair with his lips, murmured the poems of the elves in her ear. He sat beside her and held her close, running his light fingers through the shining gold. No words of greetings were exchanged; they did not need to be.

They sat for some time, breathing in each other's scent. Her hands ran lightly down his spine, feeling the hard bones beneath the skin. His muscles had a life of their own; hardened from a lifetime of use, tensing and relaxing with each breath that he took. His powerful legs were clamped beneath him, solid against the damp earth.

She smiled. Times like this were so rare . . . Doubtless she would not see him for another year or more. And if her father forced her to . . . She grimaced. "You know about Dreogan?" Her voice was soft, cringing.

"Yes." He stroked her head.

"About Father's plans for me?" She shuddered. "We're to be wed in the fall."

"I know."

"I'm to stay here so that he can formally court me."

"I'll be here."

She fingered his reddened hair. The locks glowed in the starlight, and could have easily been mistaken for spun silk, so fine were the hairs. "You're not angry?"

"No," he whispered. His lips brushed against her ear. "I would rather have it be my father than a complete stranger. This way, at least, you won't be miles away."

"But your father . . . Gods know this isn't my choice!" He voice rose to a near shout. The cry echoed amongst the trees.

He whipped a callused hand over her mouth. The grip was not confining, but it silenced her instantly. "I know. The choice isn't yours to make—"

"It's his! That slime ball, ignorant, crude, woman beater, bastard—Sorry. I know he's your father." There was no meaning behind the apology.

He drew a deep breath, wiping the beads of sweat from

his brow. "It's alright. He deserves it. I deserve it. Ele—No. I should tell you something."

She froze. "What?" Her tone, suddenly wary, circled his body like a wolf, waiting to pounce.

"I'm being sent away." He rushed on. "He knows about us, my father. He doesn't want me around—I'm a threat to him now."

"You said you would be here! That we would be together!"

"We will be—"

"No, we won't! We'll be miles apart. You have no idea what it's like to be locked up with him—don't you dare say we'll be together in spirit!" She threw his arm away and struggled to rise. He pulled her down, sharply.

"You'll come with me! Oryth doesn't really want you to be tied in an ugly marriage. I'll talk to him, make him understand." He ran his fingers through his hair. "And when this is all over, when the war is won, I'll ask for your hand. Then we'll be together."

"Then why don't you ask for it now? Save us all the trouble?"

"Ele—I can't. I'm not ready. You're not ready."

"I'm ready enough to be married to some bastard!"

"A few meetings in a secluded wood over a period of several years doesn't constitute a relationship! We need more time . . ."

"We don't have more time! I'm to be married in a few weeks, sooner, and they'll want to leave soon." She sighed. A single tear of frustration trickled down her cheek. "Please."

He smiled in spite of her tears. His finger traced the damp path, catching the droplet just as it reached the curve of her chin. "Hey. It's all right. It'll be all right. You'll see. Dreogan doesn't love you, but he does need a mate. I've heard talk . . . "

"I don't want to hear! Don't you understand? He's to be my husband!" She shuddered.

He frowned. He loved her, and it hurt him to see her in so much pain. But he didn't have much say in the matter; the women of Ivindor were generally believed to be inferior to the men, and their marriage was seen only as a means of gaining wealth. He wasn't ready to ask for her hand; he had never imagined marrying her. The idea appealed to him, now that he thought about it, appeased and appalled him. She was not the run of the mill type of girl he was expected to marry. He held her close as the tears racked her body. The salty water pooled against his shoulder, leaving a dampness in the leather. "It will be all right. I promise." He hoped that he was right.

9

Alina curled beneath the cotton comforter. Outside, she could hear the birds singing from their perches in the trees, a melodious sound likening to that of chorus. Her eyes blinked open.

She was lying in a dreary room. Above her head, an intricate mosaic was inlaid in the headboard. Pictures of the Gods danced across the tiles. She straightened up to look at it properly. Nora, Queen of the Gods, sat nobly on her throne. Her husband, Zyl, was missing, but Alina didn't wonder at that. Zyl was always on the move, wandering the lands of Ivindor, protecting his people. No, it was Nora that sat upon the throne of the Gods, up in their temple in the sky. Mists swirled outside the columned walls, fading into nothingness. This was the last realm of Ivindor.

Nora's eyes gazed thoughtfully into Alina's. Dark and piercing, they seemed to burn their way into her soul. Her black hair was pulled back in a bun, and a silver crown circled her head. Her nostrils were flared, as if she was about to voice her disapproval.

Carn had told Alina the story behind this mosaic many times. It was a tale every child grew up on. If there was bully at school, or if the local king seemed to have drunk too much ale for his own good, Nora was there. She would help. It was her duty; nay, her privilege, and she would do anything she could to keep her subjects safe.

Alina snorted. Once, she might have believed this tale, but now, she wasn't so sure. She wasn't an innocent child anymore. Too many things had happened for her to truly believe that a Goddess was about to swoop down and save her. *Where were you when Arie was hung? I called for your help, but you never came. . .. And Isen? Surely you didn't approve of him. He was killing people, Your people! And yet, you have not done a thing to stop him.*

She gasped at the thoughts running through her head. *Little wonder Nora hasn't come to my aid; I'm so disrespectful.* She shook her head. *No. It shouldn't matter whether I believe in you or not. If you're up there, you should be forgiving. If not, then you don't deserve to be worshiped.*

And if you, Great Goddess, were truly forgiving, you wouldn't hesitate to help out because one girl wasn't paying you respect. You'd see that it was a fault, but that it was an understandable fault. You'd put that aside. A true Goddess does not need to be worshiped in order to help her people.

She frowned, moving away from the mosaic. *You didn't come to my aid. Why should I bother to ask for your help again?*

Turning to the rest of the room, Alina slowly donned her cloak. Its ripped hem fluttered inches above her ankle. Across a narrow rug, Elewyn's lithe form tossed and turned on another bed. Her boots, damp and muddied, stood guard beside her feet. Alina frowned. She thought she had heard someone leave the chamber late last night.

She slipped through the door. Outside, dewdrops clung to the grass like little diamonds, sparkling in the sun. A fresh cooking fire had been stirred up, and its smoke wafted her way. A lone pot bubbled over the cools. She hurried over, scooping up a bowlful with her cup. The grey substance burped pungent fumes into her face.

It will have to do. She wrinkled her nose, but nevertheless managed to gulp a portion down. Finished, she hastily wiped her mouth on a corner of her cloak. She then set about exploring Abrelyon.

She had not been able to meander the various paths the day before; by the time Dreogan had seen them off to bed, it had been too dark to see properly. She now strode down the main street, kicking at various debris. Old eating bowls, broken spoons, arrowheads: the rubble of a half dead city. Huts lined the sides of the street, reporting to duty reluctantly. Whimpers could be heard from behind some of the doors, children stirring from their sleep. Windows glared out at Alina. She hurried by, not wishing to impose.

At the next side street, she turned abruptly to follow its course. Smaller, this street also wandered between huts. It was so narrow that she could easily touch both sides with her outstretched hands. Cobblestones, loose in their sockets, clunked beneath her feet.

Mist was rising up from the end of the street. She approached cautiously. What if she was attacked? It would be all too easy for the Black Knights to sneak up on her unawares.

Her feet felt the water first. Dark and glistening, it stretched out before her. She had never seen such a lake in her life. The water was ice cold, but steam rose from its surface, obscuring the opposite shore. Reeds waggled in its ripples. She could not see the bottom, didn't want to see the bottom. This was the sort of lake a monster would lurk in.

She stepped lightly onto its bank. The sand sunk

beneath her as she walked. So this was the fabled Lake of the Mists. Carn had told her stories; wonderful tales of knights in shining armor, of a king who was raised by a wizard, and of a lake just like this. It was to such a lake that the king had come. He had ridden into the waters, and the woman appeared. She had risen out of the water, no, was part of the water. And in her hands, she had borne a sword, so pale and sharp that the king had hesitated to touch it. Excalibur, it had been called. Alina smiled at the memory. The story had been one of her favorites, once.

A piece of driftwood was floating just off shore. She watched its progress dazedly. The black water swirled around it. Small fish darted beneath it. A branch protruded into the depths beyond. Something flapped there, caught.

She waded out into the water. Her hands grasped the damp wood, and she flipped the log over. The branch swung up her face. She ducked, and then steadied it against her knee. With trembling fingers, she tugged at the clump clinging to its end.

It was not until she got out of the water that she paused to look at the thing. Sopping wet, it dripped mud down her front. The color was alike to that of tanned leather, except that it was much too thin to have been a hide. *Parchment,* she realized. She flipped the strip over. Small markings had been etched into its surface. Ink spread from each wound like blood, blotting out any distinguishing features. Only one word was visible. Upon reading it, she hurried back to her lodgings.

Once she was seated firmly on her bed, she turned the parchment over once more. What could it mean? It was not a common word, not a word she would expect to see on just any old scroll. The writing itself was also particularly intriguing. Sharp and angular, the letters cut into the parchment. Someone had run a knife over the margins, and they were silky in her hand. She ran her fingers down it, puzzling.

Raven King. The word churned in her head. A legend, a man so powerful he could put an end to King Rolan's madness. A man that both sides knew about, that both sides were fighting for. It would not do to be caught in the center. No. She tucked it away in her saddlebag. It would not do at all.

"Alina!" The voice, sharp with excitement, echoed in the small chamber. Alina pushed herself into an upright position and rubbed the sleep from her eyes. Groggily she came to her senses.

Sunlight streamed in through the windows, the brightness obscured by the moth eaten curtains. Carn strode over to them. He ripped them open, and Alina blinked at the sudden flash of light. *It's nearly midday. How could I sleep so long?*

She tugged her boots, watching as Carn threw open the last of the curtains. His cloak hung haphazardly from his neck, and the laces of his shirt swung as he walked. He grinned. Alina decided that his hair was mussed from sleep. *We were all exhausted.* She smiled back at him, tugging her own cloak from the hook beside her bed.

Carn flopped down beside her. "You're never going to guess what's happening!" His eager face beamed in childish delight.

Alina shook her head. "Course I'm not. I haven't been out all morning." She was surprised at how easily the lie came to her. The words slipped out unaided. She tried not to think about her walk on the banks of the lake.

"We're staying in Abrelyon for a few more days—"

"What's so great about that? I know it's an elven village and all, but aren't we on a time schedule?"

"Let me finish, will you?" Carn tugged his cloak. The edge slid up over his shoulder, and he brushed an invisible speck of dust from its cloth. "Like I said. We're staying a few more days, because—You know what day it, right?"

Alina nodded in exasperation. "Tomorrow's midsummer. Just tell me!"

"Midsummer." Carn emphasized the word. When Alina didn't react, he rolled his eyes. "Midsummer. Come on! The Festival of Nora?"

"Ah! We're staying for the celebration!"

Carn's head bobbed up and down. "The entire town is getting ready! You should smell the food! Liam took Leif and Alvardine hunting for boar. We'll have suckling pig! And Dreogan's arranging the games—all of the men are out practicing!" Carn's eyes narrowed. "To think, it's the most exciting day of the year, and you've spent it sleeping! What are you, some sort of mutant bear? Even Leif was up at the crack of dawn!"

Alina leapt from the bed. She grabbed the pillow and tossed it at his head. "I'm up now. Just let me find—"

"Come on!" Carn grabbed her arm. He tugged her, hard, and Alina followed him as he dashed from the room. She couldn't remember what she was searching for.

10

The Festival Nora took up all of Abrelyon's energy. Alina gave no more thought to the scrap of parchment she had found on the edges of the lake; there was too much to prepare. Already, she could smell the first tinges of the boar roasting on the spit, and the sun was just beginning to rise. Women clustered in groups on the street outside, their chatter awakening Alina well before she would have naturally. She tugged her dress over her head and turned to stare at her reflection in the mirror.

Made of polished stone, the mirror's surface was greased with oil for extra reflection. The edges were smooth and delicate, the black obsidian surrounded by white wood. Alina bit her lip, fidgeting with her dress. She wished she had something nicer to wear. In the mirror, her own dress was tattered and travel stained. She shrugged. There was nothing she could do about it now. She smoothed the worst snarls in her hair, then spun and left the room.

Outside, the crowd was raucous with preparations. Men darted back and forth between the huts carrying spears and bundles of bows. A young boy heaved a sword towards the center of town. The weapon was too large for him, nearly half his height, and the blade dragged on the ground between his legs. Behind him, his older sister and her friends burst into peals of laughter. Alina didn't need to think hard to realize what the source of the comedy was.

She stepped out onto the street. The crowd enveloped her instantly, and she found herself jostled between gossiping women and their husbands. A baby's cry pealed like a siren in her ear. She twisted, catching sight of the infant through the dense mass of bodies. The tiny face stared back at her. The mother shifted the swaddled weight to her hip, and the baby disappeared from view.

Alina couldn't help but glow with happiness as the crowds pushed her onwards. This was the day of Nora, the longest day of the year. All across Ivindor the people would be celebrating. Even the Clan, which seemed so distant and remote to her now, would glorify in the great Goddess. The thought was comforting.

An old woman kept pace with her as she walked. Alina stole glances at the wizened grandmother, surprised that she was able to walk at all. She clutched at a cane, and her gnarled fingers shook on the handle. Her white hair was an island in a sea of black. She reached for a young girl trotting at her side. A smooth hand slipped into her wrinkled one. The girl babbled exuberantly, her excitement bringing a smile to the old woman's lips. They came to a corner, and the pair veered off from Alina, leaving her alone in the crowd of people. She frowned, but let them go. They were going to the same place anyway.

The street opened into a crossroads, and Alina found herself washed into a wide throughway. On all sides, the crowds of people grew heavier. Alina breathed in, and with the air came the scent of hundreds of humans pressed together. Sweat mingled with unwashed bodies. The thunder of a thousand conversations crushed down on her, and yet Alina felt light as air. The exhilaration of the festivities swept over her.

She made her way down the street. Progress was painstakingly slow, but she hardly noticed. Street vendors had begun to set up shop for the day, laying their wares out for all to see. She slowed down to look at them. Ivory necklaces glistened beside hammered bracelets of copper and steel. Dried meat swung from racks, dangling precariously close to jars of pickled vegetables. On one stand, dozens of furs shone brightly in the sun. She ran her hand over an otter pelt and marveled at its softness. Otters were rare catches in the Clan.

Her gaze shifted to a snow-dusted fleece. The fur was thick and rugged, cut from a carcass during heavy winter. Long, spiraled horns were displayed amidst the plush. She picked one up, weighing it her hand. It was hard to believe that any animal could support so much weight.

She turned away. Once, she would have leapt at the chance to purchase an ibex skin; the animals were nearly extinct. Only a few hunters a year managed to catch one. Even the richest of the nobles never had more than one or two of the hides, and the furs were never on market. To own such a prize was a dream that many poor girls aspired to. Alina herself had once begged Arie to hunt one for her, but now she frowned at the sight. The off white coat wasn't nearly as appetizing as it had been.

She strolled to the next stand, pushing through a cluster of children on the way. They clamored in front of the big-wheeled cart, reaching with their grimy fingers for the jars on display. A young boy burst into tears when the shopkeeper swatted him back. Alina stepped closer.

The earthen jugs shuddered at her approach. She

offered a steadying hand to the vendor, a lanky, grey haired man who bumped into the cart with each turn of his shriveled body. He squinted at her as she straightened the jars.

Alina paid him no mind. She leaned in, examining the contents of each jug. The scents of the candies wafted up to her, sugar mingling alongside licorice and maple. Buttons of sugared ginger sprawled beside the red and white swirls of peppermint. In a large, open weave basket, pressed sugar had been molded into all sorts of shapes. Simple squares and spheres aside, Alina thought she could see a horse in the midst. She shook the basket slightly, and sure enough, a crude horse shifted into view. The sugar had begun to crumble at the edges; the candy would not last much longer.

"Care for one?" The vendor spoke slowly, feeling his way around the words. He wrinkled his brow, glaring at her with piercing brown eyes. His frizzy grey hair, pluming from behind his ears, gave Alina the impression that she was staring at a squirrel, and not an old man with a potentially disagreeable temper.

"Why not?" She fished around in her purse. Alvardine had given her a few coins to spend during the day, and she was hungry. She pulled out a single gold coin and laid it on the counter. "How much can I get for this?"

The man's fingers scrambled to grub up the coin. He held it to the light, frowning at it with a puzzled expression. Finally, he dropped it into his purse. "Couple pieces."

Alina nodded in agreement before turning back to the trays. The sugared horse was an obvious choice, but she had some difficulty deciding on the second. She chose a piece of licorice from a dusty jar. Licorice had always been

Arie's favorite.

She bit into the black rod as she wandered from stall to stall. The candy was warm and sweet in her mouth, and she savored the last of the licorice before slipping the horse onto her tongue. It melted instantly, flooding her senses with rich molasses.

"Alina!"

She twisted, feeling the last of the candy disappear down her throat. The speaker, hidden in the masses of people, was invisible to her. She shook her head. The stall to her left looked particularly interesting.

"Alina!"

This time, she couldn't ignore it. Someone was calling her name, and since there weren't many people in Abrelyon who could identify her, she had a pretty good idea who it was. She waited while Carn swam through the sea of elves.

"Thank the Gods. It's impossible to find anyone in this place," Carn yelled above the din. He smacked his lips, wiping his mouth with the back of his hand. Alina saw that he too had managed to find a midday snack.

"I've never seen a festival this big," she agreed. Her hands itched to try on the pair of gloves in the stall behind her. She forced them deep into her pockets.

"No kidding! But this is just the market—it's nothing compared to the main square. Dreogan's got a tent set up, and there's a huge altar. Can you believe that it's made out of one tree? And the corral . . . Did you see the animals! Not just horses and cattle, but deer and wild cats . . . But you've already seen it. I'm boring you."

Alina shook her head, not willing to admit to Carn that she had slept nearly half the morning away. "I didn't see any wild cats," she offered. "Maybe you could show me?"

Carn's face lit up at the proposal. He grabbed her hand, dragging her through the street with such frenzy that Alina feared her entire arm would rip off. The tent was visible from halfway down the road. She stared up at the enormous canopy, dazzled by the brilliant colors of its dyed canvas. Carn snorted, yanking her forward once more.

The bleating of animals rose above the general confusion of the crowd. Alina caught a glimpse of the arena, fenced in with heavy poles. Cattle lowed at her as she approached. Several horses whinnied and pranced in proud circles, showing off to the new visitors. She played privy to their demands and admired their silky coats. It wouldn't do to mention how pretty she thought Mandan was.

Carn jerked her arm. His other hand rose up, pointing at some obscurity in the back. "There! Do you see it?"

Alina saw it. The beast was chained to a stump near the center, far enough away from the people to provide excitement without danger. Its glossy fur rippled as it paced. She watched for a moment. It glared back, its yellow eyes murderous.

"A leopard," Carn breathed. His grip on Alina's arm was rapidly growing tighter.

Alina slapped his hand away. She massaged her wrist, trying desperately to persuade the blood to return. It flushed in with a painful tingling. The leopard grumbled.

Carn jumped. He reached for Alina's hand once more, squeezing it until Alina thought she could hear the bones crack. She winced. "Carn—"

"I'm not scared." His pale face was rapidly growing paler.

She wrestled her hand form his grasp and turned to look at the leopard again. It wasn't large, still a cub in all but the most literal sense of the word. The last of the baby fur was long gone, but its eyes were soft. She imagined that it still had its milk teeth, though she couldn't be certain. The cat wouldn't open its mouth. It padded across the dusty ground. Its rope jerked taut, and the kitten mewed in frustration. She watched as it twisted to resume its pacing. "Its not much of a wild animal," she noted.

Carn shook his head. He sucked in a deep breath, letting the color flood into his cheeks. "Sure it's wild! They had to tie it up, didn't they?"

Alina looked at him. Before she knew it, her hand half rose in the air, preparing to slap some sense into him. She pushed the urge away firmly. "Come on, Carn. You're the one that told me the elves are good with animals! It's probably someone's pet, put on display for the day." She rolled her eyes. "Besides. There's no way it can get out of the cage. So relax."

Carn nodded, though he didn't look convinced. He strolled slowly along the fence, his eyes never leaving the leopard. Alina followed him. It wasn't that the leopard was about to attack—she knew Carn well enough by now. A charging animal was far less fearsome than a caged one. At least with the attacking animal, you knew what you had to deal with.

She led him away from the corral. The crowds were much thicker here than they had been on the street, and she had trouble navigating her way across the square. Young children dashed after their friends. Lines snaked away from the entrance to the tent, where women haggled over ticket prices. Alina tilted her head. The flaps of the tent fluttered as people passed in and out of them, exposing tantalizing views of the room beyond. If she could just get closer, maybe she could see inside.

Carn grabbed her arm. He dragged her towards the tent, grinning mischievously. "Come on! If you want to see the Games, then we need to go inside!"

Alina dug in her heels, but Carn was much stronger than her. She threw a nervous glance at the people waiting to get in. They glared back at her. "Carn—the lines! Shouldn't we but a ticket?"

"Alina." Carn didn't ease his grip on her arm. "We're guests here. Surely they won't make us pay!"

The tent flaps flailed in front of them. Alina caught the overwhelming scent of sweat and rancid oil seeping through from beneath the canopy. She pinched her nose. "Maybe I don't really want to go in after all—"

"Nonsense!" Carn tugged a flap aside, ushering her in to the dark space beyond. The air was thick and hot. Men strode past them, wrapped in thin towels. Their skin gleamed with oil. Many sported black and blue bruises, and Alina was sure she saw one man with a bloody bandage clutched to his ear. Another set of curtains separated them from the larger arena beyond, where a crowd jeered at the competitors.

"I think I've changed my mind, Carn," she whispered, but her friend had disappeared. She whirled, searching for his sun bleached hair in the gloom. Only the long braids of the wrestlers greeted her darting eyes.

A lithe young man slipped inside from the arena, momentarily exposing the small chamber to a blast of bright light. Alina blinked. She watched as the man strode towards her. His hair glowed a fiery red before the curtain swung shut.

She backed away, stumbling over her own feet in her

haste to escape. There was only one man in all of Ivindor with that color hair. What was he doing in the middle of Abrelyon? *I thought the elves drove the Knights out!* Her hand fell on a stiff rod. She closed her fingers over the weapon, throwing it out in front of her. The movement offset her balance. She felt herself falling backwards. The tent shivered as she crashed into it.

Alina moaned. A sharp, shooting pain entered her backside, and she rubbed at it. She didn't think she had broken anything, but still . . . Her head ached from where she had hit on a support beam.

The man knelt beside her. She felt another flutter of panic, and swung the rod at him. His hand flashed in the air. He caught the weapon before Alina had time to think. He tossed the rod aside. "You okay?"

She stared at him for a moment. This close, the man didn't look like the king at all, though his hair was suspiciously similar. His face was younger, less worn from years of battle, and he moved the agility of cat. He offered her is arm, and she took it gratefully. He tugged her to her feet.

"Liam." She bit her lip against the pain in her tailbone. She massaged it, knowing that she would be sore the next day. "Thanks."

He grunted his acknowledgment. "Alvardine said you were clumsy, but . . . Never mind. You're sure you're not hurt?"

She nodded. "Carn was here—he disappeared."

Liam grinned. "I was wondering what you were doing here! This room is reserved for athletes only. So, unless you're planning on competing . . . " He led her to the curtain, pulling it aside so that she could pass through.

"I was just on my way out, actually." The odor was

stronger outside of the tiny room. She could feel it rushing through the doorway.

Liam shook his head. "Leaving? You haven't been inside yet! Come on, I'll show you around."

Alina grimaced. "Fighting's really not my thing."

"It's not fighting. These are the Games, the tournaments of the Festival! You have to stay and see them, otherwise you'll dishonor the Great Goddess."

Alina allowed herself to be led through the doorway. She knew that he was right, but that didn't make her any happier. She wished Carn would reappear, if only to lend some support as she walked into the massive room.

The tent seemed much larger inside than it had outside in the square. Circular, it was lined with benches and stands. Men and women crowded the stadium, leaning over the railings as they attempted to see the competition. Young children sat in the dust in front of the adults; there wasn't enough seating for simple minors to take it up. They squabbled with each other under the roar of their parents' cheers.

The rest of the tent was made up of an elliptical arena. The dust had been scraped smooth, and men stood ready with brooms to repair the damage after each event. Two referees waved crimson flags at either end of the arena. They shouted something, but Alina couldn't make out the exact words.

"They're calling in the wrestlers," Liam explained. He led her to an open patch of bench. "You're lucky, if you don't like fighting. The gladiators just finished. No one died, of course, but there were some severe injuries."

Alina blanched. In the Clan, gladiators were slaves, and were forced to fight to the death. She knew that the custom was different on the surface, but she was still glad she had missed the fighting. Most gladiators carried wooden swords and toy shields to defend themselves from the very real blows of their attackers.

She watched as the last pair of gladiators marched off of the arena, disappearing into the tiny room where Liam had found her. The bench was warm under her seat, and she eased into it as the wrestlers strode onto the field. Their muscles rippled as they walked. Her fear began to ebb away. The Games weren't actually that bad, now that she was settled in.

The referees stuffed their flags into their belts. They grabbed several large jugs from the corner of the arena and carried them to the line of wrestlers. One judge began pairing the men off, while the other work furiously to uncork the jug. He raised it to his lips and gripped the stopper with his teeth. It flew off with a loud pop.

Grinning sheepishly, he poured the contents of the jugs onto one of the wrestlers. The oil was slick under his fingers. Droplets stained the dust of the arena. He lathered the athlete with the slippery liquid, then turned and did the same to his partner.

"Oil, so it's harder for them get a grip on each other," Carn whispered in her ear. Alina started. She stared at him as he slid onto the bench beside her. He held up a greasy package. "I was getting kind of hungry."

He bent over the brown parchment, peeling its layers away. The paper clung to his hands. Alina leaned in and saw the delicious golden crowns of a dozen honey cakes between the wrappings.

Carn licked his fingers. "Want one?"

She grinned despite herself, choosing to select her pastry herself rather than let Carn contaminate it with his grubby fingers. The cake melted in her mouth. She licked her lips and reached for another. She couldn't remember the last time food had tasted so good.

Carn beamed. He shoved the package at her. She took it without a word, her mouth too full of fire-baked crumbles to complain. She watched as he reached for another package at his feet.

"I've never licked honey cakes," he explained to Liam. He ripped the parchment away from his trophy, revealing a rich rack of ribs. Meat hung from the bones, nearly dissolving in its own juices. He tore a single bone from the rack and offered it to Liam. "Ribs. That is how it's done." He bit into the rib, forgetting that he had meant to give it away. Juice ran down his chin in rivulets. "Ah. That's the ticket."

Alina smiled, shifting her attention back to the arena. The crowd was roaring as the match got underway. The two men circled, eyeing each other nervously. One, larger than his partner, tripped over a wrinkle in the dust. He stumbled. Pale flesh flashed as he fell to the ground. His enemy lunged.

The crowd gasped. Both fighters were fairly skilled, and the match was nearly perfect. The pair seesawed across the arena. Black hair swirled as they danced. Suddenly, the smaller of the two found himself trapped in the other's burly arms. He was thrown to the floor with a resounding thud.

Carn grimaced, and even Liam looked a little pained. "It wasn't a very good fight," Carn explained, his words thick as he wrapped his lips around another hunk of meat. "Elves aren't made for wrestling." He glanced at Liam, but the man did not reply.

They watched as the rest of the wrestling matches were carried out in much the same fashion. The crowd grew bored, and the cries slackened. Perhaps the judges sensed this, for they waved their flags.

"Archery." Liam stood. He fidgeted nervously and then turned to his companions. "I've got to go. I'm competing." He strode away.

Several large targets were rolled into the arena. Men strained to position them, their hands sweaty on the dyed canvas of the bulls-eye. They settled the barrels on the left side of the arena, and the referees began to pace out the distance. A line of flour marked where the archers would stand.

The flaps to the athletes' chamber flew open. Twenty men strode onto the field, their bows arcing over their heads as they walked. Liam's red hair was a beacon beside the black locks of his peers. He adjusted his cloak and waited.

Each archer was to receive three arrows, and thus, three attempts to hit the target. The archer who shot closest to the center of the bulls-eye would win. The referee made sure to explain the rules in a loud, clear voice. The anticipation in the crowd mounted.

The first man stepped up to the line. His arrows had been dyed a deep purple, and he fingered them anxiously. Alina tried to calculate the distance to the target in her head, but she failed. It seemed like an awfully long way.

Cocking his bow, the man fit his arrow onto the string. He took aim and fired. Alina blinked, then threw her gaze towards the target. The arrow quivered in the center of the painted circles.

She sighed. "It would have been nice if Liam won," she told Carn, who was hardly listening. He waved to her to be quiet. The tournament continued.

The next man stepped up to the line. He notched an

orange arrow to his bow and let it fly. It too landed in the center of the target. Alina gasped. A coincidence?

No. She watched as every archer shot his three arrows. Not one missed the target, and all but three managed to hit the exact center. Liam's green arrow flew true as the others. It hit the target with a thickening thud.

The referee couldn't have been more pleased. He shouted a direction to his assistants. A man ran onto the field, his arms wrapped tightly around a bundled object. He handed it off to the referee. The wrapping fell away to reveal a long tube. The judge held it in the air for all to see. "The archers will now shoot through the tube!" he cried, his voice echoing off of the tent walls. "The man whose arrows stops in the center of the tube wins."

Alina groaned. It was impossible. Not only would the archers have to take careful aim, but they would also have to calculate the strength of their shot. She continued to frown as the judge set the tube on a wooden stand.

The first arrow fell too short. It skidded into the dust several feet in front of the tube. The archer frowned, repositioning his grip on the bow. He shot again, but this time his aim was off. The arrow slammed into the edge of the tube, veering of towards the crowd. It came to a shuddering halt in the siding of the tent.

Last arrow. Alina didn't dare to breath. The bow twanged, and another flew. Alina didn't bother to watch where it fell. The archer had missed by a long shot.

The line of archers slowly began to dwindle. Arrow after arrow fell short of the mark, or flew widely off target. Some were lucky enough to shoot through the tube; their arrows thwacked into the target beyond. Liam was the last competitor to toe the line. Alina waited with baited breath as he strung his bow. The wood creaked, and for a moment, she feared it would crack.

Liam slipped the bowstring into place as the judge brought him his arrow. He stroked the emerald fletching, his eyes wandering upwards. He closed them and waited.

The crowd began to chant. Softly at first, the words gained power until reverberated down Alina's spine. "Pray to the Gods. Pray to Nora, Great Goddess of all! Nora! Nora! Nora!" The chant reached a fevered peak. Liam's eyes snapped open. He fit the arrow to his bow. It sliced through the air.

Alina saw it enter the tube. She looked expectantly at the other end, but the arrow never left. It had come to rest in the center of the tube. Liam beamed. Elewyn dashed onto the field and folded him in her arms. Alina thought she saw a glint of tears running down her cheek.

Carn answered her questioning glance. "I overheard some men talking. Liam made a bet with Dreogan and Oryth. If he won the competition, Elewyn wouldn't have to stay in Abrelyon."

Alina looked back at the scene in front of her. She had been right the first time. Tears of joy were sliding down Elewyn's cheeks.

Later that day, the company gathered in the shade of Dreogan's hut. Food had been laid out on the table, and the chairs scraped as they all sat down to eat. Sweet honey bread steamed from platters. Haunches of meat, swimming in juice, bathed in large bowls. Their goblets full of rich mead, they drank to the mission that was to come.

"You're quite sure about this, Dreogan? Losing your son, and now a wife?" Oryth looked sharply down the table at the man. His grizzled hair stuck out at odd ends from beneath his cap.

"Liam won his bet, fair and square."

Oryth sighed. "Then Elewyn will have to come with us. I am sorry, but as you say. The boy did win his bet."

"Of course." Dreogan's eyes lingered Elewyn for a moment too long. "I understand."

"And Liam will be coming along, too." Alvardine clapped the young man on the shoulder. "Two elves in one company. Now we're sure to be a target." He laughed. "Not that we weren't already."

Liam shrugged his grandfather off. He grimaced. "I'm not really an elf, Alvardine. You know that. I'm not even your real grandson. I'm a—"

"Foundling. Yes, I know all about that. How Dreogan found you wandering in the woods when you were just a babe. How he adopted you, made you his own son. No Liam, I think I can call my Grandson still."

Liam's face turned the color of his flaming red hair.

"You'll provide us with supplies?" Alvardine turned questioningly to his son. "I know times are tough, but it is for the greater good."

Dreogan nodded slowly. "I'll give you what I can. You'll excuse me if I seem to be hurrying you off, but I am expecting a delegation from the dwarves to arrive in two days . . ."

Alvardine bowed. "We'll be on our way tomorrow."

After the meal, Alina finally managed to catch Carn alone. She led him into the shadows of the hut. "I thought no one dared to visit Abrelyon, not with the Knights so close."

Carn shrugged. "They don't. Dreogan just wants to get rid of us. Though it is about time the dwarves started talking to the elves again. It's been, what, like three centuries?"

"Dunno. I never learned that stuff. But the war was a long time ago. Too long ago for grudges to still be held. You're right. It's time for forgiveness. Especially in these times." She leaned close to her friend. "Listen, Carn. I found something by the Lake the other day. Something important."

He watched as she took a slip of parchment out of her pocket. He scanned the page, and his fingers stroked the edges thoughtfully. "Raven King. I can't see any reason for Dreogan to have something like this. He doesn't even know about it. And none of our people would have left this just lying around." He raised his shoulders. "Must have floated across the water from the Black Knight camp."

"But that means that Rolan knows about the Raven King."

"Course he does. He and Alvardine discovered the legend together, remember?"

"Yeah. But he's searching for it. Actively. What if he finds him first?"

Carn stared at Alina for a long moment. "There's always that chance, but remember, No one really knows where Sir Alleyn disappeared. Even Alvardine's just guessing."

"The closer we get to the Raven King, the closer we lead King Rolan."

"That's a chance we have to take. This is our only hope, Alina. It's all or nothing. We've got to go for it."

She frowned. "You talk like you're one of them."

Carn grinned. "Thanks to you, we both are. This is too

big of a problem for us to ignore, too big of a problem to just slide off our backs. Alina, this is our problem. Yours, and mine, and the Wanderers. Like it or not, we're a part of this war."

11

Alina tapped her heels to Mandan's sides, impatient to be going. The horse fidgeted under the weight on the saddlebags, and she grimaced as a heavy sack slid over her finger. She yanked it free, nursing the throbbing tip in her mouth. Her black eyes darted beneath her escaping curls of charcoal hair, peering down at the man standing by Mandan's head.

His fiery hair made her eyes ache in the early morning light. She could just barely make out his pale fingers clutching at Mandan's halter, his lips moving soundlessly against the desperate stampings of Mandan's feet. He had set his lantern down on the moist ground, a foolish mistake that had caused the flame to flicker out. He didn't seem to mind the darkness, but Alina did. She wished he would relight the wick.

It had been their only lantern to see by, and the darkness pressed around them. The first few rays of sunlight sliced the air on the eastern horizon with precious light. She glanced up at it, trying to tell how long it would be until the sun had fully cleared the treetops. Another hour or two at least. What was taking them so long?

Out of the corner of her eye, she watched Alvardine

heft a heavy sack onto Haranee's rump. The elf worked silently in the shadows, his figure draped in an array of cloaks and riding tunics. His boots, half laced and scuffed from years of use, were tucked around his feet. A pair of riding trousers, stiff at the inseams to prevent chaffing, clung to his legs. He swung the bag over the swaying back before tying it down with nimble fingers. A quick check over of every strap and he was mounted. She saw his lips move in a near silent command to the horse, urging the mare to stretch into place beside Alina.

Alvardine swiveled in his seat. His eyes flicked over the six riders with calculated haste. He nodded to the nearest standing figure. "You're sure about this, Dreogan? The journey will not be a safe one."

Dreogan shrugged. "The decision was never mine to make. Liam is—" He stumbled over the words. "Well, he's not my true son. If his destiny calls him your way, then there is nothing more I can do."

Alvardine nodded. "Very well. Liam rides with us. And Elewyn, Oryth?"

"She has told me very clearly. There is nothing for her here," Oryth said coldly. He did not look at his daughter.

Elewyn clicked Snowberry forward. The silver stallion stamped impatiently, his hooves clattering against the gravel path. Beside her, Liam swung up onto the back of a sorrel mare. Like Alvardine, he did not ride with reins, and he leaned forward to whisper into the mare's ears.

"We're off." Alvardine took one last look at the face of his son, and then clucked Haranee into a slow trot. The other riders followed suit, and the faint clicks filled the morning air. The horses' hooves pounded the dirt into iron bars. "Goodbye, Dreogan, my son. May the Gods lead you to a happy fate." Haranee broke through to the trail.

Alvardine raised his hand in a final farewell, and was gone.

Alina urged Mandan after him, closely followed by Carn and Liam. Both eyed each other with some hesitation, dreading spending several months with the other. Alina could feel their glares even with her back turned, so forceful were their emotions. She bit back the retort that was forming on her lips. It was, after all, natural for two men of similar birth rankings to show some confusion before one proved his dominance. They were only getting the feel of the other's strength, but Alina found herself boiling with frustration. *They have hardly known each other for three days. That's too soon for them to be arguing! There are more important things a foot, things that are going to need everyone's concentration, including theirs. How can they concentrate if they are worried about something as silly as rankings? We have a kingdom to save, for Gods' sakes!* She pushed Mandan closer to Haranee's rump, trying to distance herself from the hateful glares.

In the distance, she thought she saw a light flickering. *The Black Knights' campfire?* She leaned against Mandan's neck, wishing she could disappear. The horse's sweet smell filled her nostrils. She breathed in deeply, pulling the comfort in with the air.

When she looked up, Carn was riding at her side. His blond hair hung in tatters about his face. She grimaced. With his hair hanging low around his eyes, he looked more like a boy than the man he was becoming. He stared innocently at her.

Gods, we're so young. She followed her friend down the path, watching his narrow shoulders swaying with the horse's gait. *Too young to be on a journey. Too young to have left home. If we die, will anyone remember us? When death comes to wrap us in his sweet embrace, will anyone be around to care?*

She turned to watch Elewyn riding beside her. The girl sat perched on Snowberry, the huge stallion sliding in and out of the shadows. A faint, moonlit quality came to her skin. For a second, Alina thought she was glowing. After a moment, though, she saw that her hands were cupped around a flickering candle. Her face, bent towards the light, was still. White, frozen, she was a corpse on top of the horse.

When the world bears you away,
And death comes to take your hand.
Do not be afraid.
For I shall be at the tree,
Waiting.

The song floated from her stagnant lips. Silently, Alina watched Elewyn extinguish the candle. The flame flickered and then died. She couldn't help but think that life could be vanquished just as easily.

Shadows loomed out of the trees. The elf froze, watching the shapes come. He had been expecting this, but now? What if some one saw?

He glanced around hurriedly, but there was no one in sight. He had ridden far ahead of the party, and only their voices existed in his world now. He was alone to face the terrors of the night.

His eye caught sight of the torch, sweeping out of the

shadows. Haranee jumped under him, and he put a steadying hand to her neck. "Hush. They're coming." He was not talking about Oryth and the others.

Silent, he watched several figures step out of the trees. The torch burned steadily, and yet he could not make out their faces. He didn't need to; he knew who was coming for him.

"My lord." He refused to kneel at the man's feet. The man was on horseback, anyway, and was too high up for Alvardine to look him in the eye. He inclined his head slightly.

The man looked down at him for a moment, considering. Wisps of red hair stuck out rebelliously from beneath his hood. His face, of course, was in shadow, but his clothing was not. Brilliant purple, it glistened like the finest of silks. "You're late."

Alvardine nodded, not daring to look up. "The festivities kept me waiting."

"I do not forgive lightly," the man whispered. He leaned close to Alvardine's ear. He laughed as the elf realized what he was saying. "However. You may be of use to me yet."

"My lord?"

"Come, Alvardine! You know perfectly well what I'm talking about. I need to know where *he* is. You can tell me . . ."

Alvardine bristled. "I have no intention of doing that."

"Ah, yes. I thought we might run into this little difficulty." He motioned to one of his guards. "Have you forgotten why you came to me?"

The man paused just outside the ring of torchlight. He threw something down in front of Alvardine. The thing moaned.

Hesitant, Alvardine approached. The figure lay sprawled on its back, black hair spread wildly across his face. An ugly knife wound festered in his side; when Alvardine bent to touch it, it seeped blood.

"It's still fresh."

"Oh yes, I'm quite aware of that. You see, Alvardine, this is a new recruit. I picked him up, oh, shall we say, five minutes ago?"

Alvardine started. His fingers trembled as he reached for the figure once more. He brushed the hair aside. For a moment, he could not bear to look. When he did, the pleading eyes of Dreogan stared back at him. "Son," he whispered. He wiped the side of the man's mouth, dabbing away the bloody froth that accumulated there. He stroked the fine brow, the delicate features, so similar to his own. His face hardened.

"You wouldn't. You gave me your word!"

Laughter. "An eye, for an eye, Alvardine. You took the one I loved, so I shall take yours." He flicked a bit of dust off of his sword hilt. "That is, unless you cooperate."

Alvardine shook his head. "Cere never loved you. She would never have chosen you. All I did was expose you for what you are." His lip curled. "A traitor. Growing up among us, as my best friend! And now you threaten me with the life of my son? When they let you into that school, they did it out of the goodness of their hearts! And now you'll kill them?"

The man kicked Alvardine hard in the ribs. He watched as the elf curled up in agony. "When they took me into that school, I had been wandering for days without my parents. Because your people killed them! When I was accepted into that school, I was promised a future, a new beginning. I trusted you. And you took that away!" He swooped upon Dreogan. A knife glinted in the torchlight, and red blood welled up where the blade was pressed. "You'll tell me where the Raven King is, Alvardine." He sheathed his knife. "I don't think the boy will last as long as this one. You have three weeks."

And with that, the king of Ivindor strode away.

12

Sometimes, when Alina was quiet enough, she thought she could hear her brother's screams. She could see his capture flashing before her eyes, his beating, and his death. The hangman's noose strained around his neck, his eyes bulged. He opened his mouth as if to scream, but he died with a whisper. "Alina," he had said.

She shook the feeling aside. Arie had died months ago, and though the two siblings had been close, there was no reason for her to be mourning now. She had seen enough death. To her, it was an ordinary thing.

But Arie had been an idol to her. Strong, the leader of a rebel gang on the outskirts of the Clan territory, Arie hadn't been around much. He had always been busy with one thing or another, a new mission to complete. And for the most part, he had been successful. *Except for that last mission.*

There was no reason for it to go so wrong. There'd been assassination attempts before. . . It was only a matter of time before Isen was dead, and Carn was crowned king. But Isen was waiting. Someone, or something, warned him. She frowned, remembering the shouts of terror. Moments before Isen shown himself, Arie had ordered a retreat. He had sensed something was wrong. *That was when the first arrow struck.*

Not deep, not hard enough to kill him. Just wounded him, brought him down while the rest of the group escaped. No one stopped to save him. And then Isen appeared. Arie was tied up, and. . . She blanched. She had avoided thinking about her brother's last moments.

She stood, pushing aside the tent flap. Wind ruffling her hair, she surveyed the fields beyond the camp. Tall spruces bordered one side, and a creek bubbled on the other. Behind her, the horses grazed contently, pulling out the fresh grass by its roots. A few birds chirped in the brush near the outskirts, but otherwise all was still. When she stepped out of the tent, Mandan looked up.

The horse had grown strong in the few weeks since they left Abrelyon. Tall, dark, and handsome, he trotted towards her, prancing with his feet held high. He flung neck in the air, sending his mane cascading over his eyes. He snorted the hair back.

Alina laughed. She scratched him on the nose, feeling the warm skin beneath her fingers. His chocolate eyes stared into hers, and she gazed into the depths. The horse nodded wisely, and dipping his head, pranced in circles around Alina.

Still smiling, Alina hurried to the center of camp. Ash swirled in the breeze, hiding a few remaining embers of last night's fire. She stirred the cinders, blowing. Soon, a fire crackled in the ring.

She set a pot of water on to boil and broke open a pack of elven bread. It crumbled in her mouth, melting away with such intensity that she had to ration herself. A bite here, a bite there. There wasn't enough to gorge herself. By the time she finished, her stomach was still rumbling.

Perhaps there were some berries down by the river? She wandered down to its bank, watching as the water roiled at her feet. The sound was crisp, like the words in Carn's stories. It filled her ears with a pleasant buzzing noise.

Downstream, the bank was bare and devoid of life. A small, rocky beach bordered its edges, a perimeter that no plant dared to cross. She turned upstream. It was choked with brush, but a narrow gap in the brambles beckoned. She squeezed in.

The trail cut through away from the bank. She followed it, snatching her cloak hem away from the outstretched branches. Her feet stumbled on the few stones that littered its surface.

Several minutes later, the trail opened into a small glen. Long, cool grass carpeted the floor. Overhead, a flowering cherry tree arched its way into the sky, the pink blossoms glowing against the blue backdrop. In the center stood its trunk, small and worn by constant rubbing. She could have easily fit one hand around its circumference.

However, she did not move towards it. There was something wrong here. A feeling of expectancy. She wasn't wanted. She turned to go, but a sound stopped her. High and clear, it rose through the cold air.

She ducked out of the glen, crouching behind a large holly bush. *Silly. Who would be out and about at this time? Black Knights don't sing.*

She was about to move away, but then the words filled her ears. She froze, gingerly clutching a spiny branch.

Meet me by the tree
So tall and oaken white
Growing in the land of cold.

A stone ring circles it,
A girth for its mantle,
A bowl for its blood,
When it spills.

Meet me by the tree
Where we will be given
The chance to repay our sins!
Strange things happened there,
Once upon a night.
My love, meet me there again.

Elewyn emerged. Her golden hair was braided tightly down the nape of her neck, and her skin, soft and pale, was freshly washed. She glanced around the sheltered area once, as if checking to make sure she was truly alone. She began to hum the melody again, but something stopped her.

Alina heard it now, the cracking of twigs under foot. Someone was coming. She held her breath, afraid that Elewyn's sharp ears would catch the sound of her exhalation.

The bush rattled. A tall figure stooped into the glen. His red hair flashed in a patch of sunlight.

"Liam!" Elewyn threw herself at him, hugging him around the neck. "Gods, you scared me!"

"Scared you? You were calling for me, weren't you?" He plucked her lightly off her feet and set her down against the trunk of the cherry tree. "There's not much time—"

"Hush." She pressed a finger to his lips. "I need to talk to you." She waited while he sat down. "There is something wrong with Alvardine. I looked into his dreams... his dreams last night—"

"Looked into his dreams!"

"My father's a wizard, isn't he? I can enter the Realm of the Faeries if I want to. Anyways. He was dreaming."

"Go on."

She grinned. "Did you know that he once had a wife? He met her at an elven school. She was beautiful, Liam."

"So what was the problem? Why aren't they still together?"

"Someone else loved her. Someone with red hair, like yours, and a taste for adventure. Red hair, Liam. That man killed her out of spite." She swallowed. "Liam, I don't know if I should be telling you this, but Alvardine isn't the innocent man we know him to be."

"Well, of course not. He's, what, 150 years old? Elves age slowly, but he's still an old man in their terms."

"That's not what I mean. Liam, that other man was King Rolan."

Alina crept away. She had heard more than she had bargained for.

13

The company pulled to a halt. The horses snorted in the gloom, stamping their feet against the gravel path. Mountaintops towered overhead, their black crags biting the thin air like teeth. Trees lined the slope on either side, their tips waving in the slight wind. The air had grown surprisingly cold for summertime, and their breath rose into the night, reaching the stars in barely discernible plumes. Lanterns were held to the black, the bearers gripping the handles with numb fingers. They tried to ward off the night, hoping against hope that the sun would return in just enough strength for them to continue. It did not, and they watched as the last of the bright rays disappeared over the rocks.

Alvardine held up his hand, the signal for those that could see to stop and make camp. He slid from Haranee's back, tossing the saddlebags onto the path. It had grown too dark to pick the way from among the rocks, and he realized that the travelers would have to spend the night huddled in the narrow trail. He spread a thin blanket over the sharp gravel, his back to the grazing Haranee. There was no need to tether her, for she was not one to wander far from the protective orb of the lanterns. He clucked, whispering in the language of the elves to Oryth. Liam pricked up his ears, but Alvardine was speaking too softly for him to hear.

"The mountains grow larger every day. We do not have long to wait."

"We never did, Alvardine. Our waiting grows shorter. The King is on the move; I can see his armies in my mind's eye. The genocide grows. The Raven King remains hidden."

"The mountains call for us to cross them, and we shall have to meet their demands before we can concentrate our efforts on the Raven King. But that is not what I'm concerned about." He whipped a small sheet of parchment from his pocket. "I found this in the girl's possession."

Oryth looked the document over. When he looked up, his expression was grave. "You think she is involved, then? You think the girl, the one who calls herself Alina, carries this letter on orders of the King?"

"I do not know what to think. The girl does not reek of evil as most of the King's people do, but she has been around evil since birth. It would not be against her nature to challenge all that is good. We must watch her, and the boy too."

"What do you have against the boy? He is not as serious as the girl, not as capable of keeping secrets."

"He keeps secrets well enough. I am sure he knew of this letter; he is cleverer than he appears. I suspect that he might be able to read it, and has read it. He will have told the girl its contents, yet she has not come to us for advice."

"You expect her to? She hardly knows us. She would tell the boy first."

"I'm sure that she knows the contents of the letter, either because the King revealed it to her himself, or because of the boy." Alvardine pushed Haranee's inquisitive nose away from his lantern. His low whispers dropped until they could hardly be heard. "Remember that we do not know anything of the girl. We are not sure of her intentions for joining this mission."

"And yet you say that she acted admirably in Daedalyus." The word was a harsh guttural sound in the midst of the fluidity of their language.

"Acted. That is all. She seems to be trustworthy, but— this document would not have fallen in her hands by accident."

Oryth sipped from his flask. He did not like the tone of this conversation; it was hard to hear Alvardine speak in conniving tones. The elf had been his friend since before Finestal fell, and it was only in the direst of situations that Oryth was told of his friend's suspicions, as Alvardine was not quick to judge. The fact that Alvardine had chosen to form opinions about the newcomers was troubling indeed. "I don't think either the girl or the boy is in league with the King. They have seen enough evil in their lifetimes, and their soul spirits have always kept them from inflicting harm. Why would they start now?"

"You forget that we do not know if they have refrained from evil. We know only what they have told us, and what our sources are able to come up with. We know that they are from the Hawthorn Clan, for that is the only group of coremen near the surface in that area at the time. We also know that the Hawthorn are led by a corrupt leader, one who is corrupt enough to kill innocents and brainwash young ones. How do we know that these two have yet to conform to this leader's standards?"

"We don't, Alvardine. We really have no complete set of data in either of these children. They are children, which you seem to forget. The girl is sixteen; the boy can only count one more year. They are too young for the King to have their allegiance."

"Oh? I am afraid, Oryth, that you are forgetting that you offered your pledge to the Wanderers at the age of twelve. You were not the youngest to make your vows. " He stared down at the paper. It had been in water at some time for another, and most of the ink was blotched. The word 'Raven King' gleamed brightly, along with a signature at the foot of the page. If he squinted, he could just make out the jutting 'R' and rolling 'N' that made up King Rolan's name. "So you agree? Alina and Carn are not to be trusted."

"Very well. Do as you think is best."

14

The pass cut through the mountains, a jagged path opening to a view of the sea. Swirling snow all but covered the faint blue glimmering just below the horizon, but it was there. Her first sight of the Briginwald Sea.

And with the coming of the sea came the sight of Twedrig, the island that floated just off shore. She could just make out its hazy shape, the brilliant burst of green. It was hard to imagine that such a peaceful place could be home to King Rolan's palace.

She urged Mandan forward, carefully steering him around the gaping craters at his feet. The mountain path was worn down from the icy conditions, and great chunks were missing from the dirt. Rocks slid and tumbled as Mandan's hooves knocked them. They clattered down the side of the mountain.

Alina grimaced. She forced herself to look up, to check how far behind she was. Siv's swinging tail was just in sight; Carn was riding around a bend in the path. In front of him, the rest of the company stretched out. A gust of wind blew up a drift of snow. The flakes fluttered across her face.

Mandan snorted at them, and she grinned. *Silly. You don't like this any better than I do.* They passed a frozen stream, cascading over the side of a cliff. Icicles jutted out in all directions, some perilously close to Mandan's wobbling flank. She broke them off one by one, and felt the coolness in her ungloved hand. Without thinking, she stuck the largest in her mouth. She sucked at, and was rewarded with a burst of cold water.

A stretch of clear ground opened before them. Mandan broke into a jogging trot, tossing his head in delight at his freedom. As he approached the bend, he leaned forward, increasing his speed. He swung around it, his hooves flailing on unseen ice. For a moment, Alina was sure they would fall. She could feel his weight slipping out from under her. She was floating in midair.

Mandan's hind legs caught hold of stone. He launched himself into the air, leaping over the last bit of ice. Alina reached for his reins, and settled herself more firmly on his back. *Stupid horse.*

She pulled beside up beside Carn. The boy glanced at her, shifting his eyes beneath his blond hair. His fingers twitched on the reins. "Hey."

"Hey yourself." She bumped Mandan against his leg, playfully. "Alvardine says we'll be off the mountains be nightfall."

He nodded. "It'll be warmer down there, that's for sure. The lands west of the Tortallions are all desert, fields of sand and scorching sun. We're going from the freezer to the frying pan." He shifted uncomfortably. "Look, Alina, I need to talk to you."

The two fell back from the rest of the group. Their horses snorted in frustration.

"You remember Arie?"

Alina rolled her eyes. "How could I not? He was my brother. He only died four months ago. Why?"

Carn sighed. "You remember how he died, how Isen knew he was coming? Like someone told him?"

"Yeah. It's funny. When Arie was leader of the rebel gang, we swore we'd never be a part of one. But here we are, walking hand in hand with the largest rebellion in all of Ivindor." She smiled. "He used to take me up to the surface, you know. Not often, maybe once a year. We'd go up in the fall, sit in the sunlight, and eat apples. They were always really sour. But that was how he liked them.

"And sometimes, in the spring, he'd bring me flowers for my birthday. Big pink ones with yellow centers, and little blue forget-me-nots. I was always disappointed when they dried up, but Arie would laugh. He told me that 'good things aren't meant to live in evil places.' And then he would promise to take me out of the Underworld, once and for all, when everything was ready."

"Mmm." Carn frowned. "Don't you ever wonder what would have happened if he won?"

"You'd be king. Isen would be dead, and the Clan would be happy. I'd still be a member, and Mother would be alive. Maybe she could have come to the surface, too."

"King." He licked his lips, running his tongue over the dry edges. "I'd be king, if Arie was still alive." He glanced at her. "I'd need a queen," he whispered.

Suddenly, there was shout from up ahead. Alvardine was swinging his sword high over his head, motioning them to hurry up.

When they joined him, he pointed at the section of trail up ahead. Narrow, it was bordered on both sides by tall rocks. A shadow shifted amidst the boulders.

"There's something in there." He hefted Areslaine in hand. "Swords out."

"A snake, maybe?" Alina moved forward, as if she was

162

about to investigate. Her fingers clenched around her sword hilt. Snake or not, she wasn't going to take any chances.

Alvardine threw out a hand to stop her. "Snakes don't like this altitude." He motioned them all in closer. "I should have told you all sooner, but I didn't want to worry you. Something has been following us for the past few days. Gods take me if it is a simple snake."

"Knights?" Oryth whispered. He pulled himself up straighter. His staff clunked heavily against the frozen ground. "There's no other way to go around. We'll have to force our way through."

Liam shook his head. "We don't know that it's Knights. There isn't any reason for them to be up here—likely it's just a scouting party. But all the same." He strung his bow slowly, easing the string into the notch. He studied the landscape. "Watch the sides of the trail. It wouldn't do for anyone to fall off." He fit an arrow to his bow and nodded at Alvardine.

The elf frowned, but he did not say any more. He stepped out of the circle, edging towards the bottleneck. His feet slipped on a patch of ice. Alvardine wavered, his hands reaching for support. He fell with a heavy thud.

Almost immediately, shadows emerged from behind the boulders. Black armor glinted in the sun, and sword tips snaked into view. The closest of the Black Knights reached forward, grabbing Alvardine by the hair.

Oryth leapt into the fray, his staff shooting green sparks at Alvardine's captor. He swung his sword out of its sheath and lunged, pushing into the weak shoulder joint. The Knight screamed and wrenched the sword from his chest. He tossed it aside. The sound of clashing steel rung in Alina's ears as Leif jumped to the battle, his own blade gleaming with blood. He swung upwards, and suddenly the Knight's head was no long attached to its body.

Alina froze, unsure of how to act. She watched as Elewyn dashed to her father's aide, as Liam loaded his graceful bow, sending arrows into the Knight's midst. One struck the dull armor of a breastplate, but the others flew true. They landed with solid thunks in withering flesh. She watched Carn draw Hornet from his pocket. He slashed at the recoiling arm that held Alvardine. A sweeping blow knocked him into the constraints of yet another Knight. He yelled, burying Hornet deep into the throat above him. The Knight crumpled on top of him. He was pinned to the ground.

Suddenly Oakenwhite was flashing in front of her. She clipped through a chubby finger and whirled to drag Carn from beneath the dead body. There was no time for thanks; already her arm was up to deflect a thrown fist. She felt her bones creak under the pressure, but she didn't care, did not want to care. Her arm flailed uselessly, and she switched Oakenwhite to her other hand, sweeping upwards to meet a black blade. She was so short that she could easily slip unnoticed through the thick legs, so soon she found herself caught beside Leif's grunting battle.

He flipped Goblincleaver over her head, stabbing at Alvardine's captor. The Knight dropped the elf and flew into a terrifying rage. Sparks flew over Alina's head as blade hit blade. From somewhere to Leif's right came more sparks, these a brilliant red. He shot a questioning look Oryth's way.

The wizard twirled his staff. It whistled overhead, shooting streams of light in every direction. The missiles sought out targets, worming their way through armor and slapping hands. The Knights screamed as the light burned their flesh, scorching holes in their thick armor. One Knight tried to creep up from behind, but Oryth's staff was there, its butt knocking against the Knight's skull. He muttered under his breath, and a flaming dragon erupted from his fingertips.

The dragon roared. It flew across the battle scene; it's claws scraping at Elewyn's back. The girl half turned from her opponent, and then, seeing the dragon, she whispered in its ear. It vanished in a puff of smoke.

She dropped her sword tip slightly, giving the Knight room to raise his own weapon. He slid his dagger forward, only to find that the blade had melted, searing his hands with the hot liquid. He roared in agony, flying at Elewyn. His reddened hands clutched at her hair. She cried out, and for a moment Alina thought all was lost. An arrow whizzed past her head and embedded itself in the Knight's eye.

Oryth had broken out his bigger spells. He produced an array of fiery rocks that he threw out of thin air at his foes. He equipped himself with a pot of boiling water, its contents sloshing over everything near him. His hands drizzled oil on the Knights, so that when his fireballs hit the creatures burst in flame. Around his neck appeared a honey colored stone, which he ripped off and tossed into the air. It burst into a million sparks, showering the vicinity.

Alina dodged a flaming missile. Oakenwhite danced in her hands, and she lunged to balance her blows. She tore her cloak from her back and threw it over the head of an unsuspecting Knight as he turned to pin Carn. The black head fell from his shoulders. She did not retrieve her cloak, instead taking the time to dive aside for a speeding arrow to pass. From her vantage point on the ground, she had a clear shot of several overhanging bellies. She stabbed upward, rolled, stabbed upwards, and rolled. She felt her dagger catch on sticky meat, but she ignored it, yanking it out only to thrust it in again. She lost all sense of being, wrapping herself in her adrenaline.

A hand gripped at her bundled hair. Without breaking stride she twisted Oakenwhite back, stabbing past her neck and into the warm, well blooded wrist. Her arm ached. Moving it so much was not going to help it heal, but she continued on, gritting her teeth against the pain. She swung Oakenwhite over her head, dashing the side of the blade against an armored leg. From far away she could hear Elewyn's screams of triumph, Leif's grunts of success. She could feel Carn at her side, but she could not see him, so thick was the blood falling.

And then it was over. Fifteen bodies lay sprawled on the hard ground, their killers panting over them. Leif wiped Goblincleaver in the snow, and the others followed his example. They sheathed their weapons; Liam slung his bow onto his back. All gathered as many arrows as they could salvage to slide back into the warm embrace of Liam's quiver.

"We can't just leave them here," Carn muttered. He stared at the hewn bodies. A head rolled to his feet, and he kicked at it nervously. "The dead are supposed to be buried."

"We don't have time," Alvardine answered. He whistled, long and shrill, calling the scattered horses back to his side. "There are sure to be more around. They'll have seen the battle, and they will want revenge."

Liam nodded his agreement. He tugged a slim dagger from a sheath and strode between the boulders. About halfway though, he stopped. His hands reached for a cloak, lying twisted at his feet. He picked up the cloth, turning it over in his hands. "I know this cloak."

Alina moved past him. A body lay just beyond the narrow corridor, face down in the snow. The man wore no armor, and his skin was not the pale yellow associated with the Knights. Black hair was pulled in an elven style away from his face. She knelt and turned him over.

His face was horribly mutilated. Someone had taken a knife to it, and skin hung off in great clumps. The hole where his nose should have been gaped at her, in its depths she thought she could see the brain wither.

Alvardine knelt beside the body. A small piece of parchment was pinned to the cloak. He plucked it off, reading it idly. His brows contracted. When he looked up, his face was grim. "Take him to the side of the cliff, drop him over."

They did so. The body spiraled out of sight. Alvardine took Oryth's staff and pried at the rock above its landing place. There was a crunch as the first wave of the rockslide hit the body.

"Move out." Alvardine sheathed his sword. The piece of parchment fluttered from his grasp, and he did not move to catch it. "We're done here."

As they hurried away from the spot, Alina stooped to gather up the parchment. She turned it over. The letters burned into her eyes.

Alvardine, the first bait has gone to seed. Remember your promise.

15

There would be no more secrets. Dangerous, they lurked in the corners, shadows waiting to be forgotten. She couldn't decide if they were monsters, or merely mice, not wanted, but not feared. Either way, there would be no more of them. Of that, she was certain.

She stared out over the landscape, felt the hot air rising to her face. There wasn't any snow on this side of the mountain pass. It was all just heat, bone drying, mind numbing heat, and sand. The desert stretched before her like the sea had done a few days before. It was distant, barely visible beyond the last of the foothills, but it was there. The sand bit at her face, carried by the floating breeze.

Alina turned away, striding in long steps down the path. A level plateau spread before her, a wide ledge on the side of the mountain. It was bordered with rock, strangely pitted and holed from violent weather. Campfire smoke streamed out of the multitude of holes. Footprints led in and out. Here and there a small child darted between the subterranean dwellings. She smiled. If these people hadn't lived at such a high altitude, she would have sworn they were coremen.

She slipped into the nearest of the tunnels. Small

lanterns were bolted to the smooth walls, and the light flickered ominously. Her feet felt the soft cushion of a rug, dyed red and black on the dirt floor. Occasionally, an eye peeked up at her, woven into the fabric, as if to remind Alina that the god of the Underworld, Cyn, was watching.

A door branched off to the right. She knocked, entering into the room beyond. Narrow, it was made smaller by the large amount of people gathered within. They all glanced up when she entered, their eyes staring suspiciously.

She raised her hand in a halfhearted greeting. "Nice weather out today, huh?"

The people just stared at her. Grimacing, she edged into the next chamber.

Here, the people were more welcoming. Leif lay sprawled on the hearthrug, soaking up the warmth of the fire like an overgrown kitten. At his side, Elewyn poured over a piece of parchment. Her hands moved rapidly, and even as Alina watched, the image of a horse began to emerge, the smooth brush strokes caressing its frame. Liam grunted from his place in an armchair, and Carn gave her a half smile. He hadn't been talking much.

She sat cross-legged at his feet. Elewyn worked busily, and Alina watched her with much interest. There hadn't been any artists in the Clan; Isen hadn't allowed it. Alina, like all of the children, had dabbled with mud and crushed berries, but that had ended quickly. Now she watched in wonder as Elewyn brought forth life out of the parchment.

Behind her, Carn coughed. She turned to look at him, anxiously examining him for signs of sickness. He blinked back at her, removed, but friendly all the same. She concluded that the altitude had gotten to him.

What had he tried to tell her, that day on the

mountain? If only she had listened! Alina had the feeling that it had been very important to Carn. She wondered if he would work up the courage to ask her again.

Carn. She wasn't sure what to think of him anymore. He wasn't the carefree, relaxed boy he had once been. His eyes were haunted with a type of sadness, and he was quiet for much of the time. There were no more stories, no laughter to ring in an empty room. He huddled in his cloak, as if he could hide from the world there. When he noticed her watching him, he started guiltily.

There it is again. The secret. She stared into his eyes, trying to read the meaning behind them. Carn shifted awkwardly, and she lowered her gaze. *They're everywhere.* She glanced around. Liam was pouring over a collection of maps. When he noticed her watching, he quickly folded them up and set them aside. He stared back at her defiantly.

A rift was rising between the company members. She could feel it, in the stiffness of the air, in the cold, measured looks that were tossed her way. The members had begun to withdraw. Even she had not told all.

"We'll leave tomorrow morning." Liam's words broke the awkward silence. He glanced around, drawing their attention with his darting eyes. "We don't know how long it will take for the Knights to find us again."

Leif nodded, but Elewyn looked startled. Her wide eyes swept over Liam's features. "You think they'll come again."

"Absolutely. Rolan has always known about the Raven King. He just wasn't aware that we were searching for him. Now that he knows . . . Well, anything is fair game. The ambush up on the pass should have told you that."

Alina frowned. "How did they know we would travel through that pass? The Knights, I mean. If Rolan didn't know that we were hunting the Raven King, then how did he know to ambush us?"

Liam drew a deep breath. He leaned forward, and when he spoke, his voice was hardly more than a whisper. "Some one told him, of course." He stopped.

"Alvardine and Oryth will want to hear this." Leif got to his feet. He darted from the room.

Alina watched him leave, her eyes following his movements without really seeing. Some one had told Rolan about the Raven King. About the Wanderers. But who? She racked her brain, trying to decide. Not Liam. He was too honest for such a thing. And Elewyn couldn't have. She wouldn't, not with the lives of millions at stake. Alvardine and Oryth were out of the question; she pushed them from her mind. That left Carn, and Leif.

It wasn't Carn. Even as the words came into her head, she wondered at them. *Do I really him well enough to say that? A few weeks ago, I would have said yes, but now. . . He's changed a lot. And so have I.*

Leif. She turned the name over in her head, mulling. She had never really liked the boy. After all, he had spoken out against her at first. *But that's not evidence.*

But it had to be Leif. She started, as if about to bar the door. *It would be so easy. . .* Her fingers twitched on her sword hilt. *He would deserve it.*

The door clanged open. She pulled her hand away from the blade, slicing her finger on the edge. Blood seeped up, and she sucked at it hurriedly. Only then did she pause to look at the intruder.

Leif, a pale white, was shuddering in the doorway. He braced himself against the frame, trying to pull himself up to his full height. He failed miserably.

Alina was shocked. Leif never showed any emotion. In

fact, she had thought him incapable of doing so, but there he was, looking like he had seen a ghost.

"Alvardine and Oryth . . ." His words, barely a murmur, penetrated the silence. "Gone."

"What do you mean, gone?" Elewyn jumped to her feet. She pulled Leif inside, tugging him into an open armchair. "You mean that you can't find them. Father does have a way of wandering off."

Leif shook his head. "Gone," he gasped.

Without a word, Elewyn dashed from the room. A few moments later, they heard her cry out. She was shouting something just outside the door, her words muffled by a veil of emotions. They heard her storm down the hallway.

Liam turned to Leif. "Speak, and be quick about it."

Leif shivered. "No one has seen them since this morning. And even then, it was just a little girl; awake to milk the family cow. She says she saw two men riding away. Their saddlebags were full."

The words took a moment to sink in.

"You checked the horses? Haranee and the pony?"

"Gone." Leif reached out his hand, and they saw that he was clutching a scrap of parchment.

Liam tugged it from his grasp. He smoothed it against his thigh and began to read aloud.

Information has arisen that causes us to fear for the safety of all involved. We leave at once, and hope that you will understand. Return to the Wanderings. We will meet you there when all of this is over.
The Elf and the Wanderer

"They didn't fear for our safety," Liam whispered softly. "At least not for two of us. I overheard them talking, a while back. They feared that Alina and Carn were traitors." His words sunk into the rest of the group as if in slow motion. "Alvardine had seen a letter in Alina's possession, a letter that made him believe that she was of King Rolan's belief systems, maybe even a supporter. He decided it was not worth risking the time to find out whether his suspicions were true."

"Do you have such a letter?" Leif spoke after a moment. He grabbed at the saddlebags. "I can look if you don't tell the truth."

Alina gulped back her tears of frustration. "Of course I have a letter! I found it in Abrelyon, and I showed it to Carn . . . Well, most of it was waterlogged and I couldn't read it. I was going to tell someone . . ."

"We couldn't show it to just anyone," Carn added. He glanced at Alina, his brows furrowed in worry. His face twitched. "Could we?"

"No, I don't suppose you could have. You found it?" Elewyn muttered from the doorway. Her face was ashen. "So they left for no reason."

Alina shivered, allowing the reality to wash over her. The air beneath the blankets grew cold, as if the last of the elven warmth and hospitality had already left the world. Her toes were numb now, though the weather was fairly warm for such a mountainous region. She pushed her hair from beneath her head and recoiled against Carn's legs, sinking as far away as she could from the world outside. Not only was the world of Ivindor turned upside down, with a corrupt king ruling by brute force, but she was also no longer safe in the safety of her friends. She had trusted Alvardine and Oryth, had trusted them to make decisions best for the group, and had trusted them to support her. Now they were gone, lost in the swirling mists of traitors and nonbelievers. She did not expect to see them emerge anytime soon.

"They must be past the desert by now," Carn whispered. He had shrunk into the quilts at the foot of the bed. His watery eyes stared morosely. "We've no hope of catching them."

"No, we don't. The moment they left this place Alvardine made sure of that. Whatever his reasons, he doesn't want our help." Leif sank in the chair.

"But he needs us! They both do. Two people have no chance in finding the Raven King. It'll take too long."

"Alvardine obviously thought that was the better option compared to being turned over to Rolan. You can't find fault with his logic," Elewyn murmured. "He didn't have to take Father, though."

It was only then that Alina realized that she might never see the wizard or elf again. "We have to follow them. They might be resting in Drogonburg, as planned. We can still catch up, if we leave right now. Once they understand why we kept the letter . . . They can't believe that Carn and I were out to kill them. They just can't. Oryth will forgive us if Alvardine won't. We have to leave." She threw a glance around the room, staring into the drawn faces of her companions. "Why aren't you moving?"

"They won't have stopped in Drogonburg. You have to remember that Alvardine and Oryth both thought they were fleeing for their lives. They could be well into the forest by now, or near to crossing into it." Liam shook his head. "It's like Leif said: they have left for good."

Alina scowled. "So why didn't Alvardine take you along, too? And why did Oryth leave Elewyn here to deal with the supposed traitors?" She bit her lip, tasting the metallic blood welling beneath the skin. A single, dagger like movement, and that blood could be coursing through her mouth. A single movement and she would have a real sort of pain to contend with, one she had control over, unlike this new hurt Alvardine's departure had brought. She slipped her tooth along the ridge of dryness, searching out a soft spot hat was ready for puncture. She bit down, hard. "Why didn't he?"

"He didn't dare. He thought we were too attached to you. Maybe we still are." A chilling thought entered the room with his words.

No." Alina said aloud. But even as she spoke, she wondered. What would have happened to her and Carn if the others hadn't been attached? Would they have been left for the vultures? Stretched out with their heads bashed in? She shuddered.

"But how did Alvardine find that letter?" Carn wondered aloud. "He wasn't one for snooping, and neither was Oryth. Both of them trusted us. Someone must have tipped them off."

"Don't be ridiculous, Carn," Alina said between clenched teeth. "Let's not spread any more rumors."

"No, I'm serious. And there's only one person here who didn't trust us." He turned to look at Leif.

"No!" Elewyn threw the saddlebag into the corner of the room. She almost bared her teeth as she took up a fighting stance. She glared around protectively. "No! Leif didn't do it. He couldn't have . . . "

"Elewyn, he does have a point," Liam whispered. "No one else in here did it. No one in here would have."

She threw her hands up in exasperation. Her appearance took on that of a frenzied mother bear. Her legs stood wide and firm, she drew her body up to her full height. She shook her head violently. "He didn't do it."

"Elewyn . . . " This time it was Leif who tried to comfort her.

She shook his words away. "If I say you didn't do it, then you didn't do it." She turned to the rest of the group. "You don't understand him like I do."

The room fell silent. Elewyn, lost in her own memories, stood in a dazed trance. She hadn't thought about it before now. Could it be?

She had been born in Finestal, having been carried to the city by her pregnant mother, who was in turn being carried in Oryth's arms. She had been born six years before the attack on the city, and her mother had given birth to a young boy two years after her. The boy had been lost, though, killed by the Black Knights during the fall of the city. His body had never been recovered, but it wasn't needed. A four-year-old boy did not have a chance of survival during that hectic night. What had been his name? Oh yes, the boy's name was Leaf.

Elewyn stumbled in the dark. She hit her toe on the rough wood of one of her father's crates, and whimpered at the pain. It was not a loud whimper, but it had been enough to jar her senses. She blinked from her half dazed state, coming into the dark world with sleep-encrusted eyes. Her feet padded softly on the worn rugs as she wound the rest of the way through the maze she had built for herself. It was her habit to build a wall between her bed and the door. She was terrified by the stories of nighttime raids, the stories her father told her about the child-stealers before he tucked her into bed at night. In her six-year-old mind, the walls she built out of old boxes would protect her if those stories happened to be real.

She crept into the hallway, letting the door creak behind her. She slipped through the shadows and into the moonlight that streamed through the hall window, fresh and silver. The door to her parent's bedroom appeared on her right. She paused at the threshold before continuing on. The rumbling snores comforted the last of her startled fright away. She climbed onto the wide window ledge, her custom when she woke so late in the night.

From there she could see the last lights of the city twinkling away to blackness as their wielders extinguished them, one by one. The houses on the other side of the street loomed in front of her eyes. She could clearly see the illuminated windows in the dark, silhouetted by the figures of a man and woman in the throes of passion. She glanced at the pair curiously, and then turned her face away. She was only six years old, but she knew what she was not meant to see. She gazed out over the rooftops towards the waving forest beyond.

It was a noise that startled her from her half sleep. A loud clattering at the front of the house that echoed down the hallway and filtered into her ears. She wiggled her fingers like she had once seen her father do before a fight, the only fight she had ever seen him engage in. Her father had lost the brawl badly, but that did not matter to Elewyn. She was sure the technique would work for her. She pretended to clutch at the imaginary dagger slung around her slim hips. Burglars, she told herself, though she was quite aware that it could only be her father returning from work. She promised herself that she would be brave while defending her family. The noise grew louder. It encroached upon the end of the hallway. She braced herself, then, at the last moment, dashed back to her bedroom. The door closed with a snap.

Leaf rolled over in is sleep as she crawled back into bed. She tore the blankets from his grasp and huddled beneath them. Her fingers reached out to pull a play sword alongside her. She was not hiding, merely waiting in ambush. The burglars would come, and when they did, she would be ready.

The door slid open once more, and Elewyn froze, her hands lying forgotten on the wooden sword hilt. She watched as a figure appeared in the doorway, crouched as if ready to spring. She recognized the bushy beard and almost laughed with relief before she caught herself. Her father was playing burglar. It wouldn't do to give up the game so soon. She curled back under the covers and waited for the tickling to begin.

It didn't. She peeked out from her dome of warmth. Leaf squirmed as the cold shafts of air penetrated his tiny body. Her father stood over her, staring down. She could not see his face, but she guessed he was trying to hide his laughter beneath his full graying beard. His cloak was thrown over his left shoulder. On his right, she could make out the outline of two smaller cloaks, that of Leaf's and her own. Oryth stroked her forehead for a moment, and Elewyn lay still, relaxing under his touch. This was no longer a game of burglars. This was her father come in to say good night, to whisper his love to herself and her brother.

Oryth pulled the blankets down from her chin, down to her ankles so that she shivered and Leaf yelped in his sleep. He stood them both up and dressed them, bringing their foreheads to his lips for a kiss. He told them both that he loved them, told Elewyn to hurry with her brother to Alvardine's house, the house of their family friend. These were not pretend burglars. They were real, and much, much worse. He patted her head one last time and took her hand.

They crept back through the house. They did not stumble like Elewyn had the first time, for now their need for silence was great. They trespassed along their own hall, to the front of the house, away from the resounding thumps. Her mother met them halfway. They continued, out through the back door and onto the lawn, out onto the dusky street. Oryth hugged his daughter one last time. Both parents returned to the house, with Elewyn gazing after them, her heart aching. She was only six years old, but she was fully aware that she and her brother would never return to the house again. She was aware that returning to the house was dangerous now, that this was no longer a silly game. And yet she watched her parents walk through the door in mute silence.

The two children hid in the bushes across the road. Leaf was too sleepy to walk much further, and the cold night air threatened to put both asleep in seconds. Finally Elewyn was the only one staring with frightened eyes from beneath the branches, Leaf crumpled at her side, snoring softly. She held tight to her brother, felt his pulsing heartbeat, and was comforted. Her chubby hands rested around his shoulders. She promised herself that she would not cry out, no matter what happened. Tears trickled down her cheeks, tears of fear and abandonment. Her parents were inside that thing, that booming, shaking monster that had become of her house.

The front door opened, spilling lantern light onto the lawn. Huge dogs leapt at the chains around their necks, masters hardly trying to constrain them. The barks filled the night. And then, quite suddenly, a crumpled body fell out onto the lawn. The Knights watched her for a few moments, drawing their swords silently. When the figure wriggled in the grass, the tallest of the men stepped forward.

Her mother spoke, soft and urgently, her voice rising to a keening wail. She was pleading for her life, for them to show mercy. Elewyn could hear her words clearly from across the street. She turned away. The stars glowed brightly.

When she turned back, a pale body lay sprawled on the grass. Blood spilled from the wound in her chest. The Knights nodded in their silence and left, leaving her mother dead *upon the cold earth. Elewyn stood, brushing the twigs from her jacket. She did not wail, but walked steadily towards the body that had once been a loving mother. She left Leaf behind the bush, sleeping. He was not there when she and her father returned.*

Elewyn shook away the memory. She stared at the people gathered around her. "He was not responsible for the letter."

"Fine." Liam looked at her one last time, but he did not question her word. If Elewyn said that Leif did not bring the letter, than he believed it. "We leave in an hour. If we hurry, we could still catch up to them."

Alina nodded glumly. She sat back in her bed, watching as her friends departed. She huddled under the blankets, just as Elewyn had done twelve years before. As she watched, trust bounced just out of her grasp.

16

Alvardine strode across the clearing. His cloak swayed as he walked, sweeping the grass with long, even strokes. He had polished Areslaine the night before, and the sword gleamed. He touched her hilt, feeling the metal pulsing beneath his fingertips. How long had it been since he had drawn this blade against a true enemy? Years? No. This enemy could not be destroyed. The enemy he now faced was himself.

He clipped his pace, stopping short of the narrow bottleneck passageway. The clearing seemed to have been tailor cut to the inhabitant's purpose; the tree line swerved in and out to give the space two separate chambers. The larger of the rooms had been set aside as the receiving camp. Alvardine passed through the guards, weaving his way between the scurrying servants. Stable boys bumped into each other as they went about their daily work. Young girls dressed in flowery gowns giggled at the young noblemen, the gangly youths that haunted the edges of the clearing. A cook waggled her finger in the air, trying to cool a furious burn. Her assistant laughed, and then hurried back to work. The strong scent of roasting meat tantalized all who passed by. Alvardine sniffed, but he would not allow himself nourishment until he had seen his lord.

The burly guards nodded as he reached the passage. They stepped aside, instantly recognizing the brilliant colors of his cloak. Their spears thudded in their eagerness to remove themselves from his way. He slipped through the corridor. His feet moved soundlessly on the grass.

"My Lord." He knelt upon sighting the figure, seated in a throne of jagged metal.

Curly red hair sprouted at odd angles across the man's broad head. His face was all but obscured by a bushy beard, his teeth a perfect white crescent in the tangles. The man was not one to be impressed by a customary bow; he was too powerful for that. His shoulders rippled as he shifted in his seat to regard the elf. His scarlet tunic shone like blood. He tapped his fingers. "Well?" King Rolan cocked his head.

"It is done, my lord. As you asked." Alvardine raised his head to glance into Rolan's blue eyes. "They are passing through the gates of the Tortallions even as we speak."

"Yes? I don't expect you managed to lose the wizard along the way? Our sorcerers are not strong enough to deal with him."

"Indeed, the wizard is safely tucked into the arms of sleep." His brows furrowed. Alvardine had not liked leaving Oryth alone in the desert, his frail body bruised and parched. The wizard would survive; he knew that, though he did not tell Rolan. Letting his friend escape alive had been the most he could do. His hand still tingled from where he had struck Oryth down with the flat of his sword. "You will have no trouble from him."

"Good." Rolan paused, choosing his words carefully. The elf would have to be dealt with, but not yet. "The Wanderers are on the move."

"Yes, my lord," Alvardine grimaced. "They move towards the Raven King."

"And the Raven King? Where is he?" He suddenly seemed tall and imposing.

"My lord. You know my feelings on the matter—There is no use questioning me any further. We agreed not to speak of the Raven King, and I, at least, intend to keep my word. *I* am not a traitor to the people who raised me."

The King slammed his fist against his throne. "That was unnecessary, Alvardine," he said softly. "The Prophecy of the Raven King is just as much mine as it is yours. Need I remind you?"

Alvardine glowered. "You will keep your promise, though. My son will be safe?"

His question was greeted with laughter. "*Your* son? How can you possibly still believe that? After nineteen years? Gods, he even has my hair!"

"It doesn't matter. He's Cere's son, and I want him safe."

Rolan shrugged. His pushed his silver crown back from his forehead, twitching his hair into messy snarls. His low cheekbones gave him the appearance of one who had indulged too heavy on the honey cakes, though in fact the king was in his prime. His body was used to swinging a heavy sword in battle, for his was not lean, but muscular. His legs were stout and full of flesh, the perfect instruments to carry him over the hill, to carry him charging ahead of his men. His head was rounded to fit into a war helmet; his skull was thick to stop the lighter of blows.

He plucked a loose thread from his cloak. The crimson strand wrapped around his finger like a line of blood. He pulled it tight before looking up.

Alvardine was staring at him. Rolan allowed himself a

moment's time to reflect on the man, to study his pained features and wrinkled brow. *He's old.* The thought was pleasing. This man had betrayed him, and now he would pay.

Rolan reached for his dagger, feeling the blood stained blade running through his fingers. *Cere hated him. He tricked her, made her marry him. Because of him, she rejected you. Because of him, she is dead!* He considered throwing the knife. *No. Not yet. You can still use him. Revenge will be yours, if you take it slow. And you will be the one to cause his pain. You will repay him for betraying you. When he dies, yours will be the last face he sees.*

Another face swam before his eyes. Pale and deathly white, she stared at him. Her eyes, the merriest of grays, were not laughing anymore. He watched as she fell, hurtling towards the depths of the pit, her hair floating about her face. She did not break eye contact with him. Just as she passed out of sight, her voice echoed in his head.

'Why?'

And Rolan could only shake his head in answer. *I was saving you. He's evil. He would have destroyed you. I tried to tell you, but you didn't listen. You chose him over me. I did what I had to do.*

He sighed, blinking back the tear. He had told her, explained everything. So why had she chosen the elf? Anger boiled inside of him, and he hurtled back to the present.

Alvardine was still kneeling in front of him. Rolan blinked. "You're still here."

"The boy! Will you spare him?"

"Get out! I have no wish to associate with you." Rolan ignored the memories of laughter, the good times they had

had. "I said, get out!"

Alvardine rose to his feet. He quickly kissed the proffered hand, grazing his lips across the large ring. He tossed his cloak behind him to regain his dignity. He hurried from the clearing.

Rolan frowned after him. Speaking with the elf always left a foul taste in his mouth, a taste not unlike that of fresh dragons blood, lying hot and bitter on the tongue. He brushed a nonexistent speck of dust from his shoulder. He was not a handsome man, considering that he was five years younger than his father had been when he had been killed. His red hair showed signs of being brushed into a courtly disposition, but it still retained the shape of a war helmet. He wore his sword at his waist, a great black blade that could slice through the solidest of armor. And it had, many times. His hands were stained with the blood of not only the elves, but also with the life force of a thousand of his own men, men whose deaths he ordered simply because he was in need of entertainment.

He waggled his fingers, allowing the jade ring to catch the sunlight. He considered it to be of some value, though the gem was so large that it restricted his movements. It had taken twenty years of hard labor in the mines in order for the gem to found. He had called for the best gem cutter in all of Ivindor to cleanse the stone, and had been furious when the man cut away half of the green emerald. He had the stonecutter executed. The gem he claimed as his own, though he had never set foot within a mile of a mine. The palace jewelers had set the gem on a ring of solid gold. It was now his most prized possession, and he guarded it jealously.

He stood. His boots clicked on the scattered stones as he paced. The elf had refused! How much leverage would he need, in order to pry the information from Alvardine's lips? He had already killed his loved ones, Alvardine's wife. All that was left was the boy, with his crowning mane of red hair. One word, and he could finish the deed. He grimaced at the thought, but kept pacing.

The Raven King. He was the one person that stood in his way. Dispose of him, and he could punish the elves for the cruelties they had wrought. If his power fell into the wrong hands, the elves would walk free. And he could not have that. Not after what they did to his parents. Not after what Alvardine did to him, and to Cere.

17

Their long legs sunk into the sands, leaving hollow dips in the shifting dune. Behind them, their horses trudged, splay-legged, noses grazing the dust at their feet. The company stretched out in a long line, a snake winding across the desert. At its head, Alina strained to see through the haze. She shifted the weight of the saddlebag on her shoulders, allowing the straps to trail in the sand behind her. The tips carved narrow tracks into the dune.

She glanced to the right, catching sight of Carn laboring to keep up with her. He met her gaze, and nodded. They could not keep up this pace for much longer.

Eyes narrowed, she scanned the horizon. Heat waves rose up in glittering streams, creating a shroud that hung over the desert. Overhead, the sun circled like a hawk, waiting to swoop down on the few creatures that toed this vast wasteland. A few cacti stood guard against the coming of the night, silhouetted against the pale sky.

A shadow. She started, and her feet slipped on the sand. She fell heavily to her knees, crumpling at the base of the dune. When she looked up, the horizon was empty. She was starting to see things; she had to be. If one thing was certain, it was that she would never see the stooped figure of Oryth again.

She shook her head, allowing Carn to drag her to her feet. He plucked her saddlebags from the sands and swung them over his shoulder before leading the way to the top of the mountain of sand. His head covering flapped in the wind.

Alina hurried to catch up. Wordlessly, she tugged at the straps of her saddlebag. Carn shrugged them towards her, and she settled them across her shoulders. He reached to help her. His fingers brushed hers momentarily, and he yanked them away. Alina frowned; now she was sure her imagination was getting to her. Carn had no reason to blush, and yet a guilty pink stole up his cheeks. He glanced away, avoiding her eyes.

She worried her lip. It wasn't as if the idea hadn't occurred to her, but it had seemed so ridiculous in the past. Carn was her *friend,* and nothing more. She was pretty sure that he felt the same way.

So why is he embarrassed? She watched as the pink slowly faded. *He has nothing to hide from me.* She snorted at the thought, but she couldn't brush it aside. Not after what Alvardine had done to them.

Carn strode away, and she let him go, turning to watch the rest of the company plod towards them. Alvardine's disappearance had been hard on them all. Even Leif had been snarly than usual. The line of travelers seemed empty without the tall grace of the elf. In the front, Elewyn led the horses, two or three lead ropes in each hand. She had blindfolded most of them, and still they stuttered and halted. Snowberry walked freely behind her, tail swatting Leif carelessly in the ribs.

Leif scowled, giving the horse a sharp slap on the rump. For an instant, it seemed that Snowberry would bolt;

his nostrils flared, and cracked his mane in the wind.

But before he had the chance, Liam was at his nose, stroking his muzzle. Taking the horse's head firmly in his grasp, Liam wrenched his nose down, staring into the dark eyes. He flicked a strand of forelock out of the way before releasing the horse. He pressed forward, coming to stand beside Alina.

Soon the entire company was gathered at the summit of the dune. In all directions, sand stretched like an empty sea. Shielding his eyes, Carn glared out over the landscape. He took a step forward, wedging himself between Liam and Alina. Liam shot him a warning look, but Carn's attention was elsewhere.

He pointed, his finger rigid in the heat. "Alina. Your eyes are sharper. Can you make out what that is?"

Alina followed his gaze, her eyes focusing on a slight shadow in the sand. It could have been a simple depression, but something spurred Alina on. She slid down the side of the dune and knelt beside the shadow. Her fingers wormed their way into the sand's warm embrace.

A slight, bluish tint gleamed through the layers of sand. She brushed the sand away, scooping huge handfuls out in her hurry. Her fingers found the smooth texture of cloth, and she dragged the object to the surface.

"A cloak." She turned it over in her lap, running her fingers along the ragged hem. Brilliant blue, the cloak was oddly familiar. The hood was embroidered with faint traces of silver, small stitches that swirled in a labyrinth of patterns. Along the sleeve, a golden circle stared back at her. In its center was a triangle, and for a second, she thought she saw the eye wink. Something about it was very familiar.

Elewyn tugged the cloak from her grasp. She stared at

it wordlessly for a moment, then rolled it up and stowed it her bag. "We should keep moving."

The others agreed, and so the company set out once more. They scurried across the hot sands, sandals flapping, heads bowed against the torrent of the wind. Alina glanced back at base of the dune. The sand was already sifting back over the hollow where the cloak had been. What was a cloak doing in the desert?

Carn had explained that the desert wasn't completely unoccupied, that there were several nomadic tribes roaming the sands, but Alina didn't believe him. She couldn't. The desert was so devoid of life. It was hard to imagine any creature choosing this place as its home, much less humans. *And anyway, what would the desert people be doing with a cloak?* She watched the last of the depression disappear. Its sand walls crumpled into piles of lose dirt.

"Come on!"

She spun at the sound, but her feet didn't move. The company drew farther away, and she watched them leave. Carn wavered in the back, waiting.

She waved at him. He was just a speck in the distance. He raised his arm, and his voice wafted in the wind.

"Come on, Alina! We don't have all day!"

Grinning, she raced to catch up. He held out his hand for her to slap.

"Took you long enough," he teased, but his face was worried. He glanced back at the base of the dune.

She spun on her heels. "What is it?" Her eyes tore across the landscape. Whatever it was, she couldn't see it. The desert was empty.

"There." He nodded towards the place where she had dug out the cloak. A figure darted in the dune's shadow.

Alina frowned, tugging at her sword hilt. In this vast wilderness, it seemed unlikely that this was chance meeting. The thought of black armor flashed in her mind, and she slid Oakenwhite out of her sheath.

Carn took note of this, and followed suit. The two swords gleamed brightly in the sunlight.

Liam stepped to their side. He raised his bow, and with a swift movement strung it, at the same time casting an arrow onto its string. A slight amount of pressure on the bow, that was all. Enough to deliver a deadly stroke in less than a heartbeat.

Snowberry stamped nervously, and Alina turned to see Elewyn mounted. She too, had drawn her weapon—a thin, delicate dagger was balanced in her hands. She leaned against the horse's neck, and he quieted. The silence was a heavy weight on he company's chest.

"Do not give him time to draw his sword," Liam whispered. "There's no telling what sort of strange creature this might be. And even if he isn't a threat, better dead, and us safe, then him alive and us at risk."

Elewyn drew a sharp breath, but she held her tongue.

Leif stepped out towards the figure. "In the name of the king, show yourself." He raised his sword menacingly.

A deep chuckle came from the shadows. "That all depends, doesn't it? To which king do you refer?"

Leif waved his sword. "Come out, and maybe I'll tell you. But there is only one true king in Ivindor."

Another chuckle. The shadows began to shift, and the creature crept from his hiding place. A grey cloak flapped at his feet, pulled tight across his chest. The hood was drawn up, obscuring his face from view. Long, slender fingers were wrapped around a grey staff. "Only one true king." He smiled. "People are hung for that, boy."

Somewhere, from the depths of the hood, a glimmer flashed.

Leif motioned to Liam, and the two advanced. "People are hung for lies." He licked his lips. "But for the truth, they are tortured."

Liam cocked his bow. "Who are you? State your name and business. And put the stick on the ground at your feet."

Was that a smile Alina detected within the depths of the hood? Surely the man was not laughing at them!

The man shook his head. "Give me one good reason."

Leif acted before Liam had a chance to intervene. He swung his sword up, the blade a flash of white as he flew at the man. His muscles bulged. Alina looked away, not wanting to see the white sands stained with blood. She waited for the scream.

It never came. She turned back. Leif was cowering at the man's feet. Beside him, the hilt of his sword smoked. The remainder of his blade curled into the air as black smoke. He reached hesitantly for the weapon, but he dropped almost immediately, cursing under his breath. His fingers began to blister. "Wizardry," he murmured.

Liam heard him. An arrow shot past Alina's head. She whirled, just in time to see it vanish in thin air. Liam reloaded, but his arrow seemed stuck to the string. No matter how hard he pulled, the arrow would not release.

The man raised his staff, and the arrow dropped to the ground at Liam's feet. "And who is the true king?"

"Allyen, or his heir." Elewyn swung off down from Snowberry's back. "What?" she glared at Leif. "I don't think that this man is in Rolan's employment. When has Rolan trusted any non-human? A wizard? Baloney."

Liam nodded. "Yes, you have a point." He turned back

to the man. "Fine. Alleyn was the last true king of Ivindor."

The man raised his hand. Leif ducked his head, fearing another spell. But the man simply lowered his hood.

"Father!" Elewyn crossed the space between them in seconds. She flung herself at him, clutching Oryth's frail frame to her. Oryth smiled, and his fingers stroked her hair.

"Oryth." Leif nodded, coldly. "Given up on the elf?" His face was turning red in his fury.

Oryth shook his head. "No—"

"Then why are you here? Did you and Alvardine have a fight?" Leif was voice was tight. He sneered mockingly. "Why did you come back?"

"I—"

"You left, old man! You left us for no reason! And now you want to come back? Did you expect us to welcome you with open arms?"

"Leif!" Elewyn glanced at her father, but Alina could see the growing distrust there. She grimaced. "Why?"

Oryth looked pained. He shifted his staff to his other hand, reaching for his daughter with the other. "Elewyn—"

She stepped out of his reach. "You left. I think we deserve an explanation." She had back up until she reached Leif. Brother and sister glared at their father, impatient for his words.

Liam stepped up beside Elewyn. He held out his hand, and she took it gratefully. Their fingers wove together. His face was stern. "I agree. We deserve better than this."

Oryth nodded. "Of course, you do, you idiot!" He drew in a deep breath, steadying himself. He struggled to remember why he was here. "Sorry. That was unnecessary."

"What? Your insult, or your betrayal?" Leif's eyes seemed to shot fire.

Alina stepped around her friends. She stopped a few feet away from Oryth, waiting. "I'm not a spy," she said finally. "Neither is Carn.

Oryth smiled wanly. "Of course you're not. I was a fool to believe Alvardine when he told me."

She frowned. This didn't make any sense. "Alvardine didn't really think we were spies either," she realized. "It was all a ploy."

Oryth nodded. "Alvardine is gone. He will not be attempting to find the Raven King."

They all nodded; this much was obvious.

"How do I show them what I have seen," Oryth mumbled. He cast a searching glance across to Elewyn, but the girl didn't understand. His fingers twitched on the staff. For the first time, Alina noticed a throbbing bruise in the shadows of his hair. He touched it gingerly.

"When you say that Alvardine isn't after the Raven King anymore," Alina said slowly, "you don't mean that he's given up."

Oryth shook his head. The thought of Alvardine giving up was unthinkable, blasphemy. "He's shifted his priorities. The battle is between Rolan and Alvardine, now."

"You mean that Rolan hadn't forgotten about Cere, and he wants revenge." Leif cradled what was left of his sword in his arms, the hilt still smoking with molten steel. "We all knew it would happen eventually. But gets me is, why did Alvardine leave?"

The company fell silent. At last, they had come to the heart of the matter, and for the question that hung in the air, there was no answer. Only one thing was clear. Alvardine, their leader and hero, had disappeared from their ranks. All that was left to do was move on and hope for the best.

18

"We'll have to leave the horses here."

The group glanced up. Their weary faces focused uneasily on the speaker, their eyes darting nervously.

"We can't take them into the city."

Yes, the travelers knew that this was true. The tunnels were no place for any creature, and the darkness was sure to spook even the hardiest warhorse. There would not much food, and not near enough water. Creatures would be hungry, and waiting for prey. A horse's scent was sure to draw them in.

But they had not expected to have to leave the horses so soon. Drogonburg was still four days' walk away, the tunnels maybe two. There was a village beside the tunnel entrance, and that was where they had expected to sell the their faithful friends.

"Taking them directly to the tunnels has always been a risk. We can't afford to take that risk now."

The group nodded, but no one rose to untie the horses from their post. Only a few glanced in the general direction. Behind them, the scree covered slope whistled.

Finally, a young man stood. He swung a bow onto his back, and the flinted arrow tips were bold against the blue sky. "He's right, you know."

They knew. One by one, the travelers stood. A pair of young women clung tightly to each other, one short enough to have been the other's child. They walked shakily over to the rest of the group and helped two other adolescent boys to their feet.

Nearby, the speaker shook his head. He gripped his staff more firmly in his right hand. The wind whipped his blue cloak out behind him. "We need to hurry." His white beard jutted anxiously.

The rest of the group paused. Then the leather lead ropes were unfurled, and the ends dropped to the ground. The various packages were slung from the horses' backs. Riding blankets were rolled away. In just a few moments, the horses stood bare in the morning light.

"They'll catch up to us once we cross over."

Alina nodded, but the tears still stung her eyes. She wound her fingers through Mandan's mane, feeling the warmth of her friend. She glanced briefly into his dark eyes. They softened under her gaze, melting from icy wariness to warmth and delight. She turned away.

The rest of the group did the same. They trooped out of the small clearing, leaving the horses standing in a thick cloud of dust.

The road churned beneath their feet. Dust milled in the air, caking their throats with a thick layer of paste. Once a well used trading route, the road was now deserted. Bandits had taken over control of the intersections long ago, but they too had disappeared, leaving the paving stones to gather dust. Water was scarce.

In the distance, Drogonburg stood tall. Its walls shot up into the mists of early morning, standing century against the enemy. The stone had yet to know that the enemy was now inside.

Children had once played along these walls. They had skipped and jumped, squealed with laughter. These walls had been the city's playground, once. But that was no more.

Now it was the guards who paced along the stone streets. They ran their armored fingers across the rock, grinding the metal hideously. They barked their orders through the small peepholes, shoved their black armor down the gullets of the stones. Swords clanged in preparation for war.

The inhabitants of the city cowered in leaking huts. They had been pushed to the very outskirts of the protective walls, crushed into the gaps between the crumbling stone, so that the corners of their bed platforms protruded into the exposed plains. If an attack were to fall on the city, they would be the first to die.

But an attack was not intimate. The plains surrounding the city were devoid of all life save the small party of travelers, and the mountainous wall behind was too steep for an army to invade. Drogonburg was alone in its struggles, now; the Black Knights were too strong for any rescue to be attempted.

The party scurried down the road. They had wrapped their cloaks about their faces in an attempt to ward off the great clouds of choking dust, but along with the protection came the heat.

It was now well past midsummer. The heat reverberated in the plains, corralled in by the steep walls of the

Tortallion Mountains. Grasses withered in the dry air. The few trees that had managed to survive the violent winter storms fried, their crisp leaves flurrying at their bases. Though autumn would not arrive for several more months, the trees would be bare in just a few short weeks. The land was dying.

Oryth glanced up at the boiling sun. The group's progress was not nearly the amount he would have liked; he had expected them to reach the tunnel two days before. *No matter now. It's too late to turn back.* He trudged on.

Leif and Liam paced side by side. As both were about the same age, they had found a sort of respect for each other. They were fellow knights, brothers, and they watched each other's backs closely. Death was their enemy, and together they would conquer.

Alina glanced up at the walls from her place behind Carn and Elewyn. She had avoided watching the mass grow larger with every step, but now the sight could not be ignored. It burned in the landscape like a great beacon, the spiraling towers out of place in the desolate flatness. The walls, once white, were stained a sooty gray. They stood out from the golden haze of the surrounding grasses. Steep embankments circled the city, perhaps forming a moat once, but now dried by the hot sun. An old riverbed crunched through a heavily guarded entrance in the walls —Drogonburg had been without a source of water for some time.

The dwarves had once fished in this river; it had run full with shimmering scales of river trout. Watermills had been a common occurrence, then. Now the banks of the Grass River crumbled from drought. Alina checked her water bag. She wasn't sure when they would find a source of drinkable water again.

Why in the world would someone build a city here? In the middle of nowhere? She swung her gaze across the plains, trying to spot what the dwarves, thousands of years before, had seen. Rocky mountains hovered just behind the city walls. In some places, the flaked cliffs dove into the city center. No trees blanketed the slopes; the soil had long ago disappeared into a bed of rock. The mountains ended abruptly. They cut down to the valley floor in straight drops, almost as if someone had taken a knife and sliced them off. Generations of pick axes and taut muscle had carved the granite into pockmarked sheaves. Large boulders clung to the sides of the cliffs.

Just below rose the first walls of Drogonburg. The city was magnificent; she had to admit, even if the shocked pallor of the Black Knights did patrol its edges. Tall turrets rose gracefully into the sky. Between them stretched long lengths of white walls. Arched doorways peered out from the uppermost levels of the fortification. A marble road strutted proudly beneath the main entrance, welcoming travelers to visit, but the oaken doors remained closed, and the shafts of arrows stared pointedly out of the windows.

Alina ducked her head slightly and moved on. They would not be entering the city through the main gates, but the sight still made her feel slightly nauseous. She hurried to catch up with the trailing heels of Carn.

For the second time since she and Carn had left the Clan, she would find herself in the comforting recess of a cave. She peered into the dust, trying to strain the entrance of the tunnel from the rocky landscape. "We're close, aren't we," she frowned. "I didn't expect it to be so near to the city."

Carn smiled. "We're not close at all. Drogonburg is much, much bigger than any city we've ever seen. It's still a good four days' walk away. But yes, we're close to the caves." He restrained a shiver. The sense of homecoming was nearly overwhelming. "Oryth says we'll be there by tomorrow, at dusk."

"And we'll camp at the entrance? Won't that be terribly risky? The Knights will be sure to find us!"

Liam heard. He turned, glancing over his sun bronzed shoulder. "We won't be camping at all. We're in for a long night, little one."

Alina bristled at the slight. "Everyone thinks we're little," she whispered to Carn. "Why, you're just as old as Leif! And I'm just a little bit younger than Elewyn. Who do they think they are? Our mothers?"

"Oh hush," Carn muttered. "He didn't mean anything."

"I'm not little! And I'm sick of it! Why don't you stick up for yourself? For our race!"

Carn shook his head. "Calm down. There's nothing for me to 'stick up' to! We are little. You just have to accept it. Everyone else has."

"No, they've accepted the idea that we're children! That we must be protected, watered, feed like infants! That we must be babysat!" Alina shrugged her pack irritably. "Even in Daedalyus—that was supposed to be our chance to prove ourselves. And yet Alvardine sent us off into the storage shed while he did the fighting! Like we couldn't fight at all!"

"We couldn't! You nearly botched the whole mission with your acting . . . " He ignored her shooting glare, "and neither of us had used a sword in our lives!"

"Yeah, well." She struggled to come up with a new argument. "Why did they bring us in the first place then? They could have just killed us and saved themselves the trouble."

Leif swung around. "Oh, will you shut up! We're not murderers. And we certainly don't appreciate the insult. When you showed up so unexpectedly, you put hundreds of lives at risk. We had no idea who you were or you wanted. The easiest way to get you out was to assign you to some quest!"

"A quest that you certainly didn't expect us to return from?"

"At that point, who cared? You were threat. We were doing our duty. Who cared if you died?"

His last sentence hung in the hot air.

Oryth gritted his teeth. "That, my friend, was not very tactful." He halted, turning to face Alina. "You've been through a lot in the past month. You have every reason to wonder why. But the point, Alina, is that we care now. No one here wishes you dead."

"Oh, that's a relief!" Alina rolled her eyes. She wasn't sure what was egging her on. Maybe it was the heat, or the stresses of the journey. Either way, she felt the anger bubbling inside her. She opened her mouth to protest.

"Enough!" Carn swung to a halt. He grabbed Alina's arm and pulled her around. "You're tired. We all are. But we can't afford to argue like this!" He motioned to the surrounding grass impatiently. "Anything could sneak up on us! Knights aren't the only things we need to be watching out for. Other creatures, creatures that rely on stealth—Pulmorta, dragons, wild cats—by being so distracted, we're only making it easier for them!" He glared at her. "Control your emotions for once!"

"And what's that supposed to mean?" Alina started forward. Her hands balled into fists. She was vaguely aware of the others backing away, receding to allow the two coremen time alone. A thought occurred to her. "At least I cried when Arie died. At least I showed some feeling! You just stood there, and let it happen! Control my feelings? Since when can you say anything about feelings? If you had protested, he might have lived!"

"Alina, I don't think this is the time," Carn mumbled. His face had turned white. "That has nothing to do with this . . ."

"Carn, you loved Arie just as much as I did, and he was my brother! Why didn't you say anything?" She sank slowly to the ground, her anger dissolving almost as quickly as it had come. She felt her heart drop into her stomach, leaving a hollow space in her chest. It thudded against her stomach, and she gagged. Carn sunk to sit beside her.

"While we're on the subject," he muttered, "there's something I should tell you. Just promise you won't shout again?"

Alina nodded, her thoughts drifting. Whatever Carn said, it didn't matter. Arie was dead, gone. Her thoughts began to drift, and she listened to her friend's voice as mumbled on.

"Gods! Why did I do it? I loved Arie, I really did. But you have to understand. Isen's my father! I loved him, too!"

Alina snapped back to the present. Her eyes narrowed. "What do you mean?"

"I know what I did was wrong. You can't imagine how I've felt—the guilt! And when he was hung, I couldn't help but feel—"

"What did you do, Carn?" Her voice rose to a shout. "What did you do?"

"I was scared. I didn't want Father to die—he was all I had. So, when I heard about Arie, I did what I had to. I loved my father." His voice was almost impossible to hear. Alina hardly heard his next words over the growing buzz of the wind. "So I warned him about Arie's plans.."

19

Alina ran. She didn't care that the wind was beginning to pick up, or that Oryth was shouting for her to come back. She didn't care that she could run into a Black Knight at any second. Carn had told Isen about Arie, and that was all that mattered.

When Arie had first been banished from the Clan, all she had felt was relief. Her brother's ideas had grown dangerously close to treason over that last year, and it had only been a matter of time before Isen found out about them. So she hadn't been surprised when Arie began to speak of rebellion. In fact, she had welcomed it; since Arie was then safely out of Isen's hands, anything had seemed possible. And even at that young age, Alina had hated Isen. So had Carn, and they both had agreed to keep Arie's plan a secret.

For months, the three of them had planned. After a while, it had become obvious that there was no way to peacefully force Isen to step down. Alina and Carn had been ready to give up, but Arie was older, and wasn't as innocent as his sister and her friend. The plan for Isen's assignation had begun to take shape.

By that time, Arie had gathered a group of supporters. He was no longer alone, and didn't need to rely on two adolescents to help with his task. Late one night, while the Clan slept, Arie and his gang crept into the village. They slipped into Isen's room, and found the man on the bed asleep. They stabbed him, multiple times, until it was plain that the man had died. But when they went creep out the door, and back into the night, they found the door locked, and the windows barred. They were trapped.

Morning came, and they were able to see the face of the man on the bed. Isen had traded sleeping places with another man. It was a mere guard that they had killed, and now their plan was exposed. Someone had warned Isen about Arie.

They were hung that morning. Alina bit back tears as she thought of that fateful day. She had been forced to watch as her brother was brutally mutilated, tortured for information. Only when he was nearly dead had Isen allowed him to be hung. Alina had cried out, struggled to save her brother. As Arie's last moments of life drained away, Alina was arrested for being a conspirator. She too, was sentenced to death. And Carn, her beloved friend, had saved her. They had run, left the Clan and the underworld behind them. They had met the Wanderers, and the rest was history.

Now Alina found herself retracing the steps that the company had taken that morning across the unforgiving desert. She was unused to running, but she ran nonetheless, glad to have the wind at her back, and Carn, her brother's murderer, far behind her. Her breath came in gasps, and sweat began to trickle down her face. She wiped it away, and ran on.

Soon she found herself battling brambles. The clearing where they had left the horses broke into view. Alina sobbed: Mandan was still standing where she had left him.

She dashed up to his neck and buried her face in his fur.

It only took a moment to find the saddles where Oryth had hidden them, tucked away beneath a large blackberry vine. She tossed one over Mandan's back, yanking the straps tight. She threw her leg over, and pressed her weight into his neck. The horse leapt forward. Over her shoulder, she saw Oryth's black pony look up, startled.

She rode hard that morning, leaving the clearing far behind. It didn't matter where she ended up, so long she was far away from Carn, and so she allowed Mandan to pick the path. The horse raced towards water, and towards the city that accompanied it.

As it turned out, the wind was not just an occasional breeze. By the time Alina had calmed down enough to dismount from her horse, it had picked up to a howling fury. Sand was beginning to hurtle in all directions. Without shelter, Alina realized that she would quickly lose her way.

She could just make out the shadow of a large rock through the sandstorm. She struggled towards it, her head bowed against the wind. Her fingers groped for Mandan's reins. The horse whinnied, the shrill sound lost in the roar that had become the storm. She pulled him forward. Together, they collapsed in the shadow of the rock.

It was sometime later when she heard the voice rising out of storm. She pulled herself into a sitting position, listening intently. This wasn't the first time she had heard a cry while she hunkered beside the rock, but she had always assumed that it was her imagination. Now, as Mandan pricked his ears at the sound, too, she wasn't so sure.

"Alina!" No, it was definitely a mortal voice that called her name.

She struggled to see through the haze. Her eyelids blinked against the constant torment of sand. "Hello?" Her voice was whipped away even as it left her mouth.

A shadow appeared, not ten feet away. Silhouetted against the blowing sand, it looked a child, with his arm raised to shield his eyes. A whinny sounded from behind him. Mandan answered it with a cry of his own.

"Alina!" The figure spotted the rock, and the girl huddled beside it. He dropped down beside her. Alina saw that it was Carn.

She turned away. She was grateful that she was no longer alone, but this boy was her enemy now. He had betrayed her brother; he was responsible for his death. That she could never forgive, and so she did not speak.

"Alina . . ." Carn reached out to her arm. His touch was light, almost feather like. "I'm sorry. I know it doesn't help, but I am."

She ignored him. It was several hours before they both dropped into an exhausted sleep.

"We can't stay here." Carn's voice sounded out of place in the untouched landscape.

She looked around, trying to recognize where they were. Had that dune been there last night? She didn't think so, but it was hard to tell. Everything was coated with several feet of sand. The tops of the grasses peeked out from beneath the desert. She fingered one thoughtfully.

He's right. We're in the middle of the nowhere, with no supplies. No food, no water. We don't even have a tent. Alina stared at the city walls that rose above her. She hadn't realized that she had wandered so close to Drogonburg. They were less than a mile away from the city gates.

She looked out over the landscape. There was no sign of the friends that she had left behind, and nothing moved on top of the mounds of sand. *How are we going to get back?* She glanced at the city once again. It didn't seem so threatening, compared with the expanse of desert that faced them from the other direction. Standing now, she grasped Mandan's reins firmly in her hand. *We'll never find them now.* She stroked the horse idly as she thought. He snorted and nosed her shoulder.

We need to get to the city. That's the logical thing to do. We need a chance to rest. There'll be water there, and maybe someone will give us some shelter for the night. Tomorrow, we can start searching for the others. They're bound to come looking for us, and the city is said to attract people of all origins. We can sell the horses for money, if we need it. "We'll go to the city. We'll be better off there."

Carn bowed his head in acceptance.

20

It was the city gates that gave them trouble. The horses balked and reared, tugging frantically at their reins. Alina clung to the bay gelding, but the horse was far bigger than her. Her hands were rubbed raw from clutching the reins, and one of her fingernails had been pulled out of its socket. She sucked the bleeding digit, grabbing with the other hand for the horse's nose. She tugged his face down to eye level and buckled the halter. The metal slipped against the leather, and she cursed. *Why did I have to run?*

Throwing a wild glare up the street, she caught sight of her friend. He had managed to throw a rope around his pony's neck, and so was not experiencing the same problem with the halter. His charge was just as unruly as hers, though, and she watched as he dodged the flailing hooves. A sizable crowd had gathered to watch them struggle towards the gates. Carn barely missed stepping on a wandering child as he dug his heels more firmly into the cobblestones. The mother lunged to grab her daughter from beneath the horse's hooves, her scolds adding to the din of merchants selling their wares. Metal coins clanged in iron pots, amplifying the terrified neighs.

A particularly loud crash bit into her ears. Mandan jumped, teeth gnashing, hooves grinding. Alina clung to the halter as he threw himself into the air. Her weight on the lead rope startled him. He dropped to all fours. This moment of peace did not last long, however, as he threw his hind legs out behind him. An old man ducked an instant before a hoof plunged into the space where his head had been.

So much for going unnoticed, she thought as she dragged Mandan forward a few more steps. *We've attracted every busybody in the city.* She scanned the crowd, searching for a flash of dark armor. *No Knights yet, though. They're not nearly as rampant here as they were in Daedalyus.*

She threw her gaze towards the city walls above. A man shifted in the opening of a window, nudging the shutters open with gnarled hands. His white hair glowed with the morning sun. She watched he navigated his precarious perch.

Her eyes slid downwards. The building stretched towards the street below, its walls sleek and smooth. Generations of dwarves had worked to perfect the building's white walls, and the marble blocks fit seamlessly together. There was hardly room for a fingernail in the cracks. It was as if the entire structure had been carved from a single block of stone.

A black etching marred the center of the wall. She strained to see its blurry edges. Someone had taken a torch to the image and attempted to burn it from the wall, and the bits of colored pottery that had once graced the image were long gone. Only the outline of the shape remained. She sucked in a mouthful of air. There was no doubt about; the black raven of the Raven King was staring straight back at her.

She tore her gaze away. The raven glared at her, and she bit her lip. She was being silly, she realized that, but she couldn't shake the notion. -She could feel its eyes following her as she dragged Mandan up the street. It was a comforting thought. Despite Rolan's best efforts to wash it away, the Raven King's image lived on. *Perhaps there's still hope.*

Mandan whinnied loudly. He reared, throwing his hooves in front of him for balance. Alina ducked as one barely missed hitting her head. She scrambled for control. The reins sliced into her hands, but she tugged down anyway. Mandan dropped back to the earth. He snorted nervously.

She stroked his nose. She could feel his quivering body through her cloak; the horse was trembling like he had a fever. His eyes rolled next to her cheek. Even her insensitive nose could smell his fear.

Elewyn would know what to do, she thought. *She'd have these horses calmed down in no time.* Indeed, Elewyn had dealt with the same nervous horses in a similar condition; Alina had seen her do it. During the first few hours of traveling in the desert, the horses had panicked, and Elewyn had raced to calm them. Somehow, she had managed to lead them back to an orderly line. *But how did she do it?*

Struggling to remember, Alina paused to straighten her hood. A wide strip of cloth swathed her neck and upper back, holding the leather flap in place. She tugged at the knots, perhaps trying to remove the garment altogether; the desert sun beat down upon her.

Ah! A spark ignited in her mind. One handed, she clumsily undid the knot, allowing the hood to fall free. She stuffed it into her bag, but kept the cloth strip out. It was just wide enough, but it would work, if only she could get into place.

She threw her arms around Mandan's head, fighting the horse as he attempted to twist free. Teeth gnashed inches from her face. Ignoring this, she flung one end of the cloth into the air. It settled over Mandan's rolling eyes, and she knotted it into place. Unable to see the city walls, the horse quieted instantly.

It didn't take long for Carn to manage the same thing with Oryth's old pony, and the crowds began to disperse. Alina glanced back up at the wall above her. The white marble gazed back with blank eyes. There was no trace of the raven on its smooth stone.

Alina shook her head. She had imagined the raven; surely it hadn't just disappeared! She threw her head back and stared up at the wall. The man in the window shifted uncomfortably, but the wall below him was completely blank. The raven, and the watchful eye of the Raven King, was gone.

On her right, Carn clucked impatiently. He grabbed Mandan's reins and dragged the horse forward, leaving Alina to rip herself away from the wall. She did so, following Carn at a snail's pace as he wove through the thinning crowd. A woman glared at them as they inched through the wrought iron gates. She held out her hand, and her daughter clutched it firmly. The girl turned and imitated her mother's piercing stare. Alina shook her head. *Like mother, like daughter,* she thought. She was glad the girl hadn't been injured when the horses panicked.

The city opened at her feet, cobbled streets peeling away like layers of skin. She was surprised to find that the marble of the city walls continued into the inner architecture. Low buildings made of the cream colored stone sprawled across the city, coming abruptly to a halt as they collided with the majestic cliffs of Mt. Goram. A fine layer of dust blown in from the desert covered everything, though during the city's prime, the streets had been kept meticulously clean. Pubs and eateries lined the crowded streets. Alina wrinkled her nose; even at a distance, the entire city smelled of alcohol.

As they worked their way into the city, a warm feeling washed over Alina. Drogonburg was most definitely foreign, there was no doubt about that, but it was familiar all the same. The constant presence of the stone was comforting, and she felt safe with the rising cliffs at her back. The people here were more familiar, too. Shorter in stature, the tallest rose only inches above Alina's head. Their faces were partially hidden by wagging beards. Black eyes peeked out from behind the fluff, and these too bore the presence of the stone. There was no laughter (times were too dark for that), but Alina felt that these were a merry folk all the same.

Dwarves, she realized suddenly. *Drogonburg is a city of dwarves!* She scanned the city once more. *Yes, I'm sure of it.* Her eyes caught sight of carving in the side of a building. It was of a pickaxe, edges sharpened for work in the mines.

Only a thousand years previously, the dwarves had lived underground permanently, moving above the surface only to obtain water when subterranean rivers were scarce. But something had changed the evolutionary course, and the race of the underdwellers, as they were then called, split into two sub groups. One group remained below the surface, eventually becoming coremen. The other had moved into the sunlight. These were the dwarves, and they still kept close ties to the earth by way of mining.

Alina examined the cliffs, trying the see the precious metals hidden in the rocky depths. Drogonburg was Ivindor's largest source of gold, and Mt. Goram was riddled with dwarven tunnels. Stockpiled in its depths was far more treasure than Alina had ever laid eyes on: piles of glittering jewels, delicate crowns, and silver lace. It was no wonder that Rolan had taken over Drogonburg as soon as he came into power.

'Taken over' isn't the right phrase, though, Alina remembered. The dwarves of Drogonburg had been all too happy to accept the Black Knights into their city. It was considered an honor, to be the host to the king's troops. The dwarves had thrown open their gates, and because of this, much of the city had been spared.

The Knights of Drogonburg kept to themselves, avoiding contact with the locals. There were hardly any killings, rebellions to be squashed by black blades, or traitors to be hung with cruel hands. Bread was never taken from a child's mouth, as it was in the eastern cities, where the Knights ran rampant. The locals were left to do whatever they wished, and so their culture flourished.

Alina examined the city once more. In the cliffs, small windows peeked out of the heights. Most likely the homes of the locals, they seemed to laugh at the poor expanse of city beneath them. A huge opening had been carved into the base of the cliff. Etched with elven designs of vines and leaves, the delicate archway seemed hardly capable of supporting the cliff face. Alina smiled. Even with Rolan in power, there were certain things that would never be destroyed. The alliance between the elves and the dwarves was one of them.

She strode ahead of Carn. They were nearing the center of city now, and huge crowds of people flushed the streets. The two horses balked at the increase in noise. Mandan snorted at a passing merchant.

She yanked the reins away from Carn. Who did he

think he was anyway? Mandan was *her* horse, and she would be the one to lead him to be sold, thank you very much. She laid a comforting hand on the horse's shoulder. The horse quieted instantly. She tried not to smile too smugly at her former friend. *He is only trying to help, after all.* She pushed the thought aside. Carn deserved more than just a cold shoulder.

They rounded a corner, and Alina caught her first sight of the Drogonburg Marketplace. A large square lined with buildings, it was bustling with people. Vendors pushed carts between stalls, shouting and ringing bells to attract attention. Children darted from stall to stall as their mothers sold bread and hand woven clothe. A man dragged a clattering rack across the cobblestones. Colorful scarves danced from the hooks. Off to one side, a group of adolescent girls clustered around a tray. They chattered as they sifted through its contents.

Alina pressed closer. She slipped into the circle, until at last she hovered at the edge of the tray. Bright, multicolored beads glared up at her. The colors flashed as the girls sifted through them, plucking the brightest from the crowd. These they strung onto bits of twine. One or two produced gold coins to pay the watching merchant, but the rest of the girls seemed unable to make a decision. They mingled freely.

Alina did not make eye contact with Carn as she turned to weave her way through the labyrinth of people. Sharp laughter rang out from behind her. She glanced back at the girls, her own age, but without a care in the world.

She shook the thought from her head. It was not her fate to grow up safe and secure; she had known that since she was old enough to think. But seeing a group of peers set off a whirlwind of longing in her heart. *That could have been me. I could have been one of them, if Carn hadn't intervened.* She stole a glance at her friend. Anger began to well up with in her, fiery rage that bubbled like lava inside her throat. Tears clouded her vision. She pushed them aside. *It's his fault Arie's dead. He should be the one crying.* With that thought in mind, she stalked behind her brother's murderer.

The bustle of the market cleared suddenly, and Alina and Carn found themselves on the outskirts of an enclosure. Dust churned beneath the hooves of hundreds of animals as they were paraded around the corral. Cows milled endlessly near the gate, lowing softly. Off to one side pranced a group of pure white stallions. They tossed their heads and lifted their feet high off the ground. A few had golden lace twined into their manes. Their faces were still, noble, bold. These were the horses destined for the Gods.

Alina watched them for a moment. The scene was familiar; every city in Ivindor had a group of such horses. They belonged to the temple, and were often housed in plain sight of the public. Every year on midwinter's eve, one of the stallions was chosen by public vote. This stallion, selected above all his peers, would be given to Nora. A priest, with a sacrificial knife, would take care of the logistics.

There was something vaguely familiar about these horses, though, something Alina had never noticed before. All were pure white, but some had a slight strawberry tint, as if they had been a different color when they were younger. It was almost as if some had been born roans.

Alina was well aware that Elewyn had not bought Snowberry off some legal market. The horse was too well bred for that sort of thing. But now she wondered if

Elewyn had even paid for Snowberry at all. A horse of Snowberry's caliber was extremely hard to come by; horses like Snowberry were always taken to the temple when they were still foals. And it wasn't hard to imagine the horse prancing beside the others. *He would be the cream of the crop, sure to win the public's vote.*

She shuddered at the thought. The punishment for stealing a horse in Ivindor was severe, but to steal one of the Gods' stallions meant a punishment even worse then death. Violators were sentenced to accompany the horse as it visited the Gods. They were sacrificed, and their bodies were strung above the temple doors as a testament to the will of the Great Goddess.

It's no wonder Elewyn was so reluctant to leave Snowberry, Alina thought. She led Mandan into the corral, not bothering to hold the gate open for Carn and the pony to pass through. *Thank goodness we didn't bring him with us today! If we were caught with one of the Gods' stallions in our hands. . . We could have been killed!*

She glanced at Carn. His face was impassive, but she knew he must have come to the same conclusion earlier. *I'll follow your lead. Keep calm, don't let on more than we can afford. Remember: we're just here to sell Mandan and the pony. Sell them, and get out of here, fast.*

Her laughter startled her. She glanced around, hoping that no one had heard. *Snowberry would the least of our concerns if we're caught! We're the Wanderers, rebels. Rolan won't even pause long enough to find out about Snowberry and Elewyn. We'll be hung like dogs, and that will be the end of it.*

She followed Carn to the back of the arena. As they squirmed through the crowd, the quality of animals grew progressively less impressing. Now the temple's stallions were replaced with braying mules. Dairy cows, so thin that their ribs seemed about to tear through their skin, huddled together. Narrow cages, lined up to form aisles, shook as their occupants struggled for freedom. Alina stooped to peer through one of the grated doors. An emaciated dog cowered in the corner of the cage. Weakly, he raised his head to glare at her. She stumbled backwards, trying to tear herself away from the cage and its occupant. There was no life in the dog's unseeing eyes.

The cages ended abruptly, once more giving way to rows of larger livestock. It was here that Carn finally halted. He stood on his toes, straining to see over the backs of the animals. "These places aren't made for little people," he grumbled.

Alina ignored him. She twisted her neck as she searched the crowd. Merchants were everywhere, identifiable by their leather aprons and black clothing underneath. They clung to the halters of various horses and darted between the animals like fish on a reel. None so much as glanced at Alina, or at the horses that she and Carn held.

"Over there." She pointed, not caring whether Carn was able to see over the back of a pony that was now passing. As she had trusted him, Carn would have to trust her. She dragged Mandan forward until she stood in front of the merchant.

The man glared at her. Alina had the uncomfortable sensation that she was being sized up like the horses around her. She drew herself up straighter. *If I'm going to be examined, I might as well have a good report.* She stuck her chin out pointedly.

The man shrugged. He turned his attention to Mandan, and to the pony beside Carn. His eyes traced Mandan's spine and followed the horse's long legs as they gave way to muscular shoulder. Finally, he shook his head. When he met Alina's eyes, he was sneering. "I don't deal in butchery. You'll find him over there." He nodded towards another merchant.

Alina followed his gaze, but she hardly noticed the boy with an apron swinging around his neck. The animals surrounding this merchant were a poor selection; one of the horses was lying on the ground, being too weak to stand. Another horse wobbled with its leg at a crooked angle. Beside it, an old workhorse stood with its head hanging between its legs. Long welts from the whip blistered across its back. Blood and puss oozed from the marks, and from a wound just below he animal's eye. No one had bothered to pull the wagon harness from its weak frame.

Alina turned back to the merchant at hand. Her face was set, and when she spoke, her voice was cold. "These two horses are hardly destined for the butchery. Perhaps you were looking at the wrong animal?" She dragged Mandan forward. "This horse has seen some labor, but he's been trained as a race horse and is in good shape. The other is fine mountain animal. You won't find another like him in this marketplace."

The man snorted. He turned his eyes back to Mandan and the pony, and though his expression remained disdainful, Alina saw that his eyes moved with renewed interest. She decided to press her luck. "We bought the horse for nearly forty gold pieces. We'll sell him to you for twenty." She had no idea whether that was a reasonable price for a horse, but was enough money for she and Carn to purchase supplies.

"Ten," the man said.

"Eighteen, and not a penny less," Carn stated. His voice was firm. "We've lost enough money as is. We're practically giving him to you for free."

"Fine." The man turned his eyes away from Mandan. "I don't suppose you'd be interested in selling the pony?"

"My friend was right when she said that you won't find another creature like him any time soon. He comes from east of the mountains, and was raised on the steppes of Mt. Ferong. There's not a steadier mount for picking your way through boulders of high altitude trail."

The man waved his hand, as if pushing the information aside. "How much, boy?"

"Thirty." Carn glared at him.

"Expensive for a pony. Expensive for a horse. And this creature has been overworked, and ridden hard in the past few days. He's lost muscle tone. How do I know he'll gain it back?"

"What he's lost in muscle, he's gained in experience. This animal knows the paths of the Tortallions like his home pasture. And he's quick to recover. He'll gain his strength back."

"I'll give you fifteen for him." The man reached for his purse.

Alina raised her hand to stop him. "Fifteen? For an animal that could earn you four times that much? Hardly. You heard our asking price. Thirty, nothing less."

The man grimaced. "I'm just a poor dealer," he whined. "I can't afford thirty gold pieces. Not for a single animal."

Carn smiled regretfully. "Well, we'll move on. I'm sure another dealer will be glad to take the pony." He turned as if to leave. His fingers twitched, and Alina turned as well. They began to move back into the crowd.

"No!" The merchant dashed around them, until they

stood face to face again. "I'll give you twenty. More than that pony's worth."

Carn seemed to consider it for a moment. "Twenty-four and you've got yourself a deal. Like I said; this is a fine animal."

The merchant bobbed his head. "Yes, yes, fine in his prime. But he's weak. It'll be expensive to gain his health back."

"I said twenty-four. You'll get your money's worth."

"I'll take both animals for forty-one."

Carn smiled. "Now you're catching on." He nodded. "We'll take forty-one."

The merchant grinned a big, toothless smile. He reached for Mandan's reins. As Alina raised her hand to stroke the horse one last time, her cloak rode up. The hilt of her sword flashed in the sunlight. The merchant quickly withdrew his hand. He reached for his purse, and proceeded to count out forty-one gold pieces.

Carn pocketed the money, and handed the pony over without ceremony. Alina lingered with Mandan for a moment, running her fingers through his mane. She rubbed the white patch on his forehead. "Be good," she whispered. She held out the reins.

The merchant snatched them away. Alina blinked, and the next instant he had disappeared into the crowd. There was no sign of Mandan or the pony anywhere; just the other livestock melding back together to cover their path.

Alina turned, and began to pick her way back to the main marketplace. Behind her, she heard Carn following. He didn't say anything, didn't question her actions. He just followed, like he had from the beginning.

21

Supplies in hand, Alina made her way out of the city. Carn followed, but at safe distance, toting the ragged tent that they had bought off a street beggar. He watched his friend closely, but she showed no signs of letting up.

Alina tugged the straps of the food bag into place. The weight of it pressed down on her shoulders, and already she felt the beginnings of a blister. It burned against the cloth of her dress.

She skimmed the landscape with her eyes, trying to ignore the pain. The desert was just as bland as it had been when she entered the city. Fresh dunes washed against the city walls. Out in the open, the wind had scurried away the sand, and patches of grass peeked through. A few wildflowers winked at her as she passed. Even the sun seemed to be smiling.

She sneered. The expression was comforting, and it released some of the pent up emotions inside her. She tried it again, and then broke out into a smile. The day wasn't turning out to be so bad after all. At this rate, they would reach the mouth of the tunnel by the next evening. *Maybe Elewyn and the others will already be there.* She turned to Carn, about to share her thoughts. But then she remembered why they were searching for the others in the first place. She frowned again, and this time the frown stuck.

I hate him, she realized. It was perhaps the first time in her life that she could accurately say such a thing. She nodded slightly. Like the frown, the words felt natural against her lips. She tried it again. *I hate him. He betrayed Arie. He killed my brother.* Yes, that was right. The day of the sandstorm came flooding back to her. Tears began to sting her eyes.

The idiot! No. . . He's more than that. A murderer, despised by the Gods. A whoreson, just like Rolan. He's not fit to walk this earth! There's nothing he can say or do to make things right. I'm finished with him. He might as well die for all I care. She twisted her head, as if to tell him to leave her alone. *No. Let him be swallowed by his guilt. He doesn't deserve death—he deserves much worse! Let him be eaten alive by the desert sun! Let him be tormented by his black soul! Better yet, let the Gods wreck their fury! Traitors, murderers. . . They're no better than the scum that floats on a pond.*

Unconsciously, her hand had floated to the hilt of her sword. She wrapped her fingers around it, surprised to find it willing in her grasp. *I could kill him,* she realized. She loosened the blade in the sheath a tiny bit, just enough to let the metal catch the sun's rays. *It would be easy, like killing a rat. And he deserves it.*

She began to walk faster. *He killed my brother. I'll never forgive him for that. Just do it! It'll be easy. One less evil man walking this earth.* She drew farther ahead, so that the front of her body was out of Carn's sight. Slowly, she pulled the sword from its sheath.

The blade seemed to glow as it drew in the sunlight. She tested her thumb on the edge. A long, red line appeared, and a single drop of blood oozed out. She put into her mouth and sucked. The blood tasted good, like a warm copper coin.

She hefted the sword in her hand, wrapping her fingers around the handle. It seemed to jump in her hand. *It's hungry. It wants blood.* This was the time; it was now or never. *Do it now, while he's not expecting it!*

She felt her body begin to turn. Her knees were stiff. It took forever for her arms to move. Her fingers, so strong just moments before, were now weak. *He killed my brother! He deserves it! I trusted him!*

Now she had come to the heart of the matter. The anger fell from her like a stone. Suddenly she was empty inside. Somewhere on the outskirts of her mind, she realized that she had stopped walking. She watched the sword fall to the sand. Her knees buckled, and she joined it as it rebounded. The sand felt warm against her skin.

A dry sob croaked from the back of her throat. It took longer for the tears to come, but when they finally began to fall, they poured. She bent over, clutching her stomach. *I trusted him!*

She was vaguely aware of Carn dropping down beside her. A quavering hand reached out to touch her shoulder. She pushed it away, hard. *What right does he have to comfort me?*

Her eyes caught hold of the sword blade, still glinting with the light. She stared hard at. The blade seemed to smile back at her.

Hands shaking, she reached for its hilt. It was heavy in her hand, and she almost couldn't lift it. *This is what it feels like to die.* The thought crossed her mind, unbidden. *I could end it.* She pointed the sword upwards, and gazed down at the tiny tip.

"Alina!" He ripped the blade from her grasp.

She shook him off. He was a mere ghost to her now, the shadow of what he once was. She found herself striding across the sand. How she had managed to get up, she wasn't sure, but it felt good to move. Anything to distract her from her grief.

She hadn't cried when Arie died. Not even when her eyes met his, as they lowered the noose around his neck. Not a single tear had come to her, as those eyes slowly began to bulge, and then went lifeless. No sobs had come when they tore his body apart, and tossed it to the dogs for disposal. She had never gone into mourning for her dear brother, the young man she had held as her idol all of her life. But now, four months after his death, she mourned.

She could remember when Arie was little, and she was just a toddler. He had grinned at her, his mouse brown hair tangled. His grey eyes had twinkled with laughter. Even when he was older, his eyes had remained Alina's favorite part about him. She had loved to look up, and see him standing there, smiling. He had never smiled for anyone else in the Clan, not even for Carn, whom he treated like a brother. His smiles were for Alina alone.

When he was old enough, Arie would beg their mother to take them to the pool. Hardly a puddle collected in a divot of stone, the pool had always seemed huge to Alina. She would watch as Arie dove in, head first. It was a while before he came up for a breath, and Alina could still feel the sudden panic that she had felt then, waiting for him surface. She would watch the water, breathless.

And then Arie would appear, his head floating just above the rocky ledge. His laughter rang out, and he would call for her to join him. Alina couldn't swim, but she would spend long hours by the pool, watching him.

Alina smiled slightly. Those had been the happiest days of her life, when she was still too young to understand the cruelty of the world. Back then, Isen had only been a stern adult, aloof, and to be avoided. The whispered rumors of rebellion had passed over her head unheeded. Maybe Arie understood, even then, the place that he had been born into. But he hadn't mentioned anything to her, and she had accepted their safety for fact. Nothing could have convinced her that in five years, Arie would be dead.

But the year that Arie turned sixteen, everything changed. Arie had become a man, and with manhood came a man's responsibilities. He spent less time at Alina's side, and more time following Isen around. When the men met for discussion, he was invited to join. Alina could remember watching them, sitting in a circle with Arie at their side. She could remember the smirks on their faces. Arie had looked back with utter devotion.

And then something had changed. The men went away on a hunting trip, and took Arie with them. When they came back, Arie was quiet and depressed. He lost his appetite, and refused to go swimming, or accompany Alina to their special place, that only they knew about. He moped beside their family hearth. One night, when Alina woke from a bad dream, she looked across and saw that he was crying.

The thoughts had started soon after that. He would disappear for days at a time, and return speaking of protest. He met with other men, outlaws, in the secret of the night. Alina was left in the dark, watching.

And so, when he threatened Isen's life, Carn showed his true loyalties. Alina kicked at the sand beneath her feet. She felt Carn's presence at her back. He was offering her something. He held out her sword, his fingers draped delicately over the blade. The hilt was free, waiting for her to take it.

She swatted it away, not caring that the blade sliced Carn's fingers as she did so. *I don't want it,* she thought. *I don't want anything that you've touched. Never again.*

Even when she and Carn stopped and set up camp for the night, she avoided touching the sword. She threw her sleeping bag on the other side of the tent and flopped down, her back to Carn.

22

By the time she managed to slip out the next morning, the sun was already high in the sky. She shouldered her rucksack, looping one of the water bags into her belt as she did so. The second water bag leaned against the side of the tent. She didn't have the heart to take it, even though logic urged her otherwise.

She peeked back inside the tent. Carn rolled over in his sleep, but he didn't wake up. She stared at him for a moment, tracing his outline with her eyes. She would miss him, but that couldn't be helped. He wasn't to be trusted.

The tent flaps fluttered quietly into place behind her. She swiveled her head, gazing out over what was left of the desert. More sand had blown in overnight, but her way was clear enough. In the south, a wide green band stretched towards the horizon. The last of the desert sands gave way to scraggly trees and scrub brush. Even at this distance, she could make out the brilliant blue of lupines shooting up through the sage.

She took one last look around camp, and then set out. The day was hot, and the sun beat down on her neck. She swatted flies as she walked. The size of her thumbnail, they swarmed her bare skin. She could feel them biting her, but her reflexes weren't fast enough; by the time she managed to slap them away, a red welt had risen in their place. Her skin itched horribly, and she busied herself with scratching as she plodded along. The bites quickly began to bleed. Later on they would drip puss, but for the moment she didn't care. The relief of scratching was almost worth it.

Before she knew it, the sand had given way to the bad lands that surrounded the Grass River. Her feet stumbled on the coarse terrain. Stones rolled underfoot, spraying dead plant matter onto her shins. Branches, bleached white by the sun, cracked when she misstepped. She looked around cautiously, but all was quiet. There was no sign of the Black Knights anywhere.

She pressed on. The sound of the wind slowly began to fade away, and the singing of birds took its place. As she walked, she watched them flit between the branches of dead bushes. Chickadees cocked their heads at her as she passed. She gave the tiny birds a faint smile.

Carn had always loved chickadees, she remembered. They were his favorite. She pushed the thought aside. *Carn isn't here right now.* For good measure, she tossed a stone at one of the tiny birds. It fluttered off in a burst of motion. *Good riddance!*

The birds reminded her of a competition she had seen at the festival in Abrelyon. An hourglass had been set on a table. Elves, some young, but mostly the elders of the village, had arranged themselves in a wide circle. The goal was to attract the most birds to ones person as possible, using any means, but before the hourglass ran out.

Most of the younger men coated themselves with birdseed and honey. They stood very still, some whistling crude bird songs to attract sparrows and finches. But it was the older elves that had fascinated Alina. One particular man, with a waggling white beard and a knobby figure, had caught her attention. He settled himself cross-legged on the ground and began to talk. It wasn't a story that he told, nor was it a string of words that Alina recognized. When he opened his mouth, he spoke in the ancient tongue of the elves. The gliding vowels had almost obscured the consonants. His lips were light, and it seemed that his tongue had danced in his mouth. It had taken Alina several minutes to notice the multitude of birds that had come to roost on his thin frame. Dozens of them hand landed there, all silent, all listening.

She thought about that old man as she watched the birds. More chickadees had come to fill the place where she had thrown the stone. She let them be. *Maybe someday you'll get to hear the Old Speech again, too.*

Something darted from the bushes on her left. She whirled to face it. *Knights?* Her eyes darted frantically from bush to bush. Alone, she would have no chance of fighting them off. She reached for her sword.

The bushes erupted in quaking movement. A huge creature soared forward, black as the midnight sky. Metal clanked as it opened its sharp, curved beak. A single feather loosened from the tip of its wing. It floated softly to the ground.

She watched as the raven wheeled away. *That's twice in two days,* she thought. Her fingers fumbled as she reached for the ebony feather. Its plume was soft in her hand. *I know they are important, but I'm starting to get sick of ravens.* She watched as the bird settled in a nearby tree. It clicked its beak closed.

Fine. Alina traced the outline of her sheath. *So the Gods want to play tricks on me. Who cares? I've got things I need to do; a bird isn't about to stop me!* Her fingers moved upwards, searching for the worn hilt of her sword. She felt her heart drop into her stomach. The sheath was empty. She had left her only weapon back at camp with Carn.

She hesitated. No doubt she would need a sword in the journey to come, but there was no way she was going back to beg it off of Carn. *He's not to be trusted,* she told herself. *I can get another one when I meet up with Elewyn and the others.* She patted the empty place on her belt gingerly. It felt foreign, suspicious. It made her feel vulnerable.

She shook her head. It couldn't be helped. She would just have to make do without it and hope that she didn't run into any sticky situations before she rejoined the others. The journey to the tunnel was a short one. She wasn't expecting any difficulties.

Still unsatisfied, but stubborn, she pressed on. Liam had shown her a map of the area before leaving the mountain city, Grisholm. Landmarks were close together, and she remembered the route to the tunnel clearly. If she hurried, she could make it before nightfall.

She quickened her pace. With night would come creeping predators, hidden pitfalls, and shadows for the Black Knights to hide in. She couldn't afford to be caught out after the sun set, not without a sword. She glanced around. A large stick lay just a few feet away. She seized it, hefting it in her hands. The end was blunted where it had rubbed against a stone. She nodded. At least now she would be able to defend herself.

The tunnel itself was not hard to find. She simply followed the strip of scraggly trees towards the river. The brush gave way to sweeping willows and reeds. A slight breeze ruffled the greenery, and Alina drew a deep breath. The comforting scent of wet earth enveloped her, and she relaxed into its embrace.

She stepped down the bank, following its slope to the

river's edge. Muddy water roiled and churned over the rocks. The river was nearly half a mile wide at its narrowest part, and she had to strain to see the opposite shore. When the river was in flood, like it was now, it was impossible to ford.

Which was why it was so vital that she find the tunnel. The dwarves had carved it centuries ago, so that even in high summer, during the snowmelt, they could cross over to visit the elves.

She turned downstream, scanning the bank. The dwarves weren't known for their ability to hide their work; they were a proud folk. The entrance to the tunnel would be obvious.

There. She slipped through the trees, trotting towards the pile of stone. Huge boulders had been stacked against the trunk of ancient tree, spiraling away from a flat, circular slab. Moss grew green and rich in the cracks. She reached out to it, stroking its surface as she examined the entrance to the tunnel.

At least, she assumed that it was the entrance to the tunnel. She couldn't be sure; there was no dark opening in sight. In fact, the pile of stones could have been a natural formation, if they hadn't been carved with strange letters. She ran her fingers over the carvings, each word etched into the rock with a practiced hand. *If only I could read dwarvish!* She shook her head in frustration. *If Carn was here. . .*

She slammed her fist against the rock. It stung, but that was not the reason why tears came to here eyes. *Shut up! He's not coming! You don't want him to come, remember?* She leaned her forehead against the coolness of the stone. Her eyes closed, and for a moment, it appeared that she was sleeping. *Carn will head back to Drogonburg. There's plenty of places there he can hide. And if worse comes to worst, and the Wanderers don't come to find him before winter, he'll be happy enough staying with the dwarves. They're almost like coremen, after all.*

Alina grimaced. She gnawed at her lip, waiting for the comforting taste of blood to spurt forth. *But Carn won't stay there. He won't go back to the Clan, either. He'll follow me.* She pounded her fist against the rock again, and then again. There was a rhythm to it, and the pounding drowned out the thoughts in her mind.

That's why I need to keep moving, she reminded herself. But she did not stir from her position against the pile of boulders. Her hand droned on. Now and then, she lifted her head just far enough to glare at the river. It glared back at her with surprising venom.

And then, suddenly, something moved. It took her a moment to realize that it was the rock that she was leaning on. The large, circular slab ground against its fellows. She took a step back. *Rocks aren't supposed to move.*

She lifted her club stupidly into the air, as if she were going to bludgeon the boulder to death. Her heart pounded in her chest. She could hear her breath coming in ragged gasps.

The stone continued to shift. A crack appeared behind it. Inky blackness seeped from its depths. She jammed her fingers into the crack and began to pull. The rock slid from its place.

She stared into the cavern beyond. No sunlight filtered into its depths. She could just barely make out to forms of more boulders, growing like jagged teeth from the mouth of the narrow corridor. The stone doorway creaked ominously.

Alina stepped back. She moved with purpose now, slinging her rucksack onto the ground beside her. She rummaged through it and finally emerged with a stone and a steel-cooking knife in hand. Putting these aside, she tore at the lantern tied to the outside of the bag. The fastenings gave way with a sudden jolt. She struck the knife against the stone in her hand. A spark flew through the air. It landed in a pile of moss, where it smoldered and burned.

She grabbed the chunk of moss and held it to her face. Gently, she blew on the spark, nourishing it into a weak flame. This she fed into the chamber of the lantern, where it caught on the oil and wick placed there. The lantern began to glow with a flickering light.

Club and lantern in hand, she gathered up her rucksack. She stood before the tunnel entrance, extending the lantern into the dark. Its light was feeble, but she could see by it. With a quick glance at the forest behind her, she stepped into the darkness.

She lifted her lantern high into the air, its light dancing a tango on the walls of the tunnel. There wasn't much to see; two walls that extended to only a few inches above her short stature, a looming stone that crouched at her feet. She took another step. *This is it.*

Something began to growl once more. She whirled, just in time to see the stone slab roll over the entrance. The last bit of sunlight was extinguished with a final snap. Alina was alone in the tunnel.

She turned back to the darkness that now loomed before her. There was nowhere else to go but onwards. She took a faltering step, and then another. The tunnel grew before her as she walked.

An indefinite period of time passed. She continued to

walk forward, holding the lantern before her to ward off the darkness. The tunnel walls grew moist from the water above. Little rivulets dripped onto her hair. She glanced up at the ceiling anxiously. It seemed like she could here the magnitude of water rushing overhead.

A faint hiss echoed from her right. She twisted to face it. A leak in the tunnel? She froze, waiting for a stream of water to hit her in the face. It never did.

She was vaguely aware of this fact as another sound bounced along the tunnel behind her. She swung her club high into the air as she turned to face it. Her ears strained for the next noise. It came softly, in the form of padded footsteps.

Something else was in the tunnel. That much was certain. She lifted her lantern higher, throwing light onto the walls.

"Hello?" Her voice sounded weak, like a child's. She was half expecting an answer, but like the water, no voice came to her. She raised the lantern as high as she could. The light bounced off the walls. For a moment, she could almost see. A dark shape rushed towards her.

She swung out blindly, throwing the lantern at the creature. It crashed against a rock, spilling oil everywhere. The last shred of light was swallowed by the gloom of the tunnel. From somewhere on her right, she heard a laugh.

The hair on her neck stood on end. She whipped her club around. Its tip crunched against the wall. The ring of metal sounded from all sides. She knew that sound; she had heard it all too often since coming to the surface. It was the clatter of swords being drawn.

She swung the club again. This time her aim was true; she felt something drop to the ground at her feet. She kicked it once, even as the air whooshed around her. In the distance she heard a familiar grinding noise, but she didn't have time to place it. She lashed out with the club, trying to follow the sounds of movement. Ragged breathing surrounded her on all sides. She raised the club.

Something hit her, hard. Her head rang. She wasn't sure if the black she was seeing was the shadow of the tunnel, or her eyes rolling back in her head. The sounds around her were muffled. She felt her knees buckle, and her hands touched dirt.

When she came to her senses, she was lying face down in the tunnel. At least, she thought it was the tunnel, and that she was lying face down. She wasn't sure; everything was black. She sat up, groaning. Her head felt awful.

She reached for her hairline. Her fingers came away sticky, and when she smelled them, she caught the metallic scent of blood. She moaned again, louder.

It all came flooding back to her: the ambush, the lantern floating down the tunnel. Something had driven her attackers away. They had left her lying here, her left side pressed against the wall of the tunnel. On her right, she could feel the shapes of boulders.

She wobbled to her feet, clutching at the wall for support. The gloom extended in all directions. She took a step forward, stumbled over a rock, and fell. She cursed in the dark.

When the pain had subsided somewhat, she craned her neck. Her eyes ached from trying to see without light. She frowned, scanning the tunnel.

Ah! Either her eyes were deceiving her, or that section of the tunnel was a slightly lighter shade of black. She stared at it for a moment, blinking. The light sputtered for a moment, but it came back, as bright as before.

She stood again, and slowly made her way through the rocks. It occurred to her that the light might not be coming from a friendly source, but she didn't care. She didn't have much choice in the matter. If she waited for the light to die before investigating, she would be stuck in the tunnel. Without a light, she could wander its length forever.

A shudder rattled her body. She bit her lip against it before moving on. The light grew stronger, and she had to shield her eyes from its brilliance. She froze, waiting for the blindness to pass.

It did. She dropped her arm from her face, though she still kept it at chest height, with her hand curled in a fist. A tiny flame wavered at the base of a boulder. Lamp oil had pooled in a depression in the ground, and the flame sucked life from the glistening liquid. Alina stared at it for a moment, reveling in the tiny miracle.

She shifted her gaze from the light. A tray of broken glass caught the rays of the tiny flame, and the pieces twinkled merrily at her. She followed their radiant path.

Something dark lay at the end of the debris. She kicked at it, and it rolled over. She could now see that the object was much larger than she had first imagined; the part that she had kicked was only a small trajectory from the greater mass. Bending down, she prodded at the heart of the shape.

It groaned. She jumped back, heart racing. The thing was alive! It was a human, sprawled on the ground. The head was hidden in the shadows of another boulder. She crept forward.

The face came slowly into view. First came the blond hair, scattered at odd angles across the smooth brow. Then the boyish nose appeared, stabbing out from the worried, scrunched up cheeks. The eyes were shut tight, but she didn't need to see them to know that they were blue. Carn lay at her feet, one hand clutching at his side. She moved it gently. Dark liquid smothered his clothing. A jagged hole gaped at the base of his ribs, oozing blood into a pool below him.

Alina gasped. She threw down her rucksack; she wasn't sure how she had managed to keep hold of it in the struggle. Another lantern swung from its side. She ripped it away and hurried to the pool of oil. Using a shred from her dress, she scooped the flame into the lantern. She hurried back to Carn.

The wound wasn't as deep as she had first feared. He was still breathing, though the movement was shallow at best. She cut the tunic away from the wound. Pale fingers of skin hung limply from the hole, but red flesh was visible in its depths. *Just a glancing blow.* She breathed a sigh of relief. *Thank the Gods.*

She had purchased a roll of bandages in Drogonburg, and as she pulled the strips of cloth from her sack, she was grateful she had. The bandage grated roughly at her fingertips. She wrapped the wound as well as she could. It wasn't a very good job, but hopefully it wouldn't need to last for long. Already blood had begun to stain the white cloth pink.

She pulled the rucksack back onto her shoulders. Carn moaned, and she patted him softly. *Not long now. Hang in there.* She grasped his shoulders and heaved. His eyelids fluttered for a second, and he moved as if to speak, but she quieted him as she hauled him onto her shoulders. She stood, holding the lantern with her teeth. One step after the other, she carried Carn down the tunnel.

"Hush. I'm here," she whispered into her friend's bruised and battered ear. "I'm here for you." And for the first time since Carn had told her the truth about Arie, she was glad she was.

23

The group stared at the entrance to the tunnel. Smashed rock and wood was everywhere. Bits of branches scattered the ground. Huge boulders had been split in two, halved like they were loaves of bread, instead of masses of solid stone. The tree that had supported the pile of stones lay crumpled over the entrance to the tunnel. Someone had moved the circular entrance slab so that it leaned against the tree's uppermost branches. Its surface was crossed out, covered in red and brown liquid. The blood looked fresh.

It was the old man who finally spoke. He did so carefully, fiddling with a crystal inset in his staff. His eyes gazed piercingly into the faces of the others. "The Black Knights."

The others nodded. They continued to stare at the ruins. A young man, his head a mess of red hair, bent to the ground. The stubble of an auburn beard colored his face. He pointed at the trampled earth. "I can see the prints of the Black Knights, but look here. These prints are almost child like. There are two sets, one small and hesitant, the other quick, and determined."

A girl crouched down beside him. Her hair cascaded in long, blond tresses. "Alina and Carn?"

"Who else?" It was other boy that spoke, his hair the

same golden blond. His face was worried, but he shook the feeling aside. "We can't follow them. That's for certain."

"If they're still alive. The Black Knights are ruthless fighters. Even you or I couldn't survive an attack like this. They were angry." Oryth grimaced.

Elewyn let out a cry. "Gods! Why them?" The sound dissipated into the forest. She glanced around nervously. "We can't stay here."

The others nodded. They took one last look at the tunnel before creeping from the ruins. As they walked, each person could not help but think of the two friends that now wandered alone. They could not help but think that the Raven King, and the hope of success that accompanied him, was now far out of their reach.

24

If the tunnel had been a living hell, than this was the world of the Gods. There was no other way to describe the arching trees, the spilling waterfalls. It was as if she had stepped out into an entirely different realm.

Trunks rose like magnificent towers from the rich earth, bark draped in plush moss. Flowering vines hung in cascades from the royal branches. Ferns the length of a large horse bloomed out of their rootstalks. They loomed high above her head as she took her first steps in to the Hawthorne Forest.

Far above the emerald roofing of ferns was a vaulted ceiling of branches. Crisscrossed and woven like a basket, they grew so tightly together that only a few droplets of sunlight dripped between leaves. But the forest was not dark. Instead, it glowed with a healthy light, as if the very earth beneath her feet was illuminated.

Alina's eye caught sight of the deepest flash of blue. Pushing through the last of the ferns, she came to the bank of a crystal pool. Twenty feet deep and glassy, the pool was a brilliant blue, almost glacier-like in color. The surface was dotted with emerald lily pads, so large that Alina could have sat on them easily. Violet flowers nestled in between the leaves, rubies in a chest of emeralds and sapphires. Across the pool, a marble wall glistened with sweet dampness. Water trickled down its surface, tumbling into the pool with a sound alike to laughter. The water swirled endlessly, lapping at her feet. It caressed the soft sand bank like a long lost lover. She gazed into the depths of the pool and saw the faintest shadows darting in and out of the rocky bottom. The fish glided to the surface of the pond. They flipped over to display the brilliant rainbows of their bellies. The wind sighed softly in the trees.

She stepped away from the pool, pulling the ferns back across her path. To her left, a tree soared towards the canopy. It was so thick that three men could have laid, head to toe, across its diameter. She stroked the bark and inhaled the tangy scent of pine.

She half turned to look back at the dark mouth of the tunnel. It gaped its rich darkness, as if it was straining to swallow her back up. There was no movement in its depths; Carn was still fast asleep.

Alina strode into the forest, watching as the trees passed her by. They grew straight and tall, arrow shafts of the gods stuck into the soil. She let her feet navigate the roots and needles without the help of her eyes. Instead, she leaned back, staring up at the canopy overhead. It had to be at least three hundred feet from the first branch to forest floor.

The forest stretched infinitely in all directions, looming off into the distance like some magical fog. How were they supposed to find the Raven King in a place like this?

She turned back towards the tunnel. There was no sense in beginning the search now. She would need Carn's help. She frowned at the thought, and a touch of anger boiled inside of her. It dissolved as quickly as it came. *He saved my life.*

She ducked into the tunnel hesitantly. Once her eyes adjusted to the gloom, she strode boldly across the entrance. Carn, curled up in a corner, snorted in his sleep. She paused for a moment, studying him. Though she wouldn't admit it, the wound to his side worried her. He was weak and could hardly walk, much less travel. Blood still seeped from the gaping hole. She changed the bandages twice a day, but they were running out of cloth to use. The edges of the wound had gone pale, and his entire side was red and puffy. He groaned.

"Carn," she whispered, hardly daring to shake him awake. "Carn. Come on. You've got to get up."

He blinked awake. "Alina?"

She ran her fingers over his forehead, but the moment she touched his skin, she jerked back. He was burning hot. Fever. She dabbed his face with a moist cloth. "Yeah, it's me."

"For a second there, I thought I was dreaming. You looked like the Goddess come to fetch me," he murmured.

Shit. Not only was he weak and injured, but he was also delirious. She struggled to pull him into a sitting position. "We've got to get moving, Carn." Even as she said the words, she wondered if travel was a good idea. She watched as his face blanched a deathly white.

"Alina . . . I don't think I can." He looked up at her, pleading. His brown eyes searched her face haltingly. "I'll only slow you down. Speed is essential now. You should go without me."

She shook her head. "And leave here like some bait for the Knights to find? No. We'll go together. I'm not going to leave you here, Carn!" She pushed a lock of damp hair out of his eyes. "I've scouted the area. We're safe for the moment. There's water nearby . . . . We can stay here until you're fit to travel."

"Alina. You know that's not going to happen anytime soon. We're running out of supplies. And I hate to say it, but you're no healer. Go!"

"No!" She swatted a tear away from her eyes. "We're staying together, Carn. Just like old time's sake. You're my best friend. I'm not about to leave you here!"

"You can't stay here, Alina. If the Knights come back, they'll kill you."

"*We* can't stay here. We'll move. This is a huge forest . . . There are plenty of places for us to hide."

"But the Raven King . . . That's our top priority, Alina. You can't just sit here! Gods! People are dying out there!"

Alina stared at him for a moment. "But Carn, you're dying in here," she whispered.

The silence that followed seemed to stretch on for eternity.

"That's why you have to go," Carn said. Blinking rapidly, he lay back down against the rock. He turned away from her, hiding his face in the corner. In the darkness, he hid his tears.

"Carn . . . " Alina stroked his arm for a moment longer, and then stood. "I'm going outside. I *will* be back." She crept from the tunnel.

Outside, the sunlight seemed to sting her eyes. Tears trickled down her cheeks in great rivers. She kicked out blindly at a log. The pain shot through her like a knife. She collapsed in a heap, letting her tears mix into the dust. "Carn . . . "

Gods! He was hurt, dying even, and all she could do was sit here and watch him. She rubbed her temples, as if trying to massage the pain from her mind. There had to be something she could do, someone in this great forest who could help! An elf, maybe? They were skilled healers. She stared wildly around, but the trees were empty.

"Alone . . . " She keened into the bark of the fallen tree. The bark pressed against her face, dug into her skin. "I can't leave him here. I just can't. Oh, Goddess, I need help!"

She lifted her face frantically to the heavens. "If you can hear me up there, know that one of your own is dying! A king, a noble! You're supposed to be protecting him!

"You created this world! You created these people! And now you're just going to sit there and let them die? Carn is dying! The elves are dying! Great Mother who birthed us, don't let the pain of the delivery go to waste. Let us live!

"Carn once told me that I will never be alone, because the Gods will always be here to help me. He said all I had to do was ask for help. Well Gods, I'm asking now! Answer me!"

The bushes rustled off to her right. Very slowly, she turned, drawing her sword as she did so. She got shakily to her feet. Brandishing the blade, she pushed aside the first layer of brush. "Who's there?"

She thrust aside the last of the brush and walked boldly into the forest beyond.

25

"So the Raven King is out of the question." The members of the group glanced at each other. Across the circle, the two boys made eye contact. They nodded, as if they had suspected this would happen all along.

The shadows danced over their faces as they huddled against the cliff side. They were not far from the tunnel now, and every once and a while they heard the sounds of the Knights, who now patrolled the area.

"And even if Alina and Carn did survive that ambush," Liam said softly, "there's no certainty that they will find the Raven King." He chose his words slowly, as if drawing them out of thick mud. He did not look at Elewyn.

Leif nodded. "We cannot wait around for a miracle. We have to act." He stood up hastily, bumping his head in the process.

"And just what do you propose we do? Try to kill Rolan without the Raven King? That's suicide!" Elewyn leapt up to meet his gaze. His blue eyes flickered in the firelight.

"Suicide? Or Sacrifice?" he murmured. "This might be our only chance—"

"To die? Are you an idiot? I can kill you right now if that's what you're after, Leif! We don't have the power to overtake Rolan without the Raven King—"

"We don't need to overtake him. Not completely. Once the people get wind of a rebellion, they'll join in."

"Just what are you suggesting? That we invade Rolan's camp? That we kill him in a single swipe of the sword and parade his head around the countryside? Miracles don't exist, Leif." Elewyn flung herself back into the dust.

"But we can't just sit here waiting for some larger force to sweep Rolan aside. We are the only group opposing him, the only rebels in *all* of Ivindor. We are the elves' last chance!" Leif gestured frantically. "Don't you see, Elewyn? This is the miracle. We're it. Like it or not, we're the people the Gods designated for this role. We have to play this part!" He spun on Oryth. "Father! Say something!"

The wizard bowed his head. "I agree with Leif and Liam. But," he said, as Leif let out a triumphant crow, "I would advise that we proceed with caution. We don't have an army to back us up. If we fail, we condemn every elf in Ivindor to death."

"Then we cannot fail." Leif murmured. "We have a small army stationed just south of the palace—volunteer soldiers from the survivors of the raided towns. Not many, but enough. With luck—"

"With luck?" Elewyn turned red in her fury. "With luck? With luck we'll all die a relatively painless death. With luck, we might kill a few of the King's men. A volunteer army can't defeat an empire, Leif. Not everyone is as eager a warrior as you."

"Then let us recruit all of the men we can." Oryth rose. He stood straight, his staff held firmly at his side, no longer for support, but as a weapon. "Grisholm will send troops. And so will Abreylon. This is our last chance. It is as Leif said: we cannot fail. The time of action has come. We ride at dawn."

"To our deaths?"

"To battle," Oryth nodded. "And perhaps to our deaths."

26

The air was humming. It was the first thing she noticed, and it struck her as odd. It was not the sound of a beehive, nor of a sword shivering. No, this was the hum of power. It rang in her ears and reverberated down her spine.

And then there was the light. Soft and sweet, the air seemed to glow. The rays centered on a single orb, floating haphazardly a few feet off of the ground. She reached out to touch it, and it bounced backwards lazily. The sound of gentle laughter filled her ears.

Alina took a step forward, her first step into this otherworldly realm. She could see now that she was in a large clearing, not unlike the one she had just left. Except that this clearing was greener, wetter, and more alive.

She crossed the bed of moss without haste, pausing to admire the fragrant wildflowers that swam in the greenery at her feet. The clearing was slightly oblong in shape, and the trees all but blocked the rest of the forest from view. At the end of the clearing stood a mother tree, huge, powerful, and nurturing. Ferns sprouted out of its sides like feathers. Its branches curved upwards, arcing towards the sunlit sky with an ancient grace.

She rounded this tree, dragging her hands softly along its bark as she went. She had no idea where she was going, only that this was where she was supposed to be.

A stone. She stared at it dimly for a moment. Flat and rectangular, it floated on the moss bed just inches from her toes. *Marble,* she noticed, unconcerned. And then— *Strange. What's a stone doing here, on top of the moss? Why isn't there moss on it as well?* For the stone gleamed without a hint of green on its surface. She tapped it. *A small puzzle.*

After a moment, she moved on. It was not until several feet later that she noticed the next stone. Rectangular and shiny, it was almost identical to the one she had just seen. In fact, it was so identical that it took her several moments to figure out what was different.

It was floating a foot off of the ground! She hurriedly waved her hand beneath it, but it did not fall. She pressed on it. No results. Hesitantly, and not quite sure why she was doing so, she clambered up onto its surface. Another stone floated in front of her own, slightly higher, then another and another. The stones floated in staircase towards the canopy.

She climbed forward. The stones were slick from rain, and she almost slipped more than once. By the time she was more than twenty feet off of the ground, she had decided that this was no time to fall.

A cliff side loomed into view. Water cascaded over its side, singing the praises of the Gods as it fell into a pool below. Vines hung like curtains around the staircase. The flowers were overwhelming.

She came to an archway of branches, and paused. Was it worth entering? Shrugging, she pushed the thought aside. She had come too far to turn back now. She climbed higher still.

Finally, a platform appeared. She staggered onto it, feeling her muscles burn in her legs. She loosened her sword in its scabbard before glancing around.

The platform appeared to be made out of woven branches, some of which were still living. It was a long, narrow balcony stretching along the utmost layer of the canopy. She could just barely see its end: a lump. Something was sitting very still.

She took several steps forward. The figure came into a focus. An old man, his hair snow white with age, sat with his back to her. His fingers, gnarled with arthritis, were folded over the hilt of a sword. The blade shone lightly in his lap.

"My daughter." The man did not look up, but Alina had the disconcerting impression that her insides were being screened. His balding head bobbed slightly. "Come."

It only took a few steps to reach his side. She stood for a moment, and then lowered herself to her knees before him. She bowed her head. "You are the Raven King."

When she looked up, the old man was smiling. He set the sword on the mat beside him. "That was my name, once. I revoked it long ago. Here, I am simply Alleyn, or Master Alleyn, Keeper of the Books." His piercing green eyes twinkled.

"And, sir . . ." Alina stumbled over the words. "Master Allyen, where is 'here'?"

Allyen rose to his feet. He stretched his lithe body, and then gracefully bent to pick up the sword. He held it delicately in his hands as he turned. He began to stride back along the platform. "Walk with me."

Alina hurried to catch up. Her slapping footsteps sounded out of place here. The sound chided her. Flushing, she slowed to the old man's gentle amble.

He led her back to the foot of the platform, where an archway of young saplings marked the way from which

Alina had come. Another set of stairs, ones that Alina had not noticed before, rose into the trees on her right. Alleyn stepped out boldly.

They climbed for some time before the old man slowed. A landing in the stairs brought him to a standstill. He waited while Alina's rapid breaths wafted in the still air.

Alina took the opportunity to stare at the legend before her. 'Master' Allyen, the First Raven King, was not a large man; in fact, he was hardly taller than Alina herself. His body belied his true age, for his joints were swollen from pain and his wrinkles were numerous, but his eyes sparkled with youth of mind. A simple cloak was draped over his thin frame. The dark fabric was almost black, but silver thread had been embroidered across the shoulders. Almost hidden from view behind the swirling cloak, one hand still held the sword.

Alleyn shifted, and a drape of the cloak fell over the hilt. Alina glanced up into his face, and saw that his eyes were full of tears. "Not yet," he said.

He stepped out from the landing, and the climb resumed. They rose high above the forest floor, floating into the canopy. The tops of great cedar trees exploded into final showers of branches on all sides. Few birds flew this high, and the air was silent without their calls. The only sound was that of the waterfall, a distant roar behind them.

The stairway ended, and they stepped across a narrow bridge. Woven from thin ropes, it swung as Alina edged across it. Her hands clutched at a railing made of the same material. The rope was surprisingly supple against her palms.

When the swaying finally stopped, Alina glanced up.

For the first time, she took in the sight of their destination. A massive redwood rose before her like a tower, its trunk far larger than any she had ever seen. Several hundred people could have easily fit inside its massive diameter. Generations of hands had rubbed its bark smooth. These same hands had cut stairs into its wood. The staircase spiraled around the tree in a graceful whorl before finally ending several hundred feet above her head. A narrow landing protruded below a door, carved into the side of the tree.

Alleyn chuckled softly. "I almost forgot how magnificent this place is. It's been so long since I've left it; I've forgotten how it looks to a newcomer's eyes." He spread his hands wide, and gestured to the great tree. As he did so, thousands of windows opened in its wood. Pale, serene faces stared out them. "Welcome to Arehhan, the last home of the elves."

27

We need to hurry. The words bit at her mind. She gnawed her lip, leaning against a balcony railing. Its sturdy frame shook slightly under her weight, and she shifted nervously.

Below her loomed the interior of the great tree, a network of spiral staircases, bridges, and passageways. She stared down at them for a moment, examining the spider web with an adoring eye. No other race could have built such a magnificent city. It was little wonder that the elves were considered the noblest of races.

Generations of architects had spent their lives perfecting the last palace of the elves. The walls of the great tree were sleek and smooth, dropping hundreds of feet to the ground floor. Arched windows let enough sunlight in to see by day, though there were brackets for lanterns and candles carved into the walls. It was not hard for Alina to imagine the tree lit by thousands of candles; at night, it looked as if the entire tree were full of stars. On some nights, it actually was, for the great roof could be opened to let the moonlight shine on the sleeping elves.

They slept in hammocks, each net of fine elven rope swaying beneath a walkway. The hulls trembled as light footsteps crossed overhead. A few of these hammocks were still stretched with the weight of slumbering children.

Near Alina's head, a girl turned over in her sleep. Her face was serene as she clutched a doll to her chest.

Light had come early to Arehhan, but it was late in comparison with the elves. It was still dark when Alina first felt her hammock shake. She stood above it now, peering down at the bustling community.

Most of the adults had already slipped out into the forest, and so Alina's eyes and ears were filled with the lives of elves her own age. A young woman, still sleepy eyed and heavy of limb, stirred nearby. She stretched, her dark hair falling flat against her fine features. She spotted a friend across the room. Alina watched as the girl leapt from her hammock, landing gracefully on a thin rope. The makeshift bridge, a single strand stretched taut from hammock to hammock, quivered as the girl danced across it. She stepped off into her friend's hammock.

On Alina's other side, several young men were gathering on the walkway below. The tallest, pale of hair and eye, squatted in front of his peers. His hands moved nimbly to arrange a bundle of bows. He laid them out at his feet, stroking the elegant curves. Another boy pulled out a quiver of arrows. His fingers rustled through the feather fletching. The squatting boy nodded, opening his mouth as if to speak. He shut it abruptly.

A young woman strode towards them. She tucked a plait of sun-washed hair over her shoulder, moving her other hand to arrange her dress. She fidgeted with it for a moment. The folds fell in line, and she smiled slightly. Her blue eyes flashed as she approached the boys.

She did not seem to notice their silence, or their awkward attempts to catch her eye. She joined the boy squatting on the walkway, and ran a testing finger over a bow. She picked it up, stringing it in a single motion. Her muscles tightened as she flexed the wood. The bow responded easily, curling backwards in a smirking arc.

One of the boys reached for the bow. She let him have it, turning her attention to the rest of the weapons at her feet. The other boys sneered suddenly, their interest no longer on the girl and the weapons. They turned towards their companion. One motioned for him to try the bow.

The boy frowned, adjusting his grip on the smooth wood. His fingers tightened on the string. His muscles bulged. The bow did not respond.

His friends burst into laughter. Their jaunts echoed in the hollow tree, and the humiliated boy turned and walked away. The girl hurried to catch up to him. She slipped her hand into his as they walked, comforting him with hushed tones. Alina nodded in approval. The girl reminded her of Elewyn.

She frowned against the flood emotions. Her stomach churned as she thought of the friends she had left behind. That day in the desert, she hadn't thought of leaving anyone besides Carn behind. Now that she had time to think, she regretted running off. Now there was a chance that she would never see Elewyn or the others again.

Elewyn. Her eyes closed. She loved Elewyn, loved her more than she had ever loved any other person. *No, that's not true. I love Carn, too. Just in a different way. With Elewyn, it's so much more. . . intense.* She thought about this for a moment. *Elewyn loves life so much—it's hard not to love her back. I'll never be her best friend, but I love being around her. She can be a little intimidating sometimes, too, but I do admire her.* Alina was beginning to feel a little sick. *I don't love her like I would love a boy. It's more of a worship thing, I think.*

What about the others? Alvardine, and Oryth? Leif and

Liam? Won't I miss them, too? She sat down, her feet dangling over the edge of the walkway. She kicked them back forth as she thought. *Alvardine's gone, probably dead, but even before that he wasn't very accessible. He and Oryth were close friends, and I never really felt like I belonged when I was around them. After two people have known each other for that long, it's hard to let another person in. Besides, they were three times my age!* She grinned at thought. *Leif could have been a friend. And Liam. But Elewyn. . . She's the one I'll really miss.*

Alina stared down at the boys below her. They were snorting hysterically at something, pointing their fingers at the retreating backs of the boy and the girl. Alina wrinkled her nose in disgust.

"So you see," a voice whispered, "even the elves aren't perfect." She spun, her feet slipping on air as she reached for her sword.

"Careful, now."

She glanced up. Master Alleyn winked at her, his hand proffered to assist. She took it gratefully.

The Raven King cocked his head, looking her up and down with a beady eye. For a second, Alina was reminded of a farmyard chicken. She smiled.

"Good. No harm done, and that's that." Alleyn nodded. "I've taken the liberty of fetching your friend, Carn, in from that little cave. He's with our healer right now."

Alina grinned. "Thank you. He'll be okay, though, right?"

Alleyn nodded his affirmation. "It was only a tiny scratch. I've seen worse in my day." He began to walk along the landing, gesturing for Alina to join him. "Come, child. We have a lot to discuss."

Alina followed him, though her steps were not as sure

as his. The height of landing was disconcerting. She felt her stomach roll over, grumbling as it shifted. She was grateful when her feet finally touched earth.

The ground level of the tree of Arehhan was hardly the delicate structure that the walkways above had been. Here, at the tree's widest point, mobs of people almost completely obliterated the circular room. The same arched windows were shoved open to tempt a nonexistent breeze, leaving the air stuffy and hot. A long banquet table had been laid out in the center of the room. The scent of warm food only added to the closeness of the place. Alina gulped down a breath of air. She followed closely behind Alleyn as he wove his way through the crowd.

"Master Alleyn!" Alina spun, following her guide's gaze. A small boy waved at them, and Alleyn waited obligingly while the child rushed towards them. The boy was not very old—Alina guessed that he could count seven years at the most—but the look in his solemn eyes was ancient. He regarded her for a moment before turning back to Alleyn. "Is she a dwarf?"

Catching Alina's eye, Alleyn winked. He ruffled the boy's blond hair fondly. "Does she look like a dwarf? Look closely before you reply."

The boy stared at Alina. He squinted his eyes, puzzled. "She's not as stocky as a dwarf. Her hair is straight, not curly, though she is nearly as short. No, she's not a dwarf, but she does look like she belongs underground."

Alleyn nodded. His reply was drowned out by a swarm of children. They shouted eagerly, waving their hands to catch their mentor's attention. Each child wore a neat tunic of blue cloth, and all looked freshly bathed. A young girl pressed down her bangs as she waited.

"These are my students," Alleyn told Alina, spreading

his arms wide to welcome them all. "Normally they're a bit calmer," He cast a stern glare towards one of the boys, who was jumping up and down in his excitement, "but they're not used to newcomers. At least, they're not used to seeing people who are neither dwarves or elves." He grinned mischievously. "Let's see what they can come up with, yes? Somer was just asking about our guest," he said to the children. "We decided that she is not a dwarf. So what is she?"

Alina felt the gaze of the children shift to her. Her face blushed a bright red.

Seeing this, the jumping boy grinned. "She certainly looks a dwarf, one that's been drinking! Look at how ruddy her face is!"

Alleyn smiled indulgently. "Manners, Lomas. Look at her carefully. What species of human is she?"

Lomas fell silent under the reprimand. Obediently, he glanced at Alina. "She's a coreman. Cousin of the dwarf, but not as interested in mining. Not as hairy or fat as the dwarf, either." He licked his lips, turning his focus back to Alleyn. "It's funny, though. There aren't any settlements of coremen on this side of the Tortallions."

"Very good, Lomas! You've been studying; I can tell." Alleyn held out his hand. Lomas took it silently, clutching it for comfort. "You're right to find Alina's presence odd, Lomas. She's traveled a very long way, and I'm sure she has had many adventures. Maybe someday she will tell you about them. But today is not the day for stories. It is a day for mathematics. Go on. You'll find your problems written on your tablets."

The children groaned, but they understood the dismissal. They began to move off, picking up their chatter as soon as they left. Only Lomas remained, clinging to his teacher's hand. Alleyn did not shake him off.

Alleyn gestured for Alina to follow him as he began to walk. He murmured something to boy, who giggled. Alina couldn't help feeling a little left out of the conversation as they strode towards the back of the arena like room.

The crowds were thinner away from the door, and by the time the dark wood of the walls loomed into view, the threesome was almost completely alone. Alleyn paused at the threshold of a door. Carved into the side of the tree, Alina hadn't seen it until Alleyn pointed it out. Its surface was covered in intricate designs, ancient runes, and stars. Near the center, a mountain had been etched into the wood. Alleyn pressed his hand against the peak, and the door swung open.

A set of stone stairs descended into darkness. Lanterns hung from a hook near the doorway. Alleyn lifted one, holding it high to throw its light down the stairs. Alina peered down their slope. She could not see the landing.

Alleyn stepped through the door. He moved slowly, but before long his body began fade into the gloom. Alina hurried to catch up; it would not do to be left alone in this strange place.

The last rays of light from the doorway dissipated quickly, leaving Alina to follow the swinging orb of the lantern. The stairs were cold on her bare feet, for the elves were not used to shoes. She had left her boots in her hammock, choosing acceptance over comfort. Now she wished that she hadn't. The stone was rough and slippery, and a pair of sturdy walking shoes could have kept her from slipping. She sighed, skidding through the darkness with quickly numbing feet.

She was surprised when Alleyn began to speak. His voice sounded out of place in the dismal stairwell. "These cellars were originally built for the dwarves. Trading parties for Drogonburg used to come pretty regularly. Of course, that was before Rolan. I don't think the rooms down here have been occupied in twenty-five years."

Alina strained to hear his voice. "Why did you bring me here?"

Alleyn chuckled. "Because we're both more comfortable when there's good layer of dirt above us. And because this a private place, where we won't be interrupted."

Alina felt the stairs end. She waited while Alleyn hooked the lantern onto a bracket on the wall, watching his face flicker in the dim light. "Layer of dirt . . . Who are you?"

Alleyn smiled. "What am I' might be a better question. You already know *who* I am. I'm the First Raven King, Sir Alleyn, teacher of Arehhan."

"You talk as if there's already a Second Raven King. You're no longer *the* Raven King—you're the First." She waited for Alleyn to speak, but when he didn't, she changed tactics. "You could be a dwarf."

She saw Alleyn grin. For a moment, she felt like an errant schoolgirl, in way above her head.

"A dwarf? Do I look like a dwarf, child?"

She stared at him. His face slid in and out of the light, the high cheekbones casting shadows over his face. The light caught in his pale blue eyes. A shadow from his hair danced over his ears, making them look delicate and pointed. "I could almost say that you're an elf. But elves are tall, and you're nearly as short as me."

Alleyn looked at her with pity. "Has it been so long, child? That you can no longer recognize a member of your own race?"

"You're a coreman."

261

"Yes. Tell me, when the Gods first created the people of Ivindor, what did they give us?"

"Um . . . Food? Water? Shelter? They gave us language. And the prophecy."

"Yes! The Prophecy! They might not have actually written it out themselves, but they gave us the ability to see it."

"A time will come, in Ivindor,
When rivers flow with blood.
And at this time, the Sacred Lore,
Will, torn, lie in the mud.
But from this dark shall come a light,
The Raven King, alone,
To lead the men, their king to smite,
And sit upon the throne.
Two times these words shall come to pass,
Two kings shall be removed.
The noble and his brother's mass,
Before the Strife is soothed."

Alina's voice was soft as she recited.

"The first time has already come to pass. King Loren was taken off the throne. Now Rolan rules, and it is his turn to be overthrown. In order for that happen, another Raven King must take the First's place, and lead the battle."

"Yes, Alvardine explained all of this."

"Alvardine is a wise man. He understood most of what the prophecy said, but not all of it." Alleyn's eyes caught hold of Alina's. She held his gaze. "He understood enough to know that the First Raven King would recognize the Second. But he did not realize at the time that the two Raven Kings would be the same."

"What do you mean?"

"I mean that the Prophecy says nothing to differentiate between the Raven Kings. When the Prophecy was first heard, race was everything."

Alina nodded. She could hear her heart beating, loud and fierce in her chest. "The Second Raven King is a coreman."

"Yes. And there are only two coremen in Arehhan at this time."

"Carn? He's the Raven King." But Alina knew that this was not true.

"Alina. *You* are the Second Raven King."

28

Alvardine's memories still haunted him. They swirled inside his mind, wisps of days past, full of sunlight. Peals of laughter filled his ears as each floated by. He peered into their depths and smiled fondly.

But there was one memory that he dreaded seeing. Black with grief, it came slowly, chasing away the other, happier images until it was the only one. There was nothing he could do to stop it from coming; he could only wait for the pain to begin.

The last laugh of joy died from his ears. A faint, muffled sound replaced it, so quiet that he had to strain to hear its voice. He turned inwards, and the memory enveloped him.

It was the sound of sobbing. He felt the cries grate against the walls of his mind, scratching as if to escape from a cage. A sharp voice echoed in the distance.

"Run! He's not after you anymore."

A woman's voice, soft, pleading answered. "No. We're a family. I'm with you until the end."

He heard the crash of a door being kicked down. Chaos reigned in his mind; he could no longer tell one sound from another. Images jumbled together. For an instant, he could see the woman's face, her eyes grey and scared. He locked eyes with her, reached out for her with his hands. But before he could reach her, she was gone. A long, piercing scream stabbed at his heart. The memory floated away.

He opened his eyes. Darkness stank around him, seeping into every poor of his body. Painfully, he shifted his manacled hands against the cell wall, pressing his nail beds into the iron. *It wasn't your fault.*

Maybe, looking back on it, he could have avoided it altogether. But then he remembered clutching her to his chest, feeling her heartbeat slow to match his own. For a single instant, they had been one. And then the heartbeat faded, and the brilliant blue eyes closed. He had held her in death as he had held in her life, but not even the strength of his love could bring her back. Cere was dead, killed by the only thing that he could offer her: his love.

It wasn't your fault. But in his heart, he knew differently. Without him, things would have turned out much another way. Cere would have fallen in love with Rolan. Without him, Cere would still be alive.

He held his face in his hands. It had begun so innocently, a simple school romance. He had had no idea that Rolan fallen for the girl as well—if he had known, he would given her to him. But Rolan had left for the palace, to serve his father, the king. By the time he returned to Finestal, it had been too late. Alvardine and Cere had married, and a son had been born.

Fifteen years passed. Rolan became king of Ivindor, taking the throne while it was still covered in his father's blood. Only then did he remember his grief at losing the love of his life. He returned to Finestal, this time with a purpose.

It was nearly a year, nine months to be exact, before

Rolan had acted in his anger. By day, another son was born, with a tuft of fiery red hair. By night, his mother was brutally slaughtered, and his father sent on the run.

Liam grew, and as the months passed, Alvardine began to recognize Cere in the tiny infant. The same eyes flashed at him, the same mouth curled upwards at the corners. He couldn't bear the constant reminder, and so he sent Liam to live with Dreogan, his first son. Liam was to be raised as a foundling, and would call Alvardine 'Grandfather.'

Later, Alvardine had tried to convince himself that it was for the boy's own safety that he gave him up. Rolan was out for revenge, and wouldn't hesitate to kill Cere's children. When Dreogan was captured, Alvardine had finally realized the danger that Liam was in. He had hoped that Rolan wouldn't recognize the young man as the infant he had nearly killed years before.

But Rolan had. He had sent a note, and Dreogan's dead body, to prove it. Alvardine knew that it was only a matter of time before Liam was killed as well. And so he had acted.

He was not proud of what he had done. No. The world had gone dark for him the moment he started to leave his friends, the moment he began to consort with their enemy. *His enemy.*

Gods! If only he had known! The countless lies, the sneaking away, the telling of secrets that were not meant to be told. His body had trembled then, but now it was racked with great heaves of remorse. He had done it for Liam, and now Liam would die anyway.

Tears painted rivulets in his ashy face, following well-worn paths. They pooled at the edges of his mouth, and he licked them away ravenously. When he took the salty water into his mouth, all he tasted was blood.

He had been stripped of his traveling tunic and cloak, those garments replaced by rags hardly suited to the freezing cold of the dungeon. His long hair was cropped to shoulder length. It hung about his face in sweaty lumps. He tugged fretfully at the heavy chains about his wrists; underneath, the skin had turned an angry red, and yellow pus dribbled onto his hands. His feet shuffled in the dust as he strained against his bonds. He blinked, hoping that the prison cell would disappear.

From outside the barred door came the heavy clangs of footsteps on iron grates. A key clattered against the cold embrace of a lock, the guard cursing under his breath. He threw his weight against the hinges, and it creaked open. He lumbered over to Alvardine and hastily unknotted the restraining ropes.

"Out. Now."

Alvardine scurried forward. He bent to avoid the worst of the stinging blows as he hurried from the chamber. His feet dragged in the thick dust.

"'Still alive? You must be a favorite of the King's. Or not!" The guard laughed harshly. "There are fifty odd prisoners in this cell block. You see that cart?" He grasped Alvardine's face and pointed it down the long corridor. A rusty wheelbarrow stood near the end. Something inside was spewing green steam. "There's only enough food for three. Be good today, and maybe you'll get lucky!"

They set off down the corridor, keeping as far away from the various prison doors as possible. Occasionally a moan echoed from inside the locked chambers as they passed, but the guard only laughed and banged on their doors. Near the end of hall, a hand squirmed out from the depths of one of the cells, its body invisible in the dark. The guard drew his knife. Alvardine tried not to look at the severed hand as they moved away.

They followed a labyrinth of tunnels, stumbling around the dimly lit corners. The guard seemed to know his way around, and he shoved Alvardine roughly whenever a change in course was required, but the elf needed no guidance. He had walked this path before.

Eventually, they came to a thick oaken door. Its handle, a large brass spike embedded in the wood, prickled ominously under the glow of a nearby lantern. The guard took a deep breath. "Stinks to high heavens," he muttered. "Smells like elves." And with that, he pulled the door open.

Alvardine was thrown roughly inside, the door slamming in the guard's haste to make his get away. Cold stone tiles thwacked against Alvardine's cheekbone as he sprawled on the floor.

He was immediately seized by several large pairs of hands and tied firmly to some hooks in the wall. His clothes were stripped away, and another set of chains was wrapped about his ankles.

"Wouldn't want you getting away, now would we?"

He dared a glance at the speaker. Dressed in billowing purple robes and a golden cloak, the man's aura took up much of the small stone chamber. A frizzy red beard protruded from underneath his tightly wound scarf. A pair of black eyes twinkled, and Alvardine suddenly found himself thinking longingly of the cell he had just left.

"Rolan," he croaked.

"Glad you remembered. I trust you've had a pleasant night?"

Alvardine licked his lips nervously. "The featherbed was not to my liking," he murmured.

The king frowned. "You dare—"

A knight immediately rose to Alvardine's right. He

lifted his sword threateningly.

Alvardine bit his lip.

"Now then," Rolan announced, "we shall proceed. I expect you've had adequate time to think things over?" He did not wait for Alvardine's reply. "Where is the boy?"

Alvardine jerked his head, first left, and then right. He clenched his jaw.

"Bring the iron."

A knight hurried to the fireplace and withdrew a long metal rod. The metal, glowing a bright red, sizzled slightly in the humidity. The knight brought it gingerly.

"You'll tell me, elf."

Alvardine did not look up. His mouth was filling with blood from his lip, coating his tongue with a sweet, metallic taste.

"Very well." The king nodded slightly, and the knight brought the iron up to Alvardine's face. It floated mere centimeters from his cheek, the heat singing his facial hair. "Last time we met, you mentioned the Raven King. You said that you didn't know who it was, but you lied! Where is the boy?"

Alvardine drew in a deep breath. He lifted his chin. "You think that Liam is the Raven King?" He laughed bitterly.

Rolan looked confused, but only for a moment. He leaned closer. Alvardine could feel his musty breath mingling with the hot iron.

"Where is the boy?" Rolan asked.

Alvardine closed his eyes, but otherwise, did not reply. His cheek was beginning to blister from the heat. Small flakes of skin peeled off and blackened.

"Elf!" The rod swung dangerously close.

Taking a deep breath, Alvardine clenched his teeth,

forcing his cheek out. Metal bit against skin, the room filling with the acrid smell of burning flesh. A gasp escaped his lips, the ghost of a suppressed scream. Something warm oozed down his chin, hot and waxy.

Somewhere in the distance, a child began to cry.

29

"So Alvardine gave up everything to save his son," Alina remarked. Raven King stared at Raven King, the elder breathless from explaining. "There's one thing I still don't understand. Who is Liam?"

Alleyn wrinkled his brow. He was growing weak; conjuring up Alvardine's image had sapped his strength. He knew that it wouldn't be long before he left this world for good. "Does it really matter? Liam himself doesn't know. He never will; Alvardine will die with that secret."

Alina nodded. She understood what Alleyn was trying to say. His vague words left nothing to doubt. "So Rolan has been trying to kill his own son this whole time."

"Perhaps. We have no way of knowing for sure."

"Why did Cere do it?"

Alleyn nodded. "It's easy to feel disgust for her. She slept with Rolan to prolong her husband's life. Maybe she thought that it would save him. In the end, though, it just intensified Rolan's jealousy. He tried to kill Alvardine because of it."

"And Cere died instead." Alina struggled to understand. "She was a brave woman."

Alleyn nodded. "Yes, she was very brave. She sacrificed her body for Alvardine. He must never know that."

Alina paused. She glanced into Alleyn's eyes. "Can I ask you something?"

"Of course."

"Carn, and Arie. It's very hard to forgive, isn't it."

Alleyn bowed his head. When he looked up, he stared Alina straight in the eye. "Carn acted for love, like Cere did. Can you hate him for that?"

Alina turned away. She stared into the dark reaches of chamber. "There's a war going on."

"Yes."

"I can end it." She faced Alleyn. Determined dark eyes met his. "They're gathering the troops. I should be there."

Alleyn reached for his cloak. He pushed the material aside, revealing the sword strapped to his belt. It was the same sword he had been holding when Alina first met him, the blade etched with entwining vines. He drew it, holding it out.

Alina took the sword. It fit her hand perfectly. She guided it into her belt. If all went right, she would not need it. She met Alleyn's eye. Suddenly, she grinned. Her eyes sparkled. "You're a magician. How fast can you get me to the palace?"

The air stank of sweat and urine. Of death, demise, and fear. Feet trampled across the earth, swords clanged in their sheaths. Shields were handed out to the men, some of whom were hardly more than boys. Spearmen gathered together. An archer let fly a practice shot. This was not the time to miss.

Horses stamped across the dusty ground. They seemed to be aware of what was about to happen, and were even more concerned than the men. They snorted fretfully and pawed at their reins. Their riders held them in check, but no one leaned down to comfort them. What comfort was there to give? Chances were that they would die that day.

There were only two women on the battlefield. Though they stood separately, both stood apart from the chaotic soldiers. One, her blond hair plaited tightly against her neck, fidgeted with the reins of a white horse. Beside her, a man flexed a great bow. Neither had allowed themselves to be dressed in armor, and the man wore only a leather vest to protect him from the worst of blows. His red hair was fiery in the sunlight.

Across the battlefield, the other woman prepared for battle as well. Her dark eyes were set as she drew a pale silver sword. The blade was elven, hardly thicker than a dagger, but stronger than any other metal. She traced the etchings on the hilt, where a silver raven arced its curved beak. The wings flew outwards to guard her thumbs. She slid her hand into the grip, and was not surprised when it fit perfectly. She had been made for this sword.

The corners of Alina's mouth twitched upwards. She knew that it wasn't the time for smiles, but she couldn't help it. There was hope after all, a desperate hope, but a hope all the same. She tried not to focus on the fact that the hope revolved around her.

She glanced over at Carn. The boy stood firmly at her side, both hands clasped around the hilt of his sword. She hadn't wanted to bring him, not with his injury, but Carn had always had a streak of stubbornness in him. She was glad that he was with her.

"They're waiting for you," he whispered. He met her

gaze, giving her a quick nod.

Alina swallowed the last of her fear. "Stay with me." She began to pace towards the center of the churning crowd. Soldiers snapped their swords into their sheaths. Shields were buckled on, the fastenings knotted into place. She watched as men lowered helmets over their heads. They were ready.

She turned away. These were seasoned soldiers, and were used to preparing for war. She was not. She could feel her stomach tying itself in knots, forcing bile up the back of her throat. Keeping it down was the least of her priorities; she was the Raven King, and was expected to lead these men.

She came to a small boy, not more than thirteen years of age. He was sitting beside his father's shield, running his fingers over the metal. Mousey brown hair curled across his bow. A single tear trickled down his cheek. He wiped it away angrily.

She knelt to meet his gaze. "This will be over soon. And then you can go home." She put her hand on his shoulder.

"Do you think," he whispered, "it will really come to fighting?" He looked up apprehensively.

"Honestly? Yes. The King is not one to give into negotiations so easily. Doubtless he has already amassed his armies . . . " She stopped when she saw the boy's look of concern. "But you'll be alright. You have your sword; it looks like a fine one. Stay close to your father. He'll look after you."

"I don't . . . " He frowned and brushed another tear from his cheek. "I don't think I really want to fight."

Alina tugged his sword lightly from his grasp. She hefted it in her hand and tested the blade against her thumbnail. "To tell you the truth, none of us do. Not even Oryth, or Leif or Liam. No one wants to fight this battle. But you know why we have to? Because in this story, we're the heroes."

"And the heroes always win, right?"

She smiled and brushed his cheek with the back of her hand. "This sword is dull." She reached for her belt, unbuckling Oakenwhite's sheath. "I have the sword of the Raven King now. Take my old one, keep it close. Pray to the Gods that you won't need it."

Carn joined her as she walked away. "Children like that shouldn't be fighting." His voice was dull.

"No," Alina grimaced, "but there's nothing we can do to stop them. There's ten or eleven of them here. They'll fight with their fathers. After all, this battle will affect them more than anyone." She put her hand to her forehead. "Why did we ever leave home, Carn?"

Carn grabbed her arm. He wheeled her around to face him, meeting her determined gaze with his light eyes. "Not too long ago, we were children just like that boy. Now we're commanding an army. At least, you are. I know you're nervous, Alina, but it's kids like him who need you right now. There's an army out there, bigger than ours, stronger. It's full of Black Knights and who knows what else. And at the head of that army is the King of Ivindor, a man who could just as easily eat breakfast as put down our rebellion."

He waved his arm at the men around them. "Look at these men. See the fear in their eyes? They need you. You are the Raven King. Be strong for them, Alina. Be strong for me."

She looked into his eyes and saw the glint of terror. She nodded. This was something she had to do.

Leif and Liam had organized the men into rows. Their horses pranced beneath them as they stared across the field at the palace. A thousand Black Knights stared back, their armor glinting in the sun. Leif had drawn his sword. Liam strung his bow. Beside him, Elewyn sat atop Snowberry, a goddess of serenity in the chaos. Alina caught sight of her. She knew what she needed to do.

The horse was waiting for her. She swung up onto his strange back, reaching down to pat a mane that was not Mandan's. His speed would not be the same, nor his courage. The horse danced under her weight. His nostrils flared; he could smell the fear in the air.

At her side, Carn leapt onto Siv's back. Oryth trotted to meet them, a cloak of pure white billowing behind him. He held his staff, muttering an incantation. "I've put protective shields around our camp. It's not much, but if we need a retreat, it'll hold."

Alina nodded. She cantered to the front of the troops. Their eyes shifted to focus on her, their faces expectant and sweaty. She bit her lip. What could she say to these men to ease their fear, to bring courage into their hearts? *There's nothing to say. Most of these men will die.*

On her left, she heard Liam's voice murmuring. He had guided his horse up alongside Snowberry, and he stretched his hand across the gap between the horses. Elewyn took it silently.

"Elewyn, if anything happens—"

"Nothing will happen!"

"But if it does, I love you." He stared into her blue eyes.

Elewyn nodded, once. She squeezed his hand before pulling away. "Now, Alina!"

Alina heard her and stared out at the faces of the tiny army. She began to trot in a long line in front of them. She was aware of Carn taking his place in front his troops, and of Elewyn wheeling to face her squadron. When she spoke, her voice carried over the wind.

"Now, I will not tell you that this battle will be an easy one, or a short one. It won't be. Chances are that this will be the battle of the century. But we must stand strong.

"Men, when I look out at you, I see an army even Rolan should be afraid of. I see the heroes of today, the heroes of tomorrow. Not all of you will live to see this day's end. But that does not matter! You are fighting for a cause worth dying for!

"Men! Today we fight for humanity! For the rights of a race long forgotten. It does not matter whether we win or lose. What will be remembered is that we fought the battle!" She drew her sword. At the sight of it, the men shifted, murmuring. "When you look upon this city, and feel the tremor in your heart, do not be afraid! The Gods are with us. They are backing us. With them at our sides, we have the power to destroy this monarchy. Let's not let those powers go to waste!"

A great cry rang out at this. The men raised their spears in acknowledgment.

"The moment we swarm that city, the gates will open. Hundreds upon thousands of men will pour out of those gates, and all of them will be trained to kill. Archers, Infantry, Black Knights even. But that does not matter. Get inside that city. Head to the castle. You know who we're looking for. If anyone asks, tell them we've got an appointment with our lord, the king!" She turned to face the city herself, her sword held high. She had returned to Carn's side. She touched his shoulder. "Are you with me?"

Carn smiled. He gripped her hand. "Until the end."

Alina nodded. She pulled her hand away, raising her

sword high into the air. It blazed in the sunlight. The Second Raven King had come. "Men, are you with me?" She screamed.

A roar rose out of the ranks. In all directions, swords were drawn. She heard Carn pull his own sword from his sheath. He nodded.

"For Ivindor!"

"For Ivindor!" The men took up her cry. Her horse leapt forward and she sped towards the rows of Black Knights. The Wanderers followed her, crying out in their fear and excitement. Oryth shouted spells into the wind.

Even as they raced across the field, they saw the black gates open. Men spilled forth waving huge battle-axes. Mounted Knights broke through the walls in waves. Their horses screamed in anger.

Alina reached the Black Knights first. She swung her sword upwards. Blood sprayed as she drew the first blood of the battle.

The rest of the men came crashing in around her. The air was filled with their cries. Armor clashed against sword, shield clashed against axe.

Beside her, Liam spun from his horse. His bow twanged as arrow after arrow leapt into the air. Elewyn positioned herself at his back, her dagger flashing as it plunged into metal. Leif and Carn were nowhere to be seen. Alina craned her neck in search of them.

A huge axe swung into her line of sight. She ducked, feeling the blade scrape the skin on her throat. The hooded face of a Black Knight followed its path.

She stabbed her sword towards him, her bones jarring as the blade jolted against armor. The Knight laughed. He swung his axe again. Alina dodged, searching for an opening. The Knight was like a turtle in his armor; there was no way her blade could pierce the iron hide.

There! As the Knight twisted, his armor moved with him. A tiny gap between the plates opened. She plunged her sword towards his neck.

The Knight screamed in agony as the blade pierced him. She thrust it in harder, twisting it for good measure. The Knight dropped to his knees before keeling over.

Alina had no time to mediate on her first kill. As the Knight fell, another stepped over his body, taking his place with a double-handed sword. She saw it sweeping towards her head.

She shoved her sword up, breaking the arc of his blow. At the same time, she slid to the left, darting between a gap in the ranks of men. When the Knight glanced down, she had disappeared.

She hurtled a fallen man as she dashed towards the palace gate. It was still open, hanging from the high stonewalls as hundreds of more Knights poured out. She saw Carn rush towards it. His size helped him; he slipped through the gate and into the city beyond. *Carn!*

Leif crashed behind him, cutting through the Black Knights. He spun, his sword nearly invisible. Alina ducked beneath it.

The swarm of Knights was thinning. Most were already out on the battlefield. The gate began to swing shut. Alina rushed towards it. She was aware of Liam and Elewyn panting at her back. Leif spun. He reached the doorway, bracing it open with his shoulders. "Go!"

Alina threw herself between his legs. A Knight pitched himself at her. She went for the neck without thinking, not even pausing when the Knight collapsed. She waved the others in.

Dozens of Black Knights rushed the company. The

group formed a circle, lashing out at the dark armor. Alina found herself facing a giant of a man. His stench was almost enough to knock her out, but if that failed, then the club that he carried would do the job. Its knobbly head flew towards her.

Alina instinctively knew that her sword was no match for the club. She rolled away from its blow. The club cracked the cobblestones where she stood seconds before.

This was a new type of fight. She had no way of defending herself; all she could do was dart away from the smashing blows. Sooner or later, she knew that her feet would tire. When that happened, death would be imminent.

She step-sided another swing of the club. If she could just get close enough! This Knight's armor was different from the others', but she could already see a slit near the underarm. With the right angle, a stab there would be deadly. She made a dash for it.

The club caught her off guard. It was an offhanded blow, but it managed to brush her shoulder. She stumbled backwards, hitting the ground with a jolt. The Knight loomed over her. He raised his club for the final blow.

He froze. A moan escaped his lips. Alina scrambled away, rising just in time to see the man flop onto the ground. An arrow stabbed out of his back, slid in between the plates of armor.

"That's the second time I've saved your life this week!" Carn drew his sword once more. His hands were bloody from shoving the arrow into flesh. He slipped his blade in through the armpit, finishing the Knight off.

Alina grinned. Suddenly, she lunged forward, stabbing her sword over Carn's shoulder. Carn turned in time to see another Knight fall to the ground behind him. Alina slit the Knight's throat. "Consider the favor repaid."

Taking advantage of the moment, they broke away from the fighting. Alina led the way, racing down a side street. Carn panted at her back. Someone cried out back in the square. "Let's go kick some honey buns!" Leif had broken away as well.

Alina did not wait for him to join them. She came across a main road and threw herself down it. Her legs burned from the slight incline. She remembered that she had had a horse. She could not remember what had happened to it.

No matter. The palace was in sight now, its doomed roof rising above the rest of the city. She twirled around a corner, and there it was. A set of steps led up to the maple doors. A squad of Black Knight marched in straggled line at their foot.

Alina waited just long enough for Carn to take stock of the situation, and then she acted. She stepped out from the corner, sucking in a deep breath. "Didn't your mothers ever teach you how to march?" she shouted.

The Knights whirled to face her. They began to run towards her, their swords drawn.

"Pitiful! I've seen people like you, but I had to pay admission!" She danced away from their swords. Her own sword flashed. A single Knight fell to the ground.

Beside her, Carn took up the fight. "You know, you really should do some soul searching," he told one Knight. "Maybe you'll find one!" He thrust his sword in, hard.

Leif jumped into the fray. His sword danced, spraying blood across the stairs. "Gods! Last time we met, you were both arrogant and obnoxious. Now you're just the opposite; you're obnoxious and arrogant!"

Liam and Elewyn were the last of the company to

reach the stairs. Liam's arrows flew in all directions. He only missed once, maiming a Knight in the face rather than killing him. Elewyn tossed her dagger at the man, and with that, the last of the Knights were dead.

Alina hurried up the steps. She knew that there would be more Knights inside, roaming the corridors and patrolling for people just like her. She smiled slightly at the thought and then threw open the oak doors. They were in the palace at last.

She did not take the time to notice the fine paintings on the walls, or the beautiful tapestries that draped both sides of the entry hall. Within moments, she had located a long flight of stairs and was racing up them. The group's footsteps thundered as they climbed, but the sound didn't matter anymore. Alina gained the landing. She dashed down a long hallway, her eyes focused at its end point. A set of bronze doors beckoned her towards them. She placed her hands on the cold metal and prepared to push.

"Hey! You!" A voice shot down the hall. She turned, just in time to see the Knight fall to the carpeted floor, an arrow sticking from his neck. With her eyes still on the dead man, she backed through the door.

Silence. It hit her hard, a ram slamming against a barricaded door. She did not dare to turn and kept her eyes on the open doorway.

"I've been expecting you."

Slowly, as if time had stopped completely, she twisted to face the speaker. She struggled to breath in the thick air.

The room was barren, save for a single, high backed chair opposite the door. A few tattered scrolls had been bundled onto a table nearby, but these pieces of furniture were the only islands that broke up the sea of dusty floor. A single Black Knight stood motionless in the corner.

Alina took this all in with a single, sweeping glance. Then she turned back to the chair.

Its seat was occupied, and the man that draped over its arms seemed to fill the whole room. From the moment Alina laid eyes on him, she forgot about the sparse furnishings, the poor housekeeping. She stared at him, and he stared back.

Immensely fat, he had wrapped himself in layers of black and gold cloth. Alina couldn't help but think of queen bee in her hive, sitting smugly among her combs of honey. A purple cloak was tossed loosely over the back of the chair, and its color clashed horrendously with his fiery red hair. His jowls quivered slightly, and his pudgy fingers reached for a plate on his lap. He lifted an olive to his lips, letting the juices run down his chin. "I would apologize for the rather cold welcoming, except I just remembered—you weren't invited."

Alina raised her eyebrows, but she said nothing. *He's just guessing; he has no idea. . .*

"The Wanderers, I presume." King Rolan spat the olive pit onto the floor. Alina watched it roll away, finally coming to rest beside a dust bunny.

"We didn't come here to chat!" Leif took a step forward, his sword pointing menacingly at Rolan. He raised it, letting Rolan take it in like one would tease a starving dog with a bone. "Prepare to die!"

Rolan snorted. "Going to kill me, little boy? Going to stick me with your needle?"

Leif's lip curled upwards in a snarl. He took a step forwards. "You killed millions! I was there when Ferrington was destroyed—I saw your Knights. I saw you! You killed the man who took me in. You killed his son—he was only twelve!" Leif lunged towards Rolan.

Before Alina could act, Liam leapt forward. He grabbed Leif's shoulders, wrenching him onto the ground with a near fatal thud. Leif glared up at Liam, his eyes burning with hate. "He deserves to die!" he roared.

Liam grabbed the scruff of his tunic, throwing him back towards the door. "That's not your place!"

Rolan chuckled. He reached for another olive and sucked at its tip. "Going to cry?" His eyes rose a fraction of a degree, catching Liam in his stare. He cocked his head, pausing to swallow before he spoke again. "But you were right. It's not his place, is it?"

Liam lifted his bow slightly, adjusting his grip on the leather handle. His other hand hung loosely at his side, but Alina knew that an arrow was only a split second away.

"That job belongs to the Raven King." Rolan stood, setting the plate on the seat behind him. Crumbs fell away from his lap. "And I'm sure you'd love to kill me now, Liam, but shall we hear some things out?"

Liam opened his mouth as if to speak, but Alina caught his eye. He clamped it shut immediately.

"It was rather easy getting in here, wasn't it? But I've wanted to meet you for a long time. The Second Raven King, here to destroy the king of Ivindor." Rolan began to pace in front of them, his cloak sweeping the dust into great clouds as he walked. "I was disappointed when I remembered that you had elvish blood. Such a pity, wasting a human father on a dirty, elvish mother!"

"I was raised by the elves," Liam said. "They took me in, when no human village would. Who's dirty now, my lord?"

"Ah, yes. But weren't you once friends with a certain elf called Alvardine?" Rolan waved his hand. The Black Knight left the room. "Didn't he betray you?"

The Knight returned, dragging an oblong object along

with him. He pulled it upright, and Alina saw that it was a ragged, emaciated man. Dark eyes swiveled frantically beneath greasy hair. They latched on to Liam, and the man's face tightened. "Liam."

Rolan smiled. He had paused beside Liam, and now he threw his arm around Liam's shoulder, a kind of lopsided hug. "What's the matter, Alvardine? Doesn't seeing a father and son reunited stir you?"

Liam ducked away from Rolan. He kept his eyes on Alvardine's shrunken form, though. "You're not my father."

"You're right, he's not." Rolan smiled. "Oh, he thought he was, yes, But then, Cere never was very faithful."

The look of confusion on Liam's face was matched by the one on Alvardine's. Both frowned, their foreheads wrinkling.

"I'd have thought the red hair would give it away, but then again . . . You did get your mother's looks." Rolan reached for Liam's cheek, stroking it gently. "Yes, I knew from the time of your birth who you were. I watched you grow into a man. I was proud of you, Liam." He dropped his hand. "But then, to go and ruin it all, and send my own son to kill me as the Raven King!" He rounded on Alvardine, advancing with steady steps. "You not only betrayed these people, but you betrayed me! And you know what happens to traitors to the crown."

"No." Alina stepped forward. She sheathed her sword, the metal ringing as it was silenced. "Alvardine betrayed no one. He did what he had to do, and that was that."

"Step down, girl! These things are way over your head."

"Are they? Sir Alleyn didn't think so." Alina took another step forward, watching as Rolan's eyes darted to her sword. He froze upon the hilt, staring at the raven. His face contorted from bewilderment to sudden understanding. "No one else needs to die tonight, Rolan. There's been enough blood shed."

"Raven King." Rolan sneered, but Alina could see a glimmer of dread in his eye. This man was afraid of her. "I should rip you to shreds."

Alina raised her eyebrows. "Cere might not have chosen you, Rolan, but this man did nothing to harm you. Neither did the elves. When you were alone, orphaned, with nowhere to go, the Elven School took you in. They fed you, gave you shelter, and taught you everything you know. In your time of trouble, they were your friends. As was Alvardine. Look at him!" She gestured to the dying elf, his eyes haunted by years past. "Look what you've done to him!

"The thing is, Rolan," she said softly, "if the elves were really so terrible, then why did you fall in love with one of them?"

Rolan kicked out, hard. His foot crashed into Alvardine's jaw, and he whirled, leaving the elf to crumple among the dust. "Guards!"

Knights streamed through the doorway. The company circled together, facing outwards with their swords at the ready. Alina drew her sword. The blade shone brightly.

"She was not an elf!" Rolan shouted above the clanking armor. "Remember that when you die!" He brought his arm down in a great arc.

The Knights leapt forward, each swinging a double-headed axe. Alina glanced towards Rolan and saw that he too had drawn a sword, the blade black from dried blood. She reacted by instinct. Her sword flashed in the air. It darted towards a Knight.

An axe swept down to par her blow. She felt the bones in her arm creak, but she gritted her teeth and stabbed again. The axe was a whirlwind of spinning blades. She watched it creep towards her neck and ducked. Her sword arm plunged up; she felt something contact the blade.

She had drawn blood. Crimson droplets spotted the armor near the elbow, the plates of black metal already closing over the tiny gap. The Knight drew back in caution. He danced away from her thrusts, for the moment playing defense.

Across the room, Liam's bow twanged. His arrows flew straight and true, but the Knights' armor was of a different design that of those outside. The arrows simply slid off of the metal. Three Knights pressed through the hail.

He spun, throwing his bow onto his back as he did so. An axe rushed towards him, but Liam ducked, easily sliding beneath its path. He drew his dagger.

But this was not the environment for knife work. The Knights' armor was thick, and with three of them on him at once, he had trouble keeping up with their blows. He ducked another swing of the axe. A sword slashed down at his shoulder, and he twisted away. The sleeve of his tunic fluttered to the ground.

"He's mine!" Suddenly, the Knights were gone, their hulking forms replaced by the queen bee. It buzzed, its stinger out; Rolan was taking his last revenge.

Liam lunged forward. As he went for the throat, his dagger was invisible, and yet, Rolan somehow saw it. He brought his black blade up, catching the dagger in midair. Liam's thinner blade shattered.

Rolan laughed. He stepped forward, and Liam stumbled as he tried to escape. He found himself crawling backwards. Rolan moved in for the kill. The black blade plunged down; there was no stopping it now.

"No!" With a cry to stop the dead in its tracks, Elewyn dashed forward. She threw herself in front of Liam, raising her sword to block the blow. Her eyes widened in horror as the metal splintered. The black blade sank into her breast.

Alina saw this from across the room. Suddenly, the Knight she had been fighting was lying dead on the ground. She crossed the room in two steps, raising her own sword above her head as she did so. Rolan twirled to face her. His sword rose up to meet hers.

Somehow, the sword that Raven King had given her held. She watched as the black blade fell away, the tip broken off. She tried to pull back, dragging her sword with her, but her momentum was too great. The blade sunk into the side of Rolan's neck. The great king fell, and in that instant, the battle was won.

The last of the Knights were rounded up without difficulties. Alina helped Carn shove them into the hall. They swung the bronze doors shut. When Alina turned back to the room, the silence had returned.

Elewyn lay near Rolan's throne. Liam hunched over her, his hands over hers. His eyes searched desperately for a movement no one else could see. His ears strained to hear a breath no one else could hear. He pressed his cheek against hers. "Elewyn, my love." His hands shook as he caressed her face.

"Liam." Her lips moved softly. Her eyes met his, and for an instant it seemed like everything would be all right again. "I tried."

"Hush, hush, my love." He smoothed her hair. "You were amazing." He drew a deep breath. "You were so, so brave." A faint smile broke through his tears, like a rainbow during a rainstorm. "You'll be all right."

"I'm scared," she whispered. Her eyes were closing, half shut to the gleam of life. "Liam . . . Sing. Sing for me one last time." Her eyes closed.

"My love." He laid her gently back against the stone. Her hair fell in disarray about her face. She was curled, fetus like, hiding her bloody wound, with her face turned upwards towards Liam's.

It is said that death makes one look like one is sleeping. Elewyn's face was not one of peaceful relaxation. Her eyes stared upwards into nothingness, blue and twinkling still.

Liam gently pushed her eyelids shut. When he began to sing, Alina had to strain to listen.

Meet me by the tree
So tall and oaken white
Growing in the land of cold.
A stone ring circles it,
A girth for its mantle,
A bowl for its blood,
When it spills.

Meet me by the tree
Where we will be given
The chance to repay our sins!
Strange things happened there,
Once upon a night.
My love, meet me there again.

Liam bent, and kissed her still warm lips. Then he turned, and with the silence that he would carry for the rest of his life, he left the room. Elewyn's body lay still behind him.

30

There was no celebration that day. How could there be? Hundreds had died, and a great heroine had sacrificed herself to save her true love. The rebel forces picked through the rubble, dragging the bodies of their friends to a funeral pyre. With damp eyes, they watched them burn.

Elewyn alone was spared. Her body was laid out in a tent, where Alina and Carn arranged her limbs and smoothed her hair. Oryth paced outside the canvas flaps; he could not bear to see his daughter's cold body. He had yet to cry, but Liam's last song haunted them all. The man himself had disappeared. No one went looking for him.

When Alina finally stirred from her vigil, the sun had sunk below the horizon. Moonlight streamed through the walls of the tent, casting an eerie glow on its occupants. Alina's knees were wobbly as she stood in the shadows beside the dead body. Carn had already left, and she found herself alone with the girl she had once idolized. She raised her eyes to look the girl square in the face. It was then that it struck her, a single thought, far more powerful than Alina had ever known. Elewyn was not asleep, though her eyes were closed as if she was. She was dead, and would never rise again.

Her leather armor had been stripped away, replaced

with a lilac dress. Alina could remember brushing her hair out the night before, pulling out the tangles so that it lay like spun gold across her shoulders. The blood and grime had been washed from her face, and with her death wound bandaged tightly, Elewyn looked whole again. It was as if the battle had never happened, though the presence of her dead body spoke otherwise. Alina stroked the soft skin of her hand. Then she turned, and without a look backwards, stepped from the tent.

Later, when she stood beside Carn, watching the flames crackle around Elewyn's body, she wished that she had known the girl for longer. It seemed like only yesterday when Elewyn was volunteering to accompany them on the journey. When she remembered that Elewyn had not wanted the battle to take place, Alina bowed her head, but she did not cry. The tears just wouldn't come.

They watched the pyre slowly dissolve, and when the last spark extinguished itself amongst the soot, they swept the ashes up. These they brought down to the sea, where Oryth sprinkled them over the gently lapping water. Alina watched as the dust swirled on the current. The last essence of her friend floated for an eternity before dissolving. Overhead, a seagull wheeled in the breeze, its spirit as free as Elewyn's while she lived. And yet, the tears would not come.

The palace was empty when she next walked though it, empty except for the fallen bodies that littered its halls. She passed silently among the dead, for she herself was a ghost among the living. Knights lay sprawled where they had drawn their last breath. Alina bent, and her face still emotionless, removed their helmets, one by one. Without the black armor, the Knights were only men.

She found herself wandering the streets near the gate.

Now the bodies were no longer just those of the enemy, but were occasionally those of the rebel soldiers. In death, all of the bodies looked the same, but she knew that these were different. These were men whom she had walked among the day before. They had followed her willingly into battle, and they had died because of it. The tears did not come.

The gates still hung open, forced back on their hinges by the struggle of the bodies that surrounded them. She slowed as she passed the fallen. Her eyes searched for a single body among the dozens, a body much smaller in size than the others. She searched for the boy that she had spoken with yesterday, just moments before his death.

She found him sprawled just outside the gates. His body was obscured by the mass of a larger man, lying on top of him. She slipped off the man's helmet. It took a great amount of effort to move the boy's father away from his son, as if even in death, the man was still trying to protect the boy. Underneath both bodies, she found her old sword. The blade was split in two, splintering upwards into the hilt. She pulled the sword free and pushed it into a sheath. Then she turned back to the boy.

She pulled the armor off of him, one piece after another, flinging it away. He would not need it anymore. Underneath the heavy chain mail, the boy wore only a simple tunic and shorts. Without the armor, he ceased to be soldier, and dissolved into a child in her arms. She bore his weight his weight silently, carrying him over the battlefield.

Near the edge, she came to a crumbling path. It led her downwards, until at last she came to the crashing shore of the sea. The water extended for miles in front of her, slipping into the horizon before it slid from view. She knelt on the dew-ridden sands and began to dig.

The grave was still shallow when it began to fill with water. She pushed dry sand into the bottom and lowered the boy in. He lay still in the shadowed pit, his mousey grey hair disheveled as if from sleep. She reached down and straightened his crumpled tunic. She had no idea what his name was, or who this boy had been before the battle, but it didn't matter. The boy was dead.

She cried, then. The tears fell freely. Her body shook with sobs, and a keening wail rose to her lips. She gulped it back angrily. She was the Raven King; she was supposed to be brave, but as Alina rocked back and forth in the sands, she did not feel brave. She was alone in her grief. Guilt racked her body. Because of her, a young boy lay dead. She stared down at his tiny corpse and as she did so, she could not help but feel afraid. She was a murderer. Because of her, one of her best friends had died.

She slammed a fist into the sand. *I didn't want anyone to die! I didn't ask them to fight—there didn't need to be a battle. I could have just as easily let myself be taken captive, and when I was taken to Rolan, talked to him then. He didn't need to die either!*

I pity him, she realized suddenly. *He may have been a murderer, but the elves weren't much better. They killed his parents and left him an orphan. They took his childhood away, and when he finally fell in love, they snatched that away, too. Cere could have loved him, but instead she spurned him because he was human.* Alina sank back on her heels. Her breathing slowed. *I only ended the suffering—I didn't start it.*

As Alina was coming to realize, the suffering caused by the split between the elves and the humans had begun long before she come onto the scene. It was an ancient quarrel, and both sides had fought violently. Blood had been spilled for centuries. The Wanderers were only a recent installment in the war, and despite their best intentions, they were only adding fuel to fire. With their support, the elves had gained strength. By their blades, the humans had been punished.

Alina frowned. Her tears were beginning to slow. Dread gnawed at her stomach, and she bit her lip. *We haven't done anything to stop this war. We've only made it worse. Someday, another battle just like this one will be fought, and more men will die.* She glanced down at the boy. Already, water was beginning to seep through the sand at the bottom of the grave. *I don't want that,* she thought, and she wasn't sure whether she was thinking of the next battle, or of the only solution she could think of. She pushed sand over the grave, leaving a mound on the beach. She stood. Finally, after traveling across Ivindor, she knew what she needed to do.

31

The day was just like any other day. Hot and bleak, the sun beat down on the island of Twedrig. Fresh grass was growing in the fields around the city, and the wind rustled its blades, leaving pathways of quavering grass in its wake. On the island's western shore, the open ocean pounded in the surf. Boats, moored to the pier, bobbed in their eagerness to set sail. The day was ripe for fishing, and yet, not a single fisherman was to be seen.

In the palace, the walls had been scrubbed. Fresh carpets lay on the floor, and the tapestries had been patched where swords had sliced through the fibers. There was nothing to suggest that, only a few weeks before, the palace had been a battlefield.

Alina leaned against the balcony railing. A wind swept up form the beach, and she smiled at the scent of the sea. Beside her, Carn shifted in his new tunic. He glanced over the edge of the balcony. "Quite a crowd."

And so it was. Thousands of people milled in the field beneath them, their voices bright with excitement. As Alina gazed down at them, she noticed the lighter features of the elves in the crowd. There were hundreds of them, and though many were still thin from their days on the run, they were there. Humans and elves, together at last.

Alina turned, a smile lacing her lips. She had never thought this day would come.

"Don't be nervous." Carn grinned at her. She thought she saw him wink.

"I don't want this, Carn. You know that, right?"

Carn smiled. "You'll be fine."

She bit her lip. When Carn offered her his hand, she took it, interlocking her small fingers with his big ones. The touch was comforting. They stood for a moment, shoulders touching, hand in hand. For that moment, they were invincible.

Then Carn gently slid his hand away. "It's time," he murmured.

Alina nodded. She turned into the threshold. Carn followed her as she slipped through the palace. They came to the entry hall, and Alina paused in front of the maple doors. She sighed. Then, she threw open the doors, and descended the steps into the crowd beyond.

An aisle had been pushed through the crowd, and she followed it. Her pure white dress did nothing to hide her from the people's watchful eyes. Within moments, the crowd's murmuring had stopped. All eyes were on her as she walked towards the ring.

Alvardine smiled at her. She returned the grin, thankful for his presence. He hadn't been hard to forgive, and as he stood beside Oryth inside the ring of spectators, it was like old times. They were the only two people in the ring; Liam hadn't been seen since Elewyn's death.

Alina stepped into the clearing in the crowd. At its center, a stone slab stood elevated on marble steps. Alvardine waited at their summit. In his hands, he held a velvet pillow. She walked up to the base of the steps. Eyes burned into her back as she slowly began to climb.

When she reached the top, she paused in front of Alvardine. She knelt on one knee.

Alvardine stepped forward. From the cushions of the velvet pillow, he took the sword Sir Allyen had given Alina. Its unsheathed blade gleamed a soft silver, throwing a patch of moonlight into the sun. He held it up for the crowd to see.

The people roared their approval. He handed the sword to Alina, who took it with both hands. She clutched it against his breast and waited.

Alvardine turned back to the velvet pillow. Apparently its cushions had not been emptied, for his hands gripped something in its midst. He produced a delicate ring of silver. Its shape was suggestive of a raven, its wings curving in a gentle arc. He slipped the crown over Alina's head.

Alina rose. She turned towards the crowd, and they met her with a deafening cry. Then, one by one, they knelt, their heads bowed.

Alina twisted. In all directions, all she could see was crown of the people's heads. Even Alvardine was bowing, and Oryth was almost invisible with his bald head. Finally, she turned to Carn. He, too, was kneeling.

She stepped over to him. With one hand, she dragged him to his feet. He kept his eye averted, and Alina reached for his chin. She made him look at her. "Carn, we've been through way too much together. You bow to no one."

Carn smiled weakly. "You'll make a fine queen."

Alina grinned. She looked him straight in the eye. "I'll need a king." She held out her hand. Carn took it, and together they returned to the center of the platform. In the distance, a horse whinnied. Alina fancied that it was Snowberry, with Elewyn clinging to her back. As she stood in the center of the cheering crowd, Alina could not help but hope that all of their sacrifices had been worth it.

THE END

CPSIA information can be obtained at www.ICGtesting.com
Printed in the USA
BVOW071647260112

281452BV00001B/6/P